CW00557234

GOODBYE HOLYHELL

MATH BIRD

MCSNOWELL BOOKS

A McSnowell Book

This edition published by McSnowell Books, 2023

For Yan

1986

PART I

HEARTLAND

1

egsy Dempster had stared death in the face more than once and, with a natural cunning and wit that favoured any grifter worth their salt, always talked his way out of it.

These days, Degsy wasn't so sure. This dust-laden bedsit, the damp-stained walls and the cigarette burns on the carpet, were stark reminders that his best days were behind him. The thunder of a passing train did nothing to lift his spirits. Neither did this young idiot who sat before him.

The kid couldn't have been any older than twenty-five, his slicked-back hair gleaming beneath the shadeless light. He was gobby and ardent, his double-breasted suit and the world in which he wore it unwittingly too big for him. He stared at Degsy, holding that annoying grin as he offered him a cigarette. Degsy shook his head and handed the kid an ashtray.

'Thanks,' the kid said and glanced across the room. 'I couldn't live with myself knowing that I'd dirtied the place. You've done so much with it.'

Degsy sighed. 'I try my best.'

The kid took a deep drag of his cigarette and blew the smoke up at the ceiling. 'Seems your best is no longer good enough.'

'Benny's been patient in the past. He knows I always pay up.'

'When you say *Benny*, I take it you mean Mr Bray? He told me you'd say that. We need to look to the future.'

'Did he tell you that, too?'

The kid sat up. 'Yeah, he did. He also said the past is the past. He's no time for the *used-to-be*.'

Degsy glanced at the empty whisky bottle on the sideboard. 'I'm just having a run of bad luck, that's all.'

The kid laughed. 'That's old news, Degsy. Most of the bookies across London could have told me that.'

'I'll get Benny his money.'

The kid shook his head, his eyes widening with exaggerated disbelief. 'And how are you going to do that, old man? You've got more chance of getting laid than coming into a windfall.'

'I've still got my contacts.'

'Such as? Everyone sees you as a bad debt. You've nothing to call in. What can you offer as collateral?' He scanned Degsy's shape, his eyes filled with furious disparagement. 'How old are you, late sixties?'

'I'll be fifty-nine this June.'

The kid dragged hard on his cigarette. 'Close enough. You must have had a hard life because I was being kind. To be honest, old-timer, I had you down as seventy.'

'I don't look that bad.'

The kid shrugged. 'Beauty's in the eye of the beholder, I guess. Maybe you don't look that bad, especially if a balding, pot-bellied, grey-haired old man is your kind of thing.'

Degsy stood up from the edge of the bed and clenched

his fists. 'Don't talk to me like that. Who the hell do you think you are?'

The kid stood. 'The name's Nick Bryant. But seeing as you will be working for me from now on, Mr Bryant will do.'

'*Mr Bryant,*' Degsy scoffed. 'What dream world are you living in, boy? You're just a bit of a kid. What makes you think I'd ever work for–'

Bryant lunged forward and stubbed his cigarette into Degsy's neck. The pain burned through his skin, anger urging him to retaliate, but Bryant dropped Degsy with three punches before he raised his hands.

Degsy lay on the floor. Dazed and bloodied, he listened to a high-pitch whistling sound. It sounded faint at first. Then, as his senses returned, he realised the noise came from the heaviness of his every breath. He reached for his false teeth and, with a trembling hand, placed them in his bloodied mouth. Tears welled in his eyes; his body was too weak to hide his embarrassment.

Bryant snapped his fingers. 'Get up, you old fool. I barely touched you.'

Degsy pressed his palms into the carpet. But no matter how hard he tried, he struggled to sit up.

Bryant grabbed Degsy's arms. 'For God's sake,' he said and lifted him onto the bed.

Degsy took a deep breath, then pointed at the sink. 'Pass me that bowl.'

'You do it.'

'I would if I could. Please, pass me that bowl.'

Bryant trudged over to the sink. 'It's full of junk.'

'Just tip them in the sink. Hurry, please. Before I puke all over myself.'

Bryant emptied the dirty cups and plates onto the draining board and tossed the grey plastic washing bowl on the bed. Degsy pulled it to his lap and stared down at it. Saliva flooded his mouth, and as the bile surged up his throat, he was unsure whether it was the beating or the putrid smell of dishwater that made him retch. He heaved out the contents of his stomach until there was nothing left. Whisky mostly, he'd hardly eaten for days, forcibly suppressing his appetite by chain-smoking cheap cigarettes. He wiped the tears from his eyes, catching Bryant's condescending smile.

'Look at the state of you,' Bryant said.

Even in Degsy's lowest moment, the kid spared him no humility. Degsy leaned back into the pillows. Lately, he'd had a few restless nights, but how he felt now, he could sleep for a week. He looked at Bryant, his heavy eyelids almost closing. 'I've got you to thank for that.'

Bryant grinned. 'You'll live.' He lit another cigarette, then threw the pack to Degsy. 'I went easy on you, to be fair. Think of it as a taster.' He slipped his hand into his inside pocket, took out his wallet, and plucked out a few notes. He tossed them onto the bed. 'Buy some whisky to lick your wounds. And have a wash and shave, for God's sake. This room isn't the only thing that's stinking.'

Degsy clawed a cigarette from the pack, flinching when Bryant threw him a light. Slowly, he placed it in his mouth. Then took out a match, striking it as though it were his last. He stared into the naked flame, drawing it close, the familiar smell of burnt tobacco nauseating. Taking a deep drag proved even worse. A rawness burned inside his throat. The emptiness inside his stomach and the lingering smoke cloud made him feel sicklier.

With a trembling hand, Degsy removed the cigarette from his mouth. He glanced across the scattering of notes. 'I don't want your money. Just leave me be.'

Bryant shook his head and sucked the air in through his teeth. 'Sorry, old-timer. I can't do that. You work for me now.'

Degsy let out a deep, exasperated sigh. 'Doing what exactly?'

Bryant shrugged. 'Running errands. A bit of this and that. All the things I'm far too busy to do.'

'And Benny's good with this?'

'It was Mr Bray's idea. I'm just following orders. I do as I'm told. You'd be wise to do the same; if you know what's good for you.'

'I'm going to speak with Benny first.'

Bryant nodded. 'Please yourself. But I wouldn't recommend it.'

Degsy agreed with silence. It didn't take a genius to know Bryant's recommendation rang true. As though reading Degsy's mind, Bryant grinned. 'Seems you're not that stupid after all.' A look of disbelief settled in his eyes. 'I was told you were quite the conman in your day. What the hell happened to you?' Bryant walked over to the door, opened it and stepped into the hall. He slowly turned around, watching Degsy from the open doorway. 'I'll be in touch. In the meantime, get yourself cleaned up.'

OVER THE YEARS, Degsy had taken more than his share of beatings. Running a con was never without risk. A black eye and a few broken ribs came with the territory. Yet, despite having more than his share of cuts and bruises, none left him feeling as low as this. He felt empty inside, a hollow shell with the guts torn out of it. A dark mood had plagued him for weeks, worsened by a run of bad luck and the residue of heavy drinking. But this was a different kind of low. It seeped beneath his skin, rooted to his bones, and weakened him to the core.

Degsy had spent the last ten minutes staring into the mirror, trying to shave. His head was all over the place, and having cut himself twice, he was making a lousy job of it. *That'll do,* he concluded with a sigh. Then he pulled out the plug, watching the bloodied soapsuds, peppered with grey whiskers, sink onto the basin as he drained the water. He dried his face with a dank-smelling towel, then tossed the stiff matted rag in the bin.

The wardrobe door opened with a tired creak, filling the air with a waft of mothballs. A year had passed since Degsy had worn his best suit. It hung like a knight's armour, waiting patiently for its master. There was a time when a double-breasted blazer with wide lapels seemed unfashionable. These days everyone was wearing them. Degsy lifted it from the rack. The clear plastic bag still covering it from when he'd last collected it from the dry cleaners. He rested it on the bed, then gathered up the scattered notes.

It had been ages since he'd clenched £100 in his fist. Money like this would keep him in drink for weeks. But he needed to remain sober to talk his way out of this one.

Degsy placed the wad of notes on the bed. He lifted his shirt from the chair and then wiped the tidemark off the collar with a damp cloth soaked in vinegar. *Clothes maketh the man,* his father always said, although no one seemed to have told Degsy's beaten old brogues about that. He would soon have them shining like new. Spit and polish were an undisputed saviour. When finished, he scoured the room for a fresh pair of socks, quickly realising the well-worn grubby ones on his feet were all he had. In times of need, a man had to make do. In his younger days, it was a philosophy that held him in good stead. But the older man struggled to cast his troubles aside, and with a heavy heart, he dressed.

Degsy didn't look that bad as he studied his reflection. A clean shave took years off him. The Brylcreem he used to slick back his hair gave it lustre and shine and made it darker. It was the best he'd looked in a while. But like his father always said, *self-praise was no recommendation*.

2

After three days of rain, the sun finally stopped sulking. It broke through the grey clouds, casting shadows as it shone across the glossy pavements. There was a freshness in the air. It lifted Degsy's spirits, turned his amble into a stride, and pushed him forward along Bayswater Road. The restaurants and cafes were in full swing, transients mostly spilling out from the cheap hotels in Queensway.

Bayswater had long lost its appeal. Degsy often questioned why he'd stayed here so long. A familiar face was quickly noticeable. Which was fine if you wanted to make friends but useless if you wanted to run a con. Not that any of Degsy's associates were worth knowing. They were mostly lowlifes and hustlers. Spending an hour in their company was enough to sway the most isolated soul towards the benefits of loneliness. Degsy had little choice. Being choosy in times as dire as these was an unattainable privilege.

Degsy held onto that thought as he entered Maggie's

Bar. It was like returning to the grave; the benefits from the afternoon sunshine diminished by this smoke-filled, dimly lit room. Degsy sat in the corner, eyeing the waitress as she hip-swayed her way over to his table.

'On a promise?' she said.

Degsy laughed. 'I should be so lucky.'

The waitress shot him a suggestive grin. 'Why are you all dressed up then?'

'A man doesn't always need a reason to look smart, you know.'

She rolled her eyes. 'In this place, he does. A clean shave and a whiff of aftershave means he's usually after something.'

Degsy remained silent, holding the pretty redhead's stare with his own when she asked, 'what are you drinking?'

'Tonic and lime.'

Her green eyes widened. 'Aren't you full of surprises?'

He placed a fiver on the table. 'You and the girls have a drink on me and fetch me a pack of cigarettes.'

She snatched the money as though he was about to change his mind, dropping her smile when Degsy asked, 'Is Clate about?'

'He's out the back somewhere. I'll let him know you're asking for him.'

Degsy flashed her a smile. 'That would be grand. Could you let him know it's urgent?'

She responded with a doubting nod, then hip-swayed her way back to the bar. Degsy glanced at his watch. Sat here at three-thirty on a Wednesday afternoon was scraping the barrel even by his standards. He took in the room, seeing the wretchedness of his own situation reflected in the tired, drunk-beaten faces. Except for French Susan, he couldn't put a name to any of them. Not that it mattered. He was inches away from defeat, unable to maintain this charade for long. A few more knocks, and he would be whisky-soaking his sorrows with the rest of them.

Degsy tapped his finger on the table and looked towards the bar. He glanced at his watch. Then tapped the table again. Repeating the routine until he saw the wondrous sight of the redheaded waitress walking towards him. He flashed her his warmest smile, his heart beating thickly as she placed his drink on the beer mat. She tossed the pack of cigarettes onto his lap. 'You weren't expecting any change, right?'

'Apparently not,' Degsy said with a wry smile. 'Did you tell Clate I was asking for him?'

'He said he'd come over later.'

'How much later?'

The waitress shrugged. 'Your guess is as good as mine. You know what he's like.' She shot him a sad smile. 'I wouldn't hold my breath if I were you.' She leaned in closer. 'Why don't you go somewhere nice. You're dressed too smart for this place.'

Degsy shrugged off the compliment. 'I really need to speak with Clate first, perhaps later.' He tore off the plastic covering from the pack, took out a cigarette and held it to his mouth. 'Did he say how long he'd be? I don't have much time, you know.'

The waitress shook her head and then walked away. Degsy put the unlit cigarette behind his ear, followed the waitress to the bar, and then through one of the side doors with a gold-plated sign that said *Private*. The wide stainless-steel kitchen glinted beneath the bright fluorescent light. The place felt hot and sticky, tainted by the lingering smell of cooking oil and bacon fat.

Clate leaned on the counter, flicking through the *Racing News*, occasionally glancing up at the window.

When the waitress caught sight of Degsy, she flashed him a look that was a mix of sadness and irritation.

'Degsy Dempster wants to speak with you,' she sighed.

Without turning around, Clate shook his head. 'For God's sake, Mary, I haven't time for that old fool. I told you to get rid of him.'

'Don't blame the girl,' Degsy said. 'Some old fools can't take no for an answer.'

Clate closed the paper and turned around. A wide smile slapped across his handsome face. 'Degsy. Degsy. I knew you were there. I could smell that cheap cologne a mile away.' He reached into his shirt pocket and pulled out a pack of Castellas. He offered one to Degsy, and after Degsy politely refused, he took a cigar and placed it into his mouth. Clate patted his pockets. 'Can you believe it? Stood in a kitchen, and I can't even get a light.'

Degsy took out his box of matches and stepped forward. 'Here, let me sort that.'

Clate drew on his cigar as its tip touched the match's flame, and once it was lit, both men exchanged glances. 'So, Mr Dempster, what can I do for you?'

Degsy cleared his throat. 'I want to talk to you about a job.'

'I thought you were retired?'

'A brief hiatus, needs must and all that.'

Clate nodded. 'Come on then, let's hear it.'

Degsy looked at the waitress. 'No offence meant, Mary. But I'd rather discuss it privately if that's okay with you?'

'No offence taken,' Mary said, and scuttled out.

Clate stood over six feet tall, ruggedly handsome, and tanned, his curly dark hair peppered with grey. There was no doubt he was a fine specimen. But for all his charms, a hint of danger lurked behind his eyes, and his big shoulders and those shovel-like hands always made Degsy uneasy. It had nothing to do with Degsy being overanxious. Clate's broken nose and scattering of facial scars came from a well-earned reputation.

Clate dragged on his cigar. 'Come on, Degsy. Time's money and all that. Don't keep a man waiting.'

Degsy swallowed against the dry lump inside his throat. 'I'm planning a big con. It needs people and finance. I was hoping you could help with that.'

Clate flashed him a condescending smile. 'Carry on, I'm listening.'

Degsy leaned against the counter. 'I was thinking we could use your club as a store.'

Clate frowned. 'A *store*?'

Degsy blushed. 'Sorry, I was using grifter-speak, a store as in putting on a front to lure in marks, so we–'

Clate cut across him with a deep sigh. 'Oh, that kind of *store*.' He rolled his eyes. 'So what are you thinking?'

'A fake gambling club,' Degsy said. 'We could use one of your function rooms to run a weekly brace. We need a few people, a couple of ropers to lure in the marks, and a few shills to get them greedy. But I'd sort all that. I'd be the manager.'

Clate shook his head. 'And what's my part in all this?'

'Firstly, you'll earn an easy cut. All you have to do is supply the room and add some convincing decor to ensure everything looks legit.'

Clate stared at Degsy in silence for a moment, and then the big man threw back his head and roared with laughter. 'Poor old Degsy. You're living in the past. The days of those types of cons are far behind us. Drug money's a steady earner, and the strip clubs and peep shows down Soho. Grifters like you are few and far between. The best conmen now are all legit. If you want a big con, run a Timeshare, or play the stock market. That's what the real players are doing these days.'

In his day, no one would have spoken to Degsy like this. He was always a top earner, living the good life when Clate was a snot-nosed kid. Not that he dared to speak out. Experience had taught him to hide his grievances behind a smile. Clate was mistaken. Nothing had changed. The wrongs men do might have become more sophisticated. But a crime was a crime, and the world was never too old for any type of con.

'If the stock market's more your thing,' Degsy said. 'We could skip the brace, still use the same setup, but run a rag instead.'

Clate shook his head.

Degsy flashed him a sad smile. 'Okay, but will you at least think about it?'

Clate nodded.

'Not too long, mind. I've other people to see. An idea like this is bound to be snapped up.'

Clate inched over to Degsy and rested a clammy hand on his shoulder. 'Bound to be, so I won't waste your time giving it any more consideration. The answer's still no, and I'd hate to deny anyone else the privilege.'

Degsy sighed. 'That's a real shame. You're missing out on a great opportunity.'

Clate took a deep drag of his cigar and blew the smoke towards Degsy. 'Oh, Degsy, if only that was the case. I've got creditors hammering at my door. Unless you can give me the winner for the three-ten at Epsom, I need something with more certainty. The money from those types of cons is mere droppings. I need a big, quick windfall to solve my problems.'

Clate slapped Degsy on the back. 'Anyway, I've stuff to do, so that's about it for this conversation. You're a good sort, and I know you wouldn't want to make me angry.' He stepped ahead, opened the kitchen door, and gestured towards a wedge of light. 'You take care, Degsy. And the best of luck with everything.'

Degsy mumbled a response and trudged through the doorway, glancing over his shoulder when Clate called after him. 'Yeah,' he said, conscious of the sad desperation in his voice.

Clate smiled. 'Tell them Clate's given you an open bar. Enjoy a day of free drinks.'

Degsy replied with a nod of thanks, undecided what cut him more, the condescending smile or the blatant sympathy.

THE SUN'S high spirits were short-lived because when Degsy stepped outside, it was raining. Not that it surprised him. These days dull clouds tainted with misfortune were to be expected. The traffic streamed past him unnoticed, his thoughts lost in better times as countless tube rides blended into one. Along the central, circle and district lines, Degsy studied his reflection; he looked grey and defeated, like the strangers' faces sat alongside him. The train rumbled through the tunnels, his aching body and that false optimism quickly tiring.

He must have visited at least six clubs, having a drink or two in each. The smell of whisky haunted him like a curse. It reminded him of every rejection, as did the insatiable thirst inside his throat. Sweat trickled down his back. The promise offered by a clean shave had withered, its memory tarnished by a stiff shirt collar rubbing his skin.

Degsy closed his eyes, feeling the pang of humiliation with every sudden burst of laughter. How was he to know that Pie-and-Mash Freddie was dead, The Red Lady Kid, Bermondsey Sue? He never would have traipsed after them if he'd known. Admittedly, he'd been out of the game for a while. But they were good friends of his. Folk knew that. They should have had the decency to let him know.

After four long hours of belittling himself, Degsy had had enough. Self-pity came cheap, like the whisky in this godforsaken place. It wasn't one of his usual haunts. An Irish bar just off Paddington Green, which he'd stumbled onto by chance. The place was packed, mostly with kids, loud and unabashed, self-awareness not their forte. Music blared from the bar into the lounge. Degsy was unable to distinguish one tune from the next. Perhaps this was a glimpse of purgatory, doomed to endure the same endless song. Kids had it easy these days. They didn't know squat. Degsy had learned the hard way. He'd worked on cons with his old man since he was eight.

Back then, all you needed was a Ha'penny Store to draw in a mark, and thirty minutes later, their money was spent, with some of them foolish enough to thank you for the privilege. Degsy's dad was the master of the Three-card Monte. He slapped three cards face down on the counter and challenged them to find the Queen. At first, it would start as a joke to pass the time while they eyed the bargains. Then, when money got involved, he drew them in.

Degsy played the shill, a cocky ragamuffin kid conniving with the unwitting victim to watch the cards, then marking the Queen when his dad turned a blind eye.

Degsy's father marked a different card with the deftness of his hand, and the victim, convinced he knew where the Queen was, lay down his bets. But when the cards didn't play as he expected, he spent a fortune trying to figure out why.

That con was a great little earner for years, and Degsy would have played it forever, given a chance. After clearing the store, he would lie on the sofa, a glass of cold milk resting on his lap, and watch his old man count the day's takings. His father had an excellent head for figures. He never missed a penny until his memory ran out on him. Degsy refused to think about that, preferring to picture his old man in his heyday. If the day had proved profitable, his father celebrated by playing Degsy a tune on the ukulele. He wasn't the best of players. But every string was plucked with soul. And his rendition of *Willie O' Winsbury* was enough to melt even the coldest heart.

Degsy wiped a tear from his eye and sighed into his empty glass. He grimaced as he stretched his neck. These stiff old bones seemed stuck in a constant ache. The pain was a hindrance at the best of times, even more so in a world that moved too fast and was ever-changing.

Degsy pushed himself up from his seat, walking towards the bar with the forced restraint of a drunk trying hard to look sober. The girl serving watched him through amused eyes. Degsy stared at her, undeterred, pointing down at his glass when she asked, 'What can I get you?'

He drank the whisky as though it was his last, and before he could order another, some kid barged in front of him.

'Hey,' Degsy protested. 'I was here first.'

The kid turned to face him, his eyes concealed behind a pair of mirrored sunglasses. He flashed Degsy a smile.

'Okay, mate, no need to get upset; simmer down, for God's sake.'

'*You* simmer down. And I'm not *your* mate.'

The kid removed his sunglasses and answered with a fierce glare. He looked to be in his early to mid-twenties. Strictly speaking, he was a grown man. But anyone under forty looked young to Degsy these days. Degsy held the kid's stare with his own. He was at that stage now. Caution and wisdom were abandoned by hours of constant drinking. Whisky made men brave, opened the filters in the brain, and allowed a foolish tongue to do the talking. These had always been strange moments in Degsy's life. A part of him knew he was drunk. But a more assertive voice urged him on, aggressive and unabashed, forcing his other self to be an observer, pushing it further into the distance.

'Stop looking at me like that,' Degsy said. 'Do something if you have a problem.'

The kid and the barmaid shared a glance, and after a furtive nod from the girl, the kid moved further down the bar, throwing Degsy one last look before turning his back on him. Degsy responded with a triumphant grin. The sense of victory was short-lived. No sooner had the girl poured his drink than she politely informed him it was his last.

'And why would that be?' Degsy asked.

She looked quite beautiful when she smiled. 'I think you've had enough, don't you?'

Degsy didn't have the strength to disagree. Plenty of other places would serve him. He answered her with a nod, downed his drink in one gulp, and slapped a pound note on the bar. 'Keep the change,' he said as she motioned towards the till.

The brief journey from the bar to the pub door proved more difficult than Degsy expected. He was unsteady on his feet. A man whose drunken merriments lay on the cusp of sickness. Somehow, he traipsed outside, taking in the cold, damp air, showing contempt for the endless rain with a loud, indignant belch.

Degsy inched along the glossy pavement. His suit was almost soaked through. He would drown before he reached another pub at this rate. Like most drunks, a dogged determination urged him on. He turned his collar up in defiance, raising a finger to the passing cars who mockingly beeped their horns. Sheltering in an alleyway offered a brief respite, and with a shaky hand, Degsy even managed to light a cigarette. The smoke burned against the rawness in his chest. He swayed from side to side, gazing aimlessly at the blur of neon shop signs and the hazy glow of the streetlights.

With his eyes closed, smoking that cigarette felt dream-like. The ebb and flow of the traffic washed over him. Voices faded in and out. Then a firm hand rested on his shoulder, and a familiar voice said, 'are you all right?'

Degsy had barely opened his eyes when a punch to the jaw put him on his arse. Someone grabbed his ankles, dragging him further into the alleyway. Muddy gravel scrapped across his cheek. He raised his arms to get up, but a swift kick in the ribs quickly put him on his back. Whisky did little to numb the pain, and each blow to the head blurred his senses. He heard himself cry out, his voice hoarse, pathetic as if it were a million miles away.

Warm beer-laced breath breezed across his skin. 'You need to learn some manners, old man. Keep your mouth shut. Stop jumping the queue.'

Degsy opened his eyes and lay like a helpless child beneath the cruel youthful face peering down at him.

'You're disgusting,' the kid said.

Tears streamed down Degsy's face, not because of the lad's words but from the big wet patch around Degsy's crotch. Degsy let out a deep breath, wishing it to be his last. He shut his eyes and thought about those long-dead summers, the distant whisper of his father's voice drowning among the shame and the humiliation.

3

L aney lay on the bed while Jay put on his shirt. It had become a ritual of theirs: Jay facing the mirror, catching glimpses of the contented look on her face while she watched him dress. It was a nice touch, to begin with, although, like everything else about them, it lulled into a routine, and Jay soon grew tired of it.

As a rule, Jay never fooled around with someone else's wife, let alone the man who employed him. Having always been a sucker for lost causes, Laney's blue eyes, aided by the sob stories, quickly lured Jay in. He studied her reflection in the mirror. Her long legs were smooth and tanned; her blonde curls shone beneath a wash of light. On the surface, she was most men's dream come true. Jay found her needy and changeable, and the cuts on her arms told another story.

Jay needed little convincing the first time Laney told him what her husband had done. Gangland boss Terry Jackmond was well-groomed and polite, but Jay knew the darkness behind his smile. Men like Jackmond took what they wanted. They were brutal and unforgiving. Traits that Jay suffered in silence. Every vocation came with a downside. Cruelty and violence were part of the territory.

Only this time, his assumptions had been premature. If Nash had taught him anything, it was never to take things at face value. In fairness to Laney, she'd reeled him in. Until one day, he'd crept back into her apartment after forgetting his wallet and caught her self-harming. He'd watched her from the shadows, the bathroom door ajar, the gap wide enough to reveal the smoothness of her skin bloodied by the razor's slice.

Jay kept it to himself, and as he sat on the edge of the bed, rolling on his socks, he noticed recent cuts across her hip. Laney caught his glance, smoothing her hand down her thigh, a forlorn look on her face, eager for it to draw attention.

Jay aided his pretence with a sigh. 'Why do you let him do that?'

Laney managed a hint of poignancy in her smile. 'It keeps him quiet. He lets me stick around while he's still getting a thrill out of it.' She glanced down at the cut. 'It's not as bad as it looks. These things soon heal.'

For all her faults, Laney knew how to spin a good lie. Without a doubt, Jackmond believed anything she told him. She duped Jay for a while too, and inwardly, without having caught her in the act, he tried reassuring himself that sooner or later, he would have cottoned on.

Even now, she held onto her story. The crackle in her voice and the low sheen in her eyes were so convincing that Jay wondered if even she had started to believe it?

Laney held back her tears with a sigh. 'Terry's golfing this weekend. Are we still okay for Saturday?'

Jay tucked in his shirt and slipped on his cream leather loafers without answering. They went well with his light grey Armani suit. As he folded his tie, Laney tapped him on the back. 'Hey, handsome, are you listening to me, or are you too busy admiring yourself?'

Jay pretended to give it some thought. 'Saturday's out, I'm afraid. My Auntie Beverley's visiting to celebrate my mam and Desmond's anniversary.'

'Can't you give it a miss?'

Jay shook his head. 'Sorry, no can do. Auntie Bev looked after me when things were rough. Mam wants me there. Desmond has been a positive influence on her life. She's been clean since they met, almost seven years now.'

Laney rolled her eyes. 'Whoopee. An alcohol-free party. It sounds quite the celebration.'

Jay stood. 'You spoil yourself when you do that.'

'Do *what*?'

'Bad-mouthing things, belittling people, trust me, it does you no favours.'

She responded with an exaggerated pout. 'I just want you all to myself,' she said in a childish voice.

Jay turned to face her. 'We need to talk about that.'

Laney sat up, more handsome now than pretty, with that pensive look on her face. 'Sounds serious, go on.'

Jay raked his fingers through his hair. 'Terry spoke to me about you,' he lied. 'He said he was worried. Asked if I knew anything about new friends. He hinted that he'd appreciate it if I kept an eye on you.'

Laney narrowed her eyes. 'I find that difficult to believe. He's not the jealous type.'

'Really,' Jay said, nodding at one of her cuts, 'wouldn't you call that kind of behaviour controlling?'

He'd cornered her with her own lie, knowing she had little choice but to play along.

'Oh, it's only a few scratches,' she said. 'They'll soon heal up.'

Jay studied her for a moment, averting his gaze as she covered herself with the sheet. 'It's pretty messed up if you ask me. You should see someone about that.'

'Like who? It's not as if I can go crying to the police.'

Jay didn't answer.

'Like who?' she persisted.

Jay shrugged. 'I suppose you're right,' he said, tempted to suggest she should see a psychiatrist, although experience kept his mouth shut. He sat beside her on the bed, holding her hand. 'I'm worried about you.'

'Well, don't; Terry doesn't know squat. Let him ask his questions.' She stroked his neck with her finger. 'It's good that he's asked you to keep an eye on me. I'll get to see more of you.'

Jay glanced down at the carpet. 'That's what I want to talk to you about. We should ease off for a while, lie low for a bit.'

She snatched her hand away, grazing his skin with her nails. 'Oh, so that's what this is all about. You're dumping me.'

'I'm not dumping you.'

She let the sheet fall from her body and stood. 'What is it then?' She stomped across the floor, and Jay chased after her as she went into the bathroom. He stood in the doorway, admiring her sleek tanned body while she rinsed her face in the sink. He could have watched her all day, basking in the dapples of sunlight across her hair, the sheen of perspiration across her skin. Jay had a thing for blondes, and he didn't have to dig too deep to know why.

Laney watched his reflection in the mirror and, with the hint of a smile, said, 'What the hell are you gawping at?'

'Just admiring the scene.'

'I find that hard to believe. Now you want nothing more to do with me.'

'I never said that.'

'Not directly, no, but that's what you meant.'

'All I was saying–'

She sprayed deodorant under her arms, down the nape of her back, and then pushed past him. He turned to face her, watching while she put on her panties and slipped into her dress. Jay glanced across at the bedside cabinet. 'Don't you think Terry might suspect something if you go back with no bra on?'

'*No bra on*,' she scoffed. 'I've had my hair done three times this month, and he hasn't noticed.' She shot him a fierce look. 'Not that you care.'

'All I said was–'

'You've said too much. I'm not some one-night stand you can dump whenever you please. I've taken a lot of risks for you.'

'And that's the point, Laney, let's not take any more before things turn nasty.'

'Listen to yourself. How stupid do you think I am? Terry never said a word. *Keep an eye on me. Who am I seeing*? That's as farfetched as–'

'As what,' Jay interrupted, 'as you self-harming.'

Laney picked up the empty wine bottle from the coffee table and threw it at Jay's face. Luckily, he was quick enough to duck, but as the bottle smashed against the wall, he felt shards of glass prickle across his skin.

'Get out,' Laney screamed. 'Get out, I said, before I do something I regret.'

Jay had the good sense not to disagree. After checking for his wallet and watch, he made a sharp exit out of the hotel room. Laney's insults hounded him down the corridor. 'Who the hell do you think you are?' she cried. 'You better watch yourself, Jay Ellis. I'll teach you not to make a fool out of me.'

IT WAS common knowledge Jay drove too fast. A collection of speeding fines swore testament to it. It felt like a crawl driving through those Liverpudlian streets. After passing through the Mersey tunnel, he drove a steady eighty. The righthand lane was his for the taking, his mind distracted by Laney's threats, oblivious to the other cars as he whizzed past.

He pictured the look in her eyes when he'd left. Only a fool would have missed their dark intention. Confession cleansed the soul, and, for a woman spurned, revenge was the sweetest thing.

Jay disliked Terry Jackmond at first sight. Jackmond was bullish and single-minded. A man who fed off fear, disrupting people's lives, either directly or through an imminent threat. Those who lived a law-abiding life most likely had never heard of him. Grifters like Jay lived on the edge of things. In this dark periphery, men like Jackmond and the sordidness surrounding them were part of the everyday.

Jackmond first introduced himself to Jay one night at the Grosvenor Casino. Jay had a good run at Blackjack, and a small group had gathered around his table. Hours later, Jay was invited to the VIP lounge to join Terry Jackmond for drinks.

'It seems it's your lucky night,' Jackmond said. He never accused Jay of being a cheat, but his dark eyes were loaded with accusations.

Jay was only a few hundred up, and coupled with the present company, it wasn't such a great night. The first thing that struck him about Jackmond was his appearance. The man certainly knew how to dress. A tailored three-piece suit helped him to stand out, and with the gorgeous Laney at his side, his every mannerism was lifted by heightened confidence. He spoke as though no one else mattered. He was a man oblivious to the lives he intruded on; any notion of others' suffering was beyond him. Even if they dared to protest, their cries would be drowned beneath his inflated sense of self-importance.

Jackmond was king of his world, and when he said, 'I might have some work for you,' Jay realised he was now a part of it.

'I've no ambition to be a croupier,' Jay said with a smile.

Jackmond nodded. 'That's a shame. A good-looking kid like you could make a lot of money from it.' He studied Jay for a moment. 'So, what is your kind of thing?'

Jay shrugged. 'I don't know; it depends on what you're offering.'

Jackmond laughed, and Jay couldn't decide what was more menacing, its raucous bellow or the way it came to an abrupt stop. 'You've got gall. I'll grant you that.' He popped a cigarette into his mouth, tilting his head slightly as one of his goons gave him a light. 'I've seen you before. Under sixteens Welsh Amateur Boxing.'

'That was a while back.'

'It wasn't that long ago. You weren't that bad. Up and coming by all accounts.'

'Just a fad,' Jay said. He shot one of the goons a glance. 'I learnt from an early age it's important to be able to handle yourself.'

'Fancy your chances, do you?'

'I never said that.'

'You didn't need to.' Jackmond took a deep drag of his cigarette and blew the smoke up at the chandelier lights. 'So why do you play the cards? Are you one of those poker losers, burning your winnings for the thrill?'

'Money, of course. Cards are just a means to an end.'

Jackmond grinned. 'Glad to hear it. That's the smartest thing you've said all night.' He flicked the ash from his cigarette. 'Come here tomorrow. There are a few serious players I'd like you to keep an eye on. I've got my suspicions. It'll be a great test for someone as flashy as you. Something to get you started.'

Jay watched the card sharps for the first few weeks, spending less time on it as Jackmond grew more convinced. Errands became Jay's thing. The friendlier face of pre-warning negotiations. A big responsibility for one so young. Jackmond took a shine to him, although the disbelievers were less gracious. Suspicion ran rife, and there was no fondness to their words as they whispered, '*here comes Terry's right-hand man.*'

Jay took the knocks in his stride. He never set out to deceive. Not that he held Jackmond in any esteem. Since their first encounter, Laney had chased after him. He refused her at first. Then he gave in, mostly because she was so sure of herself. There was no doubting her beauty. But she reminded him too much of Mich. Blondes brought nothing but trouble, and Mich and Laney were two good reasons to start thinking about leaving this place.

4

———

Jay's mother, Renee, could never be described as house proud. She'd tried hard these last few years, and although it was no palace, the house was tidy, and the added touches of flowers and a fruit bowl on the table made the place feel homely. She dressed differently, too. These days she wore pastel-coloured shell suits, a tad garish for Jay's taste but better than the denim shorts and tight vests she wore ten years ago.

She rarely spoke about their time on the Moor Estate. Renee lived with Desmond in his semi-detached. It felt like a different world even though it was only streets away. Jay found it more difficult to forget. He felt no emotion regarding his mother's old boyfriend, Shane's death. The man was cowardly and mean. Anyone who tries to hurt a kid deserves what they get. Mich lingered in his thoughts from time to time, although the face that haunted him most belonged to Nash.

Nash drifted through Jay's dreams. The image of that tall, rugged man with his 50s hairstyle and tan linen suit held Jay spellbound when he least expected it. Memories were all he had, their time spent along the estuary and Nash's pocket diary that Jay kept as a keepsake.

In moments of quiet reflection, Jay caught his mother's glance. 'You don't have to be like *him,* you know,' she'd say, as though she knew exactly what he was thinking. She was watching Jay now; the pair of them sat at the kitchen table, a worried look in her eyes while she stirred her tea.

'I know I'm beautiful,' Jay joked. 'But you don't need to keep staring at me.'

Renee flashed him a smile. 'I'll stop if you tell me what's wrong?'

Jay frowned. 'I'm fine.'

'No, you're not. I could see that the moment you walked in.'

He raked his fingers through his hair. 'I'm a bit tired, that's all.'

'Tired from what?'

'Oh, this and that.'

Renee shook her head. '*This* and *that* has blonde hair, no doubt.'

Jay laughed. 'Your trouble is you worry too much.' He reached into his pocket and took out a black velvet pendant gift box. He placed it in his mother's hand. 'Today isn't about me. It's about you. Come on, smile. Bev will be here soon. I thought today was supposed to be a party?'

Renee opened the box, took out the gold necklace and held it in her fist. 'You're too good for the life you lead.' Tears welled in her eyes. 'I should have been a better Mam to you.'

'It doesn't pay to dwell on the past.' Jay stood, slipped off his jacket and hung it over the back of the chair. He walked over to the sink and gazed through the kitchen window. 'What did you mean by the *life I lead*? I'm doing pretty good if you ask me.'

'Depends on what you mean by *good*.' Renee paused. 'Edna Bailey told me you're working at the Grosvenor Casino.'

Jay shut his eyes and sighed. 'Is that old busybody still alive, poking her nose into people's business.'

'Well, are you?'

Jay turned to face her. 'A few days a week. A man's got to pay his way.'

'There are better ways of making a living. Desmond said they're taking people on at his place.'

Jay shook his head and laughed. 'That's great news for some.' He flashed her a wide smile. 'Can you imagine me making furniture with Marshall and his dopes? I wouldn't last more than an hour in that factory.'

Renee nodded. 'I suppose you're right. Be a lot safer, though.'

'Don't worry,' Jay said. 'The casino job's coming to an end. I've been thinking about moving on.'

'To where?'

Jay shrugged. 'Don't know, might try down south.'

'London, you mean. Why on earth do you want to go there?'

Before Jay could respond, he heard a key turning inside a lock. The front door shuddered as it hit the wall, and the familiar sound of Auntie Bev's voice resonated through the hallway. Both Jay and Renee hurried out to meet her.

Bev was a large woman. She'd grown bigger over the years, and with her arms outstretched, she had plenty of room to greet them. Jay felt her warm bosom against his chest. She kept pecking him on the cheek, the smell of hairspray and the musky fragrance of her perfume taking him years back. Desmond stood behind her. He acknowledged

Jay with a wary nod, seemingly happy to loiter in Bev's shadow.

Renee guided her sister into the lounge. Desmond trudged behind them while Jay remained in the hall. 'Come and sit beside me,' Bev shouted.

'I'll take your stuff upstairs first,' Jay said, happy to be away from the fuss.

Jay stood on the landing after putting Bev's case in the spare bedroom. All these houses looked the same; with his mother's words lingering in his mind, his thoughts drifted further into the past. Even though it was only ten years ago, that troubled thirteen-year-old boy seemed worlds away. He wondered what he would make of his older self. Not too much, probably. Kids called out the pretence in people. What would he see? A young man trying to be something he wasn't or a cool guy with his act together?

Jay shook his head and smiled. Mothers had the knack of seeing right through you. Maybe he was trying too hard to be like Nash? He suppressed the notion with a sigh. Nostalgia was an older man's indulgence. Not that he got the opportunity to reminisce. He was quickly brought back to the present by Bev shouting his name. 'Jay, Jay,' she kept calling, 'get yourself down here. We're all ready to eat.'

The moment Jay stepped into the lounge, his Auntie handed him a fistful of notes. 'Here,' she said.

Jay frowned.

'It's for the food,' Bev said. 'Your mother insists on cooking.' She flashed Renee a smile. 'But I'd rather not take the chance. Jay, drive to town and fetch us a Chinese takeaway. One of those banquets for four.'

'Anything else?' Jay said sarcastically.

'Get some extras, I suppose, prawn crackers, spareribs if you like.'

'Sure,' Jay said. He handed the money back to Bev. 'But it's my treat. I'll pay for this.'

JAY HAD one foot out of the car when the green Saab 900 pulled up alongside him. Being distracted by Bev's arrival was a lame excuse; in Jay's line of work, stopping in a deserted car park was a clear sign of someone who wasn't thinking. *Mistakes cost lives*, Jackmond always said, although judging by the grim-looking men standing on either side of the car, he didn't seem too concerned for Jay's survival.

'All right, la,' the permed one said. 'Thought we were going to waste hours looking for you.'

Jay eased his foot back into the car and shut the driver's door. He flicked down the locks and gradually wound down the window. The perm's name was Mocksy, and his shaven-headed accomplice was known as Squilt. Jay had only spoken to them a few times. Mostly they just glared at him, strutting around the Casino with the rest of Jackmond's crew.

'What do you want?' Jay asked.

Mocksy grinned. 'You're a popular man.'

'I must be for you to come this far out. I thought you lads get nose bleeds if you wander too far from the Mersey.'

Mocksy pulled on the door handle. 'Gerrout.'

Jay shook his head. 'I'll stay where I am if that's okay.'

'Na, it's not. Gerrout, I said. Terry wants to speak with ya.'

Jay slipped the key into the ignition. 'Terry will have to wait till Monday. Weekends are my own. Why the rush? What's all this about?'

Mocksy kicked the driver's door. 'You know what it's about, you sly little shit.'

Jay started the engine. 'No, sorry. I haven't got a clue what you're talking about?'

Mocksy slipped his hand through the gap in the window, his greasy, tattooed fingers distracting Jay long enough for Squilt to move the Saab and block him in. Jay watched the Saab from his rearview mirror. He weighed the odds as he revved the engine, wondering if there was any benefit in reversing straight into him. The noise would draw attention, causing a nosey neighbour to call the police. The question was when? Where was Edna Bailey when you most needed her?

Jay didn't want to waste any time. Waiting too long often resulted in missed chances. He swung open the car door and slammed it into Mocksy's shin. As Mocksy's dull mind registered the pain, Jay punched him, keeping him down with a swift, hard kick in the balls. Mocksy's hard man reputation was seemingly undeserved, and for a second, Jay wondered how it had been so easy. Squilt appeared equally perplexed. Petrified by indecision, he stared at Jay through the dirty windscreen. A stupid look settled on his face as though he was expecting Jay to give him further instructions.

Squilt's hesitancy didn't last long. He didn't appear that concerned for Mocksy's welfare, throwing his Buddy a fleeting glance before reversing the Saab the length of the car park. Squilt glared at him, then drove away at the sound of a distant siren.

If only it was as easy as that. But this evening's escapade confirmed Jay's fears. Laney had sold Jackmond her story. A sad and troubled tale, no doubt. Where Laney was the unfortunate victim of a young chancer, a treacherous one at that.

Jay tapped Mocksy with his foot. 'Come on, sit up. I barely touched you.'

Mocksy sat hunched on the tarmac, pinching the soft part of his nose and smearing the blood across his chest. 'You shouldn't have done that, la. You're a dead man walking.'

'Is that right? You don't look in any fit state to make threats.'

Mocksy grinned. 'Not me. Jackmond's got people all over the shop. You'll be dead and forgotten before the end of the week.'

Jay listened as the siren drew closer. A police car wailed past, and Jay, his heart pounding inside his chest, watched until it drove off into the distance. Mocksy's expression shared Jay's relief. Jay studied him for a second. 'What's this all about?'

Mocksy shook his head and laughed. 'As if you didn't know.'

Jay shook his head. 'I haven't got a clue.'

'Come off it, la. You need to keep that dick of yours in your pants. If shagging Jackmond's missus isn't bad enough, you had to take it too far.' Mocksy narrowed his eyes. 'I knew there was something off about you. I give my missus a slap now and then, but I don't go cutting her with a knife.'

Jay closed his eyes and sighed. 'And everyone believes that?'

Mocksy got to his feet. 'Look how you reacted.'

'You threatened me. I defended myself.' Jay observed as Mocksy let his arms hang loose at his sides. His left hand slipped into his pocket, and Jay caught the perm-haired grunt with an uppercut before he reached his knife. Jay left him on the ground, throwing him one quick glance to ensure he was still breathing.

Jay got into his car and started the engine. This time, leaving town felt different. He'd been threatening to go for years. He wondered if Nash had experienced the same feelings all those years ago? As he drove, the distant estuary shone through the trees, the vast sky as vacant as the emptiness inside him, and Jay wondered if he was ever coming back.

5

————

At first, the relentless banging on the front door formed part of Degsy's dream. It started as a muted thud, growing louder as it gained momentum. Degsy placed the pillow over his face trying his best to ignore it. He glanced at his cracked watch. What could be so urgent at eight o'clock on a Sunday morning? It was probably one of the kids from the flat downstairs locking themselves out. Degsy threw back the eiderdown, slowly moving his stiff, aching body, and sat at the edge of the bed. He felt the morning's chill across his feet and squinted at the sunlight gleaming through his only window.

Degsy ignored the mirror when he walked past. Catching sight of himself only brought it all back. He rubbed his thumb across the swelling on his right eye. Even that took effort after spraining his wrist in that alleyway.

'All right,' he shouted as the knocking continued. 'I'm coming; keep your bloody hair on.'

Degsy covered himself with his old, monogrammed paisley gown. He'd bought it years ago during a lucky spell. It was a lavish spend. Something to wear during his retirement, to complement his chequered slippers and glass of vintage cognac. He suppressed the memory with a sigh and then trudged downstairs, the pain in his joints intensifying with every step. He pried open the front door. It stiffened in the cooler months, especially after the rain.

Degsy stood hunched in the doorway, the cold air prickling his skin. 'What do you want?' He said to the handsome young face smiling back at him. 'You'll wake the dead banging like that. Anyone would think you were trying to knock the door in.'

The kid gave him a look of friendly concern. 'I'm sorry about that. It wasn't my intention.'

Degsy nodded with a grunt. 'What do you want?'

'I'm looking for Degsy Dempster; does he still live here?'

'And who are you?'

The kid held out his hand. 'Jay Ellis, I'm a close associate of a man called Nash. I'm looking up some old friends of his.'

Degsy refused to shake the kid's hand. 'You're a bit late, aren't you? Nash was dead last I heard, a while back, more than ten years ago.'

The kid nodded. 'Sadly, yes. It's only now I'm able to catch up with people. I was very young at the time.'

Degsy threw the kid a scathing look. 'You're not that much older now.' He shivered against the cold. 'And why the hell are you seeking out his so-called old friends? Nash was hardly Mr Popular.'

'I couldn't comment on that,' the kid said, then slipped his hand into his jacket and took out a black pocket diary. He waved it in front of him. 'All the names in here suggest otherwise.'

Degsy grimaced. 'And Mr Dempster's name is in that?'

The kid nodded. 'Does he still live here?'

Degsy shook his head. 'He moved out years ago.'

'Interesting,' the kid said. 'Do you know where I can find him?'

Degsy shrugged. 'Your guess is as good as mine.'

'You don't know where he is?'

'Nope. I haven't got a clue.'

The kid regarded him for a moment. 'I'm staying at the Regal in Bayswater.'

Degsy chuckled. 'There's nothing regal about that dump.'

'It's cheap enough.'

'It's certainly that. You keep your clothes on in bed in that place.'

The kid smiled. 'I'll bear that in mind. Give me a shout if you hear anything.'

Degsy gave him a mock salute. 'Sure thing, boss. Trust me, you'll be the first to know.'

'Thanks. That's much appreciated.' He pointed at Degsy's gown. 'That's a nice piece of silk.'

'This old thing. I've had it years now.'

'Interesting,' the kid said. 'Quality like that is hard to come by these days.' He pointed at the two big D's emblazoned across Degsy's chest. 'Especially with the embroidered initials like that. What does DD stand for?'

Degsy gave him a stern look, then slammed the door in the kid's face.

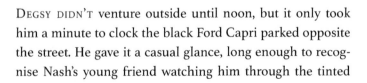

DEGSY DIDN'T venture outside until noon, but it only took him a minute to clock the black Ford Capri parked opposite the street. He gave it a casual glance, long enough to recognise Nash's young friend watching him through the tinted glass. If his body had allowed, Degsy would have quickened his pace. Instead, he hobbled along, the rumble in his stomach leading him to his favourite cafe.

Not so long ago, Degsy often imagined retiring to warmer climes, a glass of wine in his hand, contemplating life's hurdles beneath a cloudless Spanish sky. Garry's Cafe was nothing like that. Degsy's hunger didn't discriminate, and he found no argument against the virtues of a full breakfast fry-up, especially when priced below 99p.

There was a lot to be said for eggs and bacon. Sadly, Degsy's joy was short-lived, spoiled by the arrival of Nash's young friend. The kid strolled confidently to the counter and ordered a coffee, setting it down slowly as he sat at Degsy's table.

Degsy wiped the residue from his lips. 'What the hell do you want?'

The kid answered with a smile.

'Well?' Degsy said. 'Answer me then, or are you going to sit there gawping?'

The kid held the cup to his mouth, shaking his head before taking a sip. 'Good manners are cheap. You should consider that; it might make you less angry.'

Degsy stared at him and frowned. 'A man's got good reason to be vexed when someone keeps following him around.'

The kid leaned back in his chair. 'I didn't mean any harm. I was intrigued, that's all. It's not every day you meet someone who lies about their identity.'

'Who I am and who I'm not is my business.'

The kid shrugged. 'Nash once told me that–'

'Nash was a class act, and you're nowhere near that.'

'It's a shame you feel that way. I thought we could have helped each other out.'

Degsy ate the last scrap of food on his plate. 'How on earth can *you* help *me*?'

The kid gave him a scathing glance. 'Lots of ways.' He nodded at Degsy's black eye. 'Looks like you've been in the wars.'

'I'm doing fine,' Degsy said and took out a crumpled cigarette. He put it in his mouth, then patted his pockets, quickly realising he didn't have a light.

'Sure,' said the kid as he flicked open his lighter. 'A smoker who can't afford a box of matches is definitely on the up.'

Degsy ignored the dig and leaned towards the flame, dragging on the cigarette until it was lit. He released the smoke through a long, exasperated sigh. 'Hilarious. Seems you're quite the comedian.'

The kid answered with a knowing smile. 'I'm not that funny.' He placed his hands, palms down, on the table. 'To be honest with you, I'm strapped for cash, so if you're interested in helping me, you could make yourself an easy ton or two.'

Degsy held the smouldering cigarette in his hand. 'How?'

The kid glanced around the room. 'Greasy spoons have never been my kind of thing; how's about we get a proper drink?'

IN BETTER TIMES, Degsy found pleasure in afternoon drinking. Today, sat in the self-imposed exile of a corner table; this dimly lit bar brought his troubles flooding back. He sipped his whisky, listening to the kid's proposal without interruption. When the kid was done, Degsy suppressed a smile. 'Mich,' he said, mulling over her name. 'I haven't seen her in ages.' He swirled the whisky around in his glass. 'Two hundred quid is a generous amount for an address. Does she owe you money or something?'

The kid tried his best to look calm. 'What makes you ask that?'

'Ten years is a long time. When a man's desperate to find someone, it's usually about money, love or revenge; sometimes it's all three.'

The kid glanced at his glass; the orange juice and lemonade remained untouched. 'It's a mixture of those. It's complicated.'

'Life usually is. But there are easier and cheaper ways to find folk.'

'Such as?'

'Public library, births, deaths and marriages, the electoral register.'

'I considered that; however, I don't even know her full name, and as for her age, I'd have to guess.'

Degsy chuckled. 'Michelle Lancelot, Michelle Thomson, Mich Walker, Shelly Wilson. She's gone by lots of names over the years. Feel free to take your pick.'

'No need,' the kid said with a smile. 'I had a good feeling about you from the off. Seems like you're a little information goldmine.'

Degsy emptied his glass. 'Not these days, kid. You're ten years too late. You're best trying some other names from your little black book.'

'Would if I could. Your name's the only one with an address.'

'That figures. What does that tell you?'

'You and Nash were close?'

Degsy released a loud, exaggerated laugh. 'Nash never

knew the meaning of the word *close*. I'm still at the same address because I've never moved on.'

'Nothing wrong in settling down in one place.'

'There is in my line of work.' Degsy narrowed his eyes. 'You know how Nash earned a living, right?'

The kid nodded. 'Yep. I'm in the same type of business.'

Degsy laughed again, a mixture of pity and disbelief. 'Dream on. You'll never be like him.'

'Perhaps, you're right; no harm in trying, though. Isn't this the decade of the entrepreneur? The land of free enterprise?' The kid picked up his orange juice and took a sip.

'*Free enterprise*,' Degsy scoffed. 'Hand me that little book of yours.' The kid tossed the pocket diary across the table. Degsy snatched it up, shaking his head as he flicked through the pages. 'There are no entrepreneurs in here. These are lowlifes, liars, and cheats. They don't have one moral between them. Most of them are dead, probably tried to make a profit by selling their last breath.'

The kid reached out his arm, keeping it outstretched until Degsy handed back the diary. He slipped it into his pocket. 'So no one can help me then?'

Degsy glanced down at his empty glass. 'I never said that. I've still got folks in the know. But it'll cost me two hundred just for the asking. I'll need another two to make anything out of it.'

'Like you said before, that's a lot of money just for an address.'

Degsy shrugged. 'You set the prices, not me. You came knocking on my door, remember?'

'How long?'

'How long you got?'

'A few days?'

Degsy pretended to give the deadline some consideration. 'Sounds reasonable. How's about I meet you here at one-thirty this Thursday?'

The kid answered with a suspicious nod.

Degsy rubbed his hands together. 'I'll need that two hundred to cover expenses.'

The kid took out his wallet and counted the twenties on the table. 'What if you don't show?'

Degsy beamed. 'There's no reason why I shouldn't. And even if I don't, you know where to find me.'

6

A cheap room in a Bayswater Hotel was roughing it even by the lowest standards. Jay lay fully clothed on top of the bed. A musty, damp smell intensified with every breath while the endless rush of traffic roared past the open window. In moments like these, he wished he smoked. He'd hated cigarettes since he was a kid. His mother's old lighter was only a keepsake. Jay thought about her as he kept striking it, watching the yellow flame rising.

He'd said goodbye to her before he left. *Where are you going?* Was all she kept asking. Jay made up a story about a job down south. Renee hadn't believed a word, the sweat on his forehead, Mocksy's blood on his hands calling out every word of his lie. Jay ignored her tears as he stuffed a wad of twenties in her purse. *I don't want any of that money,* she insisted. Jay knew she needed it. But seeing the dejected look in his mother's eyes, he had to leave her with something.

As a boy, Jay swore to avenge Nash's death. The need

eventually dissipated over the years. Seeking out Mich became nothing but a teenage whim. He thought about her in the midnight hours, driving on the nearly deserted motorway, her face lingering in his mind, as a rare sense of loneliness took hold of him.

Now, in this wretched room, he deliberated on why he'd come here. After all these years, Mich had probably spent all the money she'd stolen. What could Jay hope to achieve, an insincere apology at best? Mich couldn't even spell the word, never mind comprehend the meaning of *redemption*. All Jay wanted was a hook. Contacts led to opportunities, a new city, and a new start; he needed a little grounding.

Degsy Dempster seemed promising. Jay didn't believe the old man would give him Mich's address for one minute. He saw the lies in his eyes from the start. The way he rubbed his hands after running a con. But losers like Dempster knew folk, and keeping a close watch on Dempster's antics had to lead to something.

With that in mind, Jay got up. He stretched his arms above his head, wiped the tiredness from his eyes and peeked out the window. These last few days, Jay managed to get his bearings. After familiarising himself with Paddington, and Lancaster Gate, he explored Hyde Park, then spent countless hours walking up and down Queensway. He wasn't in awe of these London streets. The litter, the noise, the lack of eye contact and the forlorn faces of the destitute all lived up to his low expectations.

A BATTERED BENCH beneath the overhanging branches of two old trees was the perfect hideout to watch Degsy. The old man liked his routines. He dined in his favourite cafe every day around noon. Except for the small, battered suitcase under his arm, today was no exception.

Jay didn't follow him immediately. He always let Degsy gain a little distance. The old man's pace was quicker than usual. He walked like a man with a purpose, an urgency to each step, as though he were about to break into a sprint.

Instead of taking a left to his usual haunt, Degsy headed for Queensway station. He flashed a smile as he stepped inside. A brief hint of bliss quickly turned into an expression of pale alarm when a man, not much older than Jay, stepped out from nowhere, grabbed Degsy's arm, and led him away from the entrance. The man tightened his grip, marching Degsy along the pavement like a tired parent scolding their troublesome kid.

Jay hurried after them, pausing whenever he got too close, then losing all sense of caution when the man dragged Degsy down a Chip Shop back alleyway. Jay paused at the entrance, the air a fetid mixture of grease and urine.

'What's your problem?' the stranger asked Jay when he caught sight of him.

Jay strolled towards him. 'Just what I was about to ask you.' He pointed at Degsy. 'Why have you got my friend shoved against the wall like that?'

The stranger released Degsy from his grip and turned to Jay. His slicked hair used too much gel, gleaming beneath a lighted window like the oily tarmac path. His taupe double-breasted suit looked like it had been taken straight from Burton's store rack. The shoulders were too padded; there was slight staining on the lapel and fraying around the cuffs. The stranger's eyes shone with confidence. But the scuffed unpolished shoes told Jay another story.

'*Friend*? Don't make me laugh. If you prefer his company, you're a bigger loser than he is.'

'Prefer has nothing to do with it,' Jay said. 'It's a business relationship. Degsy's doing some work for me.'

The stranger frowned. 'That's news to me. As far as I'm concerned, Degsy's on my payroll.' He poked Degsy in the stomach. 'Secrets get you hurt, old man. Have you been holding out on me?'

A red-faced Degsy shook his head. 'You've got it all wrong, Bryant. I was going to speak with you.'

Bryant shook his head. 'Course you were. Before or after your little trip?'

Degsy frowned. 'Trip to where?'

'I don't know. Wherever you're going with that little suitcase.'

Between the fearful look in Degsy's eyes and the old man's nervous laughter, Jay couldn't decide what was more belittling. He tried offering Degsy a means of escape, stepping closer to Bryant and telling him, 'You can settle any grievances later. Degsy needs to come with me now.'

Bryant stood in silence; his initial expression of amused disbelief quickly washed away by something far uglier. Rage festered in his eyes; his thin lips tightened as he swung at Jay with his fist. Jay slapped the punch away, caught the other and held on to it. A frustrated Bryant tried pulling away. Jay gripped tighter, catching the counter punch, and grabbing Bryant's wrist. A look of confusion settled in Bryant's eyes. He'd clearly run out of moves. Until today, that three-punch combination had been enough. In his desperation, Bryant lashed out with a kick. Jay let go of Bryant's hands, grabbed his ankle, and pushed him back into the trash.

Bryant lay on his back, his legs and arms sprawled out. Scrambling to his feet among the garbage and the rotten food, he looked like a back-alley bum suddenly disturbed from his wretched slumber. Men like Bryant usually had a knife, and Jay shoved him back down before he could reach for it. Jay pushed out his palms. 'That's enough. That's enough, I said. Let's not make this any worse.'

Even though the look on Bryant's face indicated he wanted another try, he didn't budge. After a few seconds, he slowly got to his feet, patting himself down.

Degsy, as though reading Bryant's mind, said, 'None of that was my fault.'

'Of course, it was,' Bryant said. 'You set it up, you scheming old goat. You wait till Benny gets wind of this.' He nodded at Jay. 'It'll take a lot more than your little flash saviour here to get rid of me.'

Jay flashed Bryant his best smile. 'You've got it all wrong. I'm not partnering with old Degsy. You're not the only one he's trying to con. I gave him some money in exchange for information. The old fox is running out on me.'

Disbelief flickered in Bryant's eyes. 'What information?'

'That's my business,' Jay said. 'But join me for a drink, and I might share it with you.'

Bryant frowned. 'You must be as senile as the old man. You seem to have forgotten what you just did. Why the hell would I want to drink with you?'

Jay smiled. 'Don't be like that. A simple misunderstanding, that's all. You look like a businessman to me. When money's involved, it pays to have a short memory.'

Bryant stared at him. The uncertain expression on his face mirrored the questions ticking over in his thick head. Jay suppressed a laugh. This guy was easier to read than a book. 'Come on, Bryant, what harm can it do? The only way is up from here on. We've already fallen out.'

Bryant agreed with a sigh. 'I suppose.' He shot Degsy a fierce look. 'I suppose you'll be bringing *him.*'

'Absolutely,' Jay said. 'After today's adventures, I'm not letting old Dempster out of my sight.'

7

To hear him talk, you would think Jay Ellis had lived in London all his life. He chatted about where he was staying and where he'd been. Speaking with the ease of a local as though he were familiar with every avenue and street. Degsy hadn't made his mind up about him yet. There was no denying the lad was sharp. The way he handled Bryant in that alleyway, he definitely had something. The question that remained was, what? Degsy had seen lots of kids like that. They all told a great story, but most failed to deliver when it came down to it.

Jay didn't seem any different. He appeared to be looking for any opportunity, grasping at any word that gave a glimmer of hope and changing direction in mid-sentence.

By the look on his face, even Bryant noticed it. 'Ten years is a long time,' he said doubtfully, 'this Mich woman could be anywhere,' his every word full of scorn and mocking the rationality of Jay's plan. 'What do you want with her, anyway?'

Jay looked down at his glass. 'Oh, this and that.'

'Money.' Bryant said, confident it was the answer.

Jay nodded.

'How much does she owe you?'

'A tidy sum, with enough to benefit anyone interested in helping me.'

Bryant scrunched his brow, a look of agony on his face like a man pained by and unaccustomed to thinking. 'You couldn't have been more than a kid ten years ago. How come a woman owes you?'

'I'll tell you more once you help me find her. For now, let's just say it's complicated.'

Bryant raised his eyes. 'If you say so.' He reached into his pocket, pulled out a crumpled fiver and tossed it onto the table. 'Degsy, go to the bar and get another round of drinks.'

Degsy sighed. 'Can't you do it?'

'No, I can't, and you need to make yourself useful.'

Degsy remained seated for a few minutes. Then he snatched the fiver off the table and stood up. He shot the kid a glance, catching a tinge of sympathy in his eyes. Emotions could get you killed. In this business, any trace of humanity was viewed as a weakness. Bryant would have noticed it too, and Degsy knew by the slight smirk on Bryant's face it had already given him an edge. Degsy sloped off towards the bar.

Degsy sat on a stool, waiting for the barman to show his face. It was darker at this end of the room, obscuring him in shadow while he watched Jay and Bryant sitting against a backdrop of grey light. He was happy to be away from them. He felt like the worst version of himself in Bryant's company; his self-respect, although at an all-time low, blossomed whenever he gained more distance.

'What can I get you?' the barman said, his sleepy-eyed nonchalance adding to Degsy's irritation. At first, Degsy answered him with an aggravated look, then said, 'same as last time.'

'What time?'

Degsy sighed. 'The time you served me last, half an hour ago.'

The barman lost his cheesy grin. 'Hey, no need to be like that. For all I know, it could have been yesterday or last night.'

Degsy remained silent, suppressing his urge to answer with a quip that likened a goldfish to the man's memory. Having paid for the drinks, Degsy sauntered back to his seat and placed them on the table.

'You forgot the salted peanuts,' Bryant said, 'go back and get them,' grabbing Degsy's arm before he had time to sit. Degsy motioned towards the bar, but Jay stood up before Degsy took one step. 'Sit down, Degsy.'

'He needs to sort it,' Bryant protested.

Jay rested his hand on Degsy's shoulder. 'Let him sit down. There's no need to make him traipse up and down like that.' He pressed Degsy down onto his chair. 'I'm happy to stretch my legs.'

'You've got yourself a protector there,' Bryant said the instant Jay was out of earshot.

Degsy slipped his hand into his jacket pocket and pulled out a cigarette. 'I don't need babysitting; I can take care of myself.'

Bryant grinned, 'of course, you can,' then leaned towards Degsy and gave him a light. He snatched the cigarette from Degsy's mouth and started smoking it. 'What do you make of his little story?'

Degsy took out another cigarette. 'Sounds plausible.'

'Everything sounds plausible. He might be handy with his fists, but he seems a bit of a soft touch if you ask me.'

Degsy couldn't disagree but remained silent. This time Bryant didn't offer him a light. Instead, he took a deep drag and blew the smoke in Degsy's face. 'If you find out anything about this Mich woman, you come straight to me first. Understood?'

Degsy remained silent.

'Understood, I said. Are you listening?'

Degsy nodded.

'Well, answer me then, you old fool. You speak to me first. Let me know everything. I'll decide where we go with this. You got that?'

'Sure,' Degsy said. 'You're the boss.'

'And less of the sarcasm.'

'I wasn't being sarcastic, just acknowledging you were in charge, that's all.'

Bryant frowned. 'Yes, I am. And you'd do well to remember that.' Bryant looked towards the door and nodded to the pretty young girl waving at him. 'Wait for me outside,' he shouted, finished his drink in two gulps and slammed the glass down on the table. Bryant stood and looked over his shoulder towards the bar. 'Your little saviour likes to talk, doesn't he.'

'He's what you call a people person.'

'Seems a bit of a bullshitter if you ask me.'

'Aren't we all,' Degsy said with a smile.

Bryant glared at him. 'There you go with that mouth again.' He scanned Degsy with a disparaging eye. 'Look at the state of you. You don't seem too clever to me.' He glanced at his watch. 'Tell Mr Chatty I'll catch him later. I'll be in Maggie's Bar after nine if he needs to speak with me.' He swaggered towards the door, checking his reflection in the bar mirror on the way out.

Degsy released a deep, exasperated sigh when Bryant was out of sight. Bryant was as pathetic as he was cruel, and Degsy didn't know whether to laugh or cry. He settled for neither, drawing hard on his cigarette and blowing the smoke up at the ceiling, repeating the pattern until Jay returned to the table.

Jay dropped the packets of salted nuts next to Bryant's empty glass. 'Where's he off to?'

Degsy shrugged. 'Spend some time with his girl, I suppose.'

'The one that waved to him by the door?' Jay frowned. 'She looks like she's still in high school.'

Degsy stubbed out his cigarette in the ashtray. 'Yeah, well, Bryant likes them young, I guess. She might be older, for all we know. Everyone looks young to me.'

Jay waved away the smoke cloud lingering in front of him. 'He seems a nasty little bastard. Why do you let him treat you like that?'

Degsy sighed. 'Because I'm an old man with few friends.' He popped another cigarette into his mouth, drawing his head forward when Jay offered him a light. 'Me allowing it to happen has nothing to do with it.' He took a drag of his cigarette and blew the smoke out through his nostrils. 'Bryant has dangerous friends. In fact, I'm in a similar position as you.'

'How come?'

'As you so aptly describe it, the situation's *complicated*.'

Jay smiled. 'Things usually are.' He tore open a packet of nuts. 'Perhaps working together can help to simplify that?'

'Is that so,' Degsy scoffed. 'It sounds like you're starting to believe that cock and bull story of yours. You're just fishing for a way into something. You've less of a plan than I have.'

Jay emptied some peanuts into his palm and scooped them into his mouth. He chewed them quickly, swallowed, and then wiped the salt from his lips. 'That's where you're wrong. Once I locate Mich, you'll see.' Jay leaned forward. 'Which reminds me, you need to return the money I gave you. You're obviously struggling with the task.'

'I'm not struggling.'

'No? You still don't know where she is, though.'

'West Brompton.'

Jay's eyes widened with surprise. 'What?'

'Mich lives in West Brompton,' Degsy said. 'She married a man called Earlston; he's a stockbroker or something similar.'

'Are you sure?'

Degsy beamed. 'Yeah. Michelle Earlston. Saw her a few weeks ago. Any conman worth their salt knows that.'

'Why didn't you tell me before?'

'I don't know you from Adam. You needed to make it worth my time first.'

'Fair enough. Why the sudden change of heart?'

Degsy slumped back into his seat. 'I enjoyed how you slapped Bryant around; I figured I owed you a favour.'

A t first, it suited Mich just fine, a lavish London townhouse, a weekly allowance, and a wealthy husband who was hardly ever at home. Even the pet Labrador, before it died, took a shine to her, its lustrous dark eyes filled with loving anticipation. Unfortunately, this could not be said for her stepdaughter. The girl was sulky and aloof, typical for most adolescents, but Jenny Earlston was more withdrawn than your average sixteen-year-old. When her head wasn't stuck in a book, this pale, almost pretty girl spent hours gazing through the window. Mich tried countless times to befriend her, yet, just like the light that rarely frequented the teenager's bedroom, the girl refused to let Mich in.

Today was no exception. Still dressed in oversized pyjamas, Jenny lay stretched on the sofa, flicking through the TV channels. Mich tried getting the girl's attention with a sigh. When that failed, she used a less subtle approach by snatching the remote from Jenny's hand and slamming it down on the table. The girl didn't respond, tilting her head slightly to look through Mich and fix her pale dull eyes on the TV.

Mich killed the picture with the remote, causing Jenny to shake her head and sigh. 'Finally,' she said with a triumphant smile.

'Finally, *what*?' came the girl's irritated response.

'Finally got a reaction. The way you've been lying there, I thought you might have slipped into a coma.'

Jenny rolled her eyes. 'What's wrong, Mich? Have we run out of drink or something?'

Mich regarded her for a moment. 'You know a smart mouth can get a girl in trouble.'

Jenny slowly nodded her head. 'I'll bear that advice in mind, knowing it's coming from years of experience.'

Mich took a deep breath, distracted by her reflection in the large mirror that hung above the fireplace. She gave herself an approving smile, although lately, a niggling voice inside her head tried convincing her she wasn't all that. Mich brushed the doubts aside, knowing she still turned heads wherever she went. Besides, no one ever asked a lady's age, and even if they dared, few would dispute she was on the good side of thirty.

Mich kept in shape and even went to aerobics classes twice a week. She'd stayed with the blonde look, her lacquered, blown-away curls never losing their style, even on a stormy day. Make-up had never been her thing, but it became more necessary every year. Late nights were the worst; these days, it took more effort to hide the aftermath of alcohol.

Mich sensed Jenny staring and turned to face her as the girl said, 'I recently read a book about Caravaggio.'

'Carra-who,' Mich said, 'what on earth are you talking about?'

'The Italian painter, he did a piece called Narcissus.'

Mich gave her a blank stare.

Jenny sighed with impatience. 'The character from Greek mythology who fell in love with his own reflection.'

'Is that so,' Mich said. She studied the girl for a moment. 'As I've said countless times, wearing your hair so greasy and lank does you no favours. Mousy brown takes well to peroxide, a bit of foundation to cover those blackheads, and you'd be transformed. Boys might take more notice of you.'

Jenny got up and walked out of the room. Mich listened while the girl stomped into the kitchen, pulled open what sounded like a drawer and slammed it shut seconds later. She returned holding a wad of twenty-pound notes. 'Here,' she said, stuffing the money into the jacket pocket of Mich's aqua and pink shell suit.

Before Jenny could walk away, Mich grabbed the girl's arm. 'What the hell do you think you're doing?'

'That's what this is all about, isn't it?'

'*This*?'

'Being a pain in the arse, giving me a hard time, switching off the TV.'

'I just want to spend some time with you, that's all.'

'Yeah, right. Since when have you been interested in me? Daddy said you'd be like this. You're always the same when you're skint.'

Mich released the girl's arm. 'Your father said that? You spoke with him about me?'

Jenny shrugged. 'Yeah. Why look so surprised. We do live in the same house, you know.'

Mich flashed her a flat smile. 'We do indeed, but there's talk, and there's *talk*. It hurts me to know you've been talking behind my back.'

'Daddy was upset. You spend money like there's no

tomorrow, and the way you disappear for days with God knows who. I guess he wanted someone to talk to.'

'Talking's fine, but some things are private between a husband and his wife.'

Jenny shook her head in disbelief. 'You're suddenly his wife now?'

'I try to be, although it isn't easy, especially when you're up against a spoilt conniving brat.'

To her credit, the girl remained calm, and Mich might have been impressed in better circumstances. Jenny traipsed over to the sofa. 'I'm not conniving. I gave you that money, didn't I? Even though Daddy told me not to.'

Mich hid her surprise. 'Really? When did he say that?'

'Early this morning before he went to work.'

'I'm surprised you were up at that time of the morning.'

'Never claimed I was,' Jenny said with a smile. 'Daddy came to see me before he left.'

'To tell you to hide this money?'

'That and other stuff.'

'What other stuff?'

Jenny grabbed the remote, slunk back onto the sofa, and switched on the TV.

'What stuff?' Mich asked again.

Jenny turned up the volume, repeatedly flicking through the channels without answering.

Mich stood in front of the TV. 'Well?'

Jenny rolled her eyes and sighed. 'Stuff between a husband and his wife. So you'll have to ask him.'

'But I'm asking you.'

Jenny stood up and stomped off to her room, slamming the door shut behind her.

9

M ich tried sitting it out. For the first hour, the money remained untouched. Then she eased open the drawer, and thirty minutes later, with a pot of coffee at her side, she counted it at the kitchen table. Two hundred pounds would barely last her the day, let alone a week. Earlston was known for being tight, but this was cheap, even by his standards. She resisted at first, then boredom got the better of her, the voice inside her head goading her to step outside, conspiring with a burgeoning restlessness, luring her to the Off-licence. If Earlston thought so lowly of her, then she might as well have a drink.

She took the wine bottles home. No matter how stifling the house was, it was better than walking the streets and drinking outside alone. Music offered some company, and flicking through the channels on the radio was a welcomed distraction. No single tune held her attention for long. Her thoughts led her deeper into the past. Every glass of wine softened her stern resolve, and her emotions weakened with every sad song.

Mich shook her head and sighed. *Too many ghosts*, she

whispered as the image of Nash's face became rooted in her mind's eye. She'd thought about him a lot these last few weeks. Perhaps these shiftless hours were to blame? Nash took her secrets to the grave. And fond of him as she was when Benny Bray was concerned, she'd felt more relief than sadness. Nostalgia was for the old; these days, guilt seldomly raised its grisly head.

Mich pushed the images aside and raised a glass to Nash's memory. No sooner had she taken a sip than she heard the sound of a key turning inside the lock. She grimaced towards the door, listening to it open, then slam shut. 'Hi, I'm home,' said Earlston's annoying voice. He called out again. 'Jenny? Jenny? Do you fancy something to eat?'

'She's in her bedroom with her headphones,' came Mich's curt reply. As Earlston walked into the lounge, Mich greeted his stare with her own. 'Did it occur to you that I might be hungry? There are more than two people in this house. You also have a wife, or have you forgotten that?'

Earlston glanced down at Mich's glass. 'That's not an easy thing to do.' He glanced at the wine bottle. 'Besides, you rarely have an appetite. Last time I asked, you made it clear that you like to eat when it suits you.' He took off his double-breasted, herringbone tweed overcoat and rested it on a chair. 'In fact, I strictly remember you instructing me not to ask you.'

'A girl can change her mind, you know.'

'Indeed, she can,' he said with a wry grin. 'And God knows you're a testament to that.' He studied the wine bottle briefly, then poured himself a glass.

'Bit early for you, isn't it?' Mich said.

Earlston took a sip. 'It's been a long day, and by the look on your face, I thought I better arm myself.'

Mich topped up her glass. 'Aw, poor little you, although in this case, I think I'm the one who's hard done by.'

Earlston sighed. 'Come on, let's hear it.'

Mich made a face of mock surprise. 'I've got little to say; you're the one with the secrets.'

'What secrets?'

'Your little schemes, plotting behind my back.'

At first, Earlston frowned, then a hint of understanding flashed in his tired eyes. 'You've been talking with Jen?'

'Too right I have. You two are always pushing me away. God knows how long you've been talking behind my back.'

'Is that what Jen told you?'

'Yeah, once I got the truth from her.'

Earlston slammed his glass on the table and pointed his finger at Mich. 'You leave the girl alone; you bully her enough.'

'*Bully*,' Mich scoffed. 'It's the other way around, more like. She's the wrong sort to be pushed around. In fact, she bullies me; she's got a smart mouth on her that one.'

'I wonder where she got that from?' Earlston rubbed the tiredness from his eyes. 'Just get to the point, Mich. I don't want to spend all night on this.'

'Fine,' Mich said. 'The point is some things are best discussed between husband and wife.'

Earlston nodded. 'Fair enough. Is that it?'

'No, it's not.' She ignored Earlston's exasperated sigh. 'Why did you tell Jenny to hide that money from me?'

'I left it for *her*.'

'And you were afraid I'd take it?'

Earlston's unhandsome face stared back at her. The years had been unkind to him; his wavy dark hair was peppered with grey, and his jawline had sprouted an extra chin. He was a lot heavier from when they first met, and being shorter than average, he failed to get away with it.

Mich studied the hint of defeat in his eyes. 'Well?' she said.

'Well, what?' came his weary reply.

'Were you afraid I'd take it?'

Earlston rubbed his hands despairingly down his face. 'Afraid is the wrong word; it implies an element of doubt. Once you knew where it was, taking that money was a fore-gone conclusion.'

'What makes you so sure?'

He nodded at the wine bottles. 'You've already spent some of it, right?'

Mich quickly refilled her glass and emptied it in a few large gulps. 'I asked you to increase my allowance. Perhaps if you took better care of me, I wouldn't need to go sneaking around.'

Earlston shot her a fierce look. 'You get more than enough from me; that's the problem.'

Mich poured herself another glass, drinking it faster when Earlston told her to slow down. 'Running a house isn't cheap,' she said, slamming her glass on the table.

Earlston's expression was a mixture of anger and disbelief. 'When have you ever run this house? We have a cleaner that comes in three times a week. I pay all the bloody bills. There's never any food here. We either have to eat out every night or order a takeaway.'

'It's what you prefer,' Mich shouted back at him. 'And who do you think chose all these fixtures and furnishings? That white leather sofa your precious daughter keeps lounging on, the paintings you love, that antique globe, the wall-to-wall bookcases, do you think all that shit just appeared here by magic and organised itself?'

Earlston's face reddened while he clenched his fists. Yet, as was his way, he didn't do a thing. Mich hated men who kept it all inside. Self-restraint was fine for a board meeting, but it was the enemy of the bedroom. Not that it mattered. Earlston's lovemaking was mediocre at best. But it came with the house. The man lacked passion, and his nocturnal fumbling had been a necessary evil for years now. Sometimes Mich wished he would take a swing at her. Anything to show he cared, a black eye, tears, a bloody nose, at least it would be something. Instead, he took a deep breath, composing himself in his usual annoying way. Earlston sipped his wine with exaggerated calm and said, 'True, you're to credit for all that. But its cost is too high, and I've yet to see a receipt.'

'What are you trying to imply?'

'I'm not trying to imply anything. I'm being quite blunt about it.'

'So what are you accusing me of?'

Earlston shook his head and let out a bewildered laugh. 'Let's say mismanagement of funds.'

'Stealing, you mean?'

Earlston waved away the accusation with his hand. 'Call it whatever you like; either way, it needs to end.'

'By stopping my allowance?'

Earlston shrugged. 'It's the only way I know. I need to break even somehow because you'll never pay it back.'

'You make me sound like one of your debtors. Whatever happened to "for richer, for poorer"?'

'I'm certainly poorer, that's for sure.'

Tears welled in Mich's eyes. She could summon them at will, and usually, that's all it took, and Earlston was holding her in his arms and begging for forgiveness. There was something different about him tonight. A look of cold detachment lingered in his eyes. His words were more direct, and his responses more brutal and quicker. As though possessed by savage confidence, he sat with his arms folded, meeting her stare with his own like a man who had suddenly found a purpose. 'Don't get upset,' he said with mock sympathy. 'You're the one who started this.'

Mich's tears vanished as quickly as they arrived. The softness in her eyes had frozen, and her expressionless face, with its smooth contours and prominent cheekbones, looked almost statuesque. 'I never started anything. All I did was ask a question.'

Disagreement flashed in Earlston's eyes, but his silence clearly showed he was happy to end the argument. He offered compromise through a smile. Mich crossed her arms in refusal. She wouldn't let him retreat without an apology; she was in no mood to lick her wounds. 'I just thought you would have discussed it with me first.'

Earlston lowered his eyes. 'I tried, but there's no getting through to you when it comes to money.'

'Well, you've certainly achieved that now. I just hope there's a way back from this.'

A look of worry passed across Earlston's face for the first time that evening. 'It's a misunderstanding, that's all. Now that everything's in the open, the only way is forward.'

Like a predator stalking its prey, Mich pounced upon the slightest hint of weakness. 'We can't move forward without trust. From where I'm standing, we don't seem to have that.'

He reached out to her, covering her hand with his. She could feel its clamminess against her skin. Judging by the tenderness of his grip, any resolve he might have had was close to breaking. 'I wanted it to stop, that's all,' he said. 'It's been getting me down for weeks now.'

'Conspiring with Jenny didn't help.'

Earlston released her hand and rubbed the back of his neck. 'I wasn't conspiring. I just confided in Jenny. She is my daughter, after all. I don't know what she told you. But it wasn't as conniving as it seemed. You know what teenagers are like. It didn't quite pan out like that.'

'It's not what you said before.'

'You started on me the moment I walked in. It's been a long day. I was in no mood not to defend myself.'

No sooner had they mentioned Jenny's name than the surly teenager mooched into the lounge. She went straight to Earlston, wrapped her arms around his waist and buried her face into his chest. Earlston kissed her forehead. 'Now that's a welcome to make any man feel at home.' He kissed her again. 'Hey, hey, what's all this,' he said as she squeezed him tighter.

Jenny released him from her clutches, linked his arm with her own and rested the side of her head on his shoulder. 'I've just missed you, that's all. I've been thinking about you all day.' She shot Mich a fierce look. 'I hate to see you upset.'

Earlston smiled. 'I'm fine; don't worry about anything.'

A reassuring tone travelled through the warmness of his voice. He always seemed different when he spoke to Jenny; his eyes shone with soft surrender. It was a love and acceptance that Mich could only ever watch from the outside; she'd always be second best while Jenny was around. This was Earlston at his most intimate, a tenderness he reserved solely for his beloved daughter.

Jenny rolled her eyes at the empty wine bottle. 'Have you been celebrating, Mich? It didn't take you long.'

'That's enough,' Earlston said before Mich could answer. 'It's all sorted now; everything's in the open.'

An aggrieved look settled across Jenny's face. 'I'm on your side, Daddy.'

Earlston sighed. 'This isn't about sides.'

'That's not what you told me last night, Daddy. I hate the way she makes you feel. She's been having a go at me all day. I know you said to hide that money from her, but–'

'That's enough, Jen.'

The girl abruptly moved away from her father's side. 'But I told her about it as a test. She didn't need to take it. All your suspicions about her are true. I tried telling you that from the start.'

Mich glared at Earlston. 'Suspicions?'

Earlston shook his head. 'It's not what I said. I was a bit down, that's all. Mostly tiredness from work. Let's move on now. Jenny got the wrong end of the stick.'

Jenny moved towards the door, stopping when Earlston grabbed her arm. 'Get off me. Let me go, Daddy.' she protested.

Earlston maintained his grip. 'Come on, don't be like that.'

Jenny tried to pull free. 'I'm not being like anything. I knew you'd be like this.' She threw Mich a scathing look. 'All it takes are a few fake tears, and you're taking her side. You promised you'd stand firm. She's making a fool of you.'

'No, she's not,' Earlston insisted. 'Mich is going to keep tabs on her spending. We've come to an agreement.'

'Of course you have,' the girl said and walked away.

'Jen, Jen,' Earlston pleaded.

'Leave her be,' Mich said when the girl didn't answer. 'She'll be fine in a few hours, especially once we order a takeaway.'

Earlston didn't answer. Instead, he looked straight

through Mich as though she wasn't there. Then, as a look of panic and regret settled in his eyes, he chased after his daughter into the hallway. Mich knew this would always be the case and, resigned to its inevitability, poured herself another drink. The wine had lost its appeal. Its ability to console diminished, its smell nauseating, aggravating the throbbing pain inside her head. Mich drank it all the same. Then poured herself another. It wasn't the worst place she'd found herself. But it was bad enough, and she'd learned from an early age the only way to cope was to numb the senses.

LATER, in the quiet hours after midnight, Earlston, naked and aroused, came to her bed. With his heartfelt apologies whispering in her ear, he pressed himself against her. Mich had heard it so many times before, and for all his protests and the day's charade, Earlston remained a weak man. Mich kissed away his tears, promising she would never leave him. Not that Mich had any choice. Foolishly she'd agreed to and signed the pre-nuptial agreements. Divorce would leave her penniless. So, unless she came into a windfall, she'd spend the rest of her days as second best in the shadow of Earlston's beloved daughter.

10

They had sat in the car and watched the large townhouse since early morning. It was a joyless activity in the rain, the drab grey sky, and the dirty wet street, worsened by Degsy's endless snoring. Jay gave him a nudge, smiling as the old man snorted, then suddenly woke up.

After gathering his senses, Degsy looked at Jay. 'What did you do that for? I didn't sleep too well last night. Surely you wouldn't deprive me of forty winks?'

Jay shook his head and smiled. 'You've been sleeping since I picked you up. I told you to stay put. But you insisted on coming along.'

Degsy rummaged inside his jacket pocket, his permanent frown easing slightly as he plucked out a crumpled cigarette. He popped it into his mouth, then wound down the window on Jay's instruction before lighting up. After taking a deep drag, he released the smoke with an even deeper breath. Jay and Degsy watched it drift upwards until it vanished into the dull sky. Degsy took another drag, his eyes bright with contentment. He turned his face towards

Jay. 'I came along to help you out. Staking a place out is easier done in shifts.'

Jay glanced at his watch. 'What the hell are you talking about? We've barely been here a few hours; it's not even noon.'

Degsy grinned. 'It's tiring work just sitting and watching, the world passing you by, filling your head with all those missed opportunities, riddling your body with pain, burdening your heart with regret.'

'Jesus,' Jay said, shaking his head. 'Just when I thought the day couldn't get any worse. I preferred you when you were asleep.'

Degsy laughed, which quickly developed into a loud, rasping cough. At one point, Jay feared the old man would choke to death, but to his relief, Degsy finally composed himself. Red-faced and teary-eyed, Degsy pointed towards the house facing them. 'You've got to hand it to Mich. This time the girl's really landed on her feet.'

Jay nodded, silenced by the sense of longing and sadness in the old man's voice.

Degsy sighed. 'Always fancied a place like this. It's Georgian.'

'How do you know?'

'Because I do. It's got all the characteristics, four storeys high, sash windows with smaller panes, hipped roofs and parapets, the list goes on.' Degsy gave Jay's battered old paperback a disparaging glance. 'You're not the only one who can get their head stuck in a book.'

'I guess not,' Jay said. 'But you best hold on to those textbook illustrations because that's the closest you'll ever get to it.'

'But I'll always be closer to it than you,' Degsy said, 'even if I'm a million miles away.'

Jay didn't answer, staring silently through the windscreen at the tall, blonde woman leaving the house. It felt strange seeing her after all these years, a ghost from the past triggering so many emotions: anger, fear, sadness, and shame charged through his veins, bombarding his mind with a slew of bad memories.

Jay watched her from his rearview mirror until she was a hundred yards down the street. He removed the car key from the ignition, pushed open the driver's door and stepped outside, catching the protest in Degsy's eyes before he slammed the door shut. 'What?'

Degsy gave him an incredulous look. 'So you're just going to leave me here?'

Jay glanced anxiously over his shoulder. 'Apart from slowing us down, Mich also knows what you look like, right?'

'Maybe,' Degsy said with a shrug. A glint of hopeful desperation flashed in his eyes. 'Or maybe not. To tell you the truth, I haven't seen her in years. In fact, the more I think about it, Mich doesn't know me from Adam. Sure, she's heard my name, but women like her only remember pretty faces.'

Jay smiled. 'She'll recognise you sure enough. I doubt you've changed that much. You stay here and look after the car. Your face isn't so easy to forget.'

Degsy grimaced. 'She knows you too,' he said, his words less of a statement and more of a question.

Jay pressed on the bonnet with both hands. 'She knew me years ago when I was a kid. I've changed a lot since then. I'd give a hundred to one against the chance of her recognising me.' He closed the car door, turning his back on the old man as he leaned across the driver's seat and wound down the window.

Jay hurried down the street, disregarding the rain and the old man calling after him. He glanced at his watch; it was barely noon, yet the petrol-like hues from the brightly lit shops and offices reflected on the wet pavement.

Jay followed Mich through the rain, stopping whenever she window-shopped, watching her askance, mindful of her every move, always keeping a safe distance. It reminded him of a game they once played. Mich, Jay, and Nash hiding and seeking along the promenade of the sunny seaside town of Rhyl. She played them both for a fool, this bewitching woman with the brightest smile who could do no wrong at one time in Jay's eyes. Jay still felt like a sucker in her presence, and no sooner had he stopped himself from drifting back into yesteryear than she was gone.

Jay didn't pay too much attention at first. Following someone required concentration, and daydreaming had its consequences. He wandered casually into the nearby stores, browsing with the well-dressed shoppers, scanning each place with one look, mindful not to linger too long.

For all his searching, there was no trace of her. Jay stood outside in the rain, wondering where she could have disappeared to, but no clues offered themselves, and he stared longingly into the midday mist.

11

J ay broke into a jog, every unrewarded step making him more anxious. When he reached the end of the street, Jay turned around. She couldn't have come this far. No one was that quick. But Mich was clever. Maybe she'd sensed him on her tail. By his own admission, Jay was new to this. Perhaps she'd spotted him from the start, saw how green he was, and decided to give him the slip. Then he saw her sitting in a wine bar on the other side of the street. Jay smiled at his own foolishness. Boyhood memories flooded his mind, and he remembered one thing he'd learned about Mich. She wasn't as cool and calculated as she made out. Admittedly, she had her own agenda. But Mich could barely plan from one day to the next. Jay remembered she was a creature governed by emotion, an insight he couldn't express when he was a kid but something he could now use to his advantage.

Jay crossed the road and went into the wine bar. He threw Mich a passing glance sensing her watching him as he ordered a drink. He sat by the bar and stared at his reflection in the mirror. The place was empty except for Jay, Mich, and a small group of office workers. *Holding Back the Years* played melodically on the radio. Jay enjoyed the tune until Gary Davies' voice blabbered over it. He shook his head in disapproval, turning to his left as a woman said, 'I'm with you there, hon. Those damn DJs spoil every song they play. The show's all about them. They just love the sound of their own voice.'

Jay answered Mich with a nod. He tried to look casual, which proved hard, considering he was staring at a ghost. 'Absolutely,' he said with a smile, then nodded at her empty glass. 'What are you drinking?'

'A dry white, please,' Mich said without hesitation. 'That's very kind of you.' She matched his stare with her own. 'Have we met before?'

Jay shook his head. 'Not that I'm aware. I think I'd remember. I don't usually forget a pretty face.'

'Likewise,' she said with a smile. Mich regarded him for a moment. 'Where do I know you from?' A hint of recognition flashed in her eyes, and then, much to Jay's relief, it withered and died. 'No doubt it'll come to me.'

She'd looked stunning from that first glance. But Jay could see that time had taken its toll. She was still more beautiful than most, yet the lines and darkness around the eyes were more visible these days. The illusion of her, which he'd carried around all these years, faded rapidly now that he stood this close.

'That's an intense stare,' Mich said.

Jay blushed. 'Sorry, I didn't realise. I–'

'That's all right. I don't mind. You look even more handsome when you're thinking. I've never been attracted to dullards. Luckily for you, there seems to be a lot going on in that pretty head of yours.' She adjusted her earring. 'Listen,

I've never liked propping up bars; everyone earwigging.' She pointed at one of the booths. 'How's about we go somewhere more discrete.'

After paying for the wine, Jay followed her to the booth. He handed Mich her drink and then sat opposite her.

Jay thought how surreal it was to be sitting together after all these years, the music playing in the background, the optics across the bar reflecting the soft golden hues of the lights. Part of it felt like a dream, and he longed for such moments when he was a kid. He pictured Mich all those years ago, dancing in his old front room, Nash watching coolly from the sofa while his mother's former boyfriend, Shane, threatened him through gritted teeth.

Shane's face lingered in his mind's eye; the man's eyes were brutal and cruel, and Jay sighed against the slew of dark memories flooding back. Shane had left his mother for dead after Mich played him for a fool and ran out on him. '*Never been attracted to dullards*,' Jay whispered under his breath. Mich certainly made an exception when she bedded Shane; describing him as slow was an understatement.

Mich narrowed her eyes. 'What was that you said?'

'Dullards,' Jay said with a smile. 'You rarely hear the word used these days.'

'I guess not. You used to hear it a lot ten years ago.'

'So, why aren't dullards your thing?'

Mich shrugged. 'Are they any girl's thing? I imagine most women want a sharp man who has a bit of nous about them.'

'Probably, but some women prefer a dullard too. They like to have someone to manipulate.'

Mich sipped her wine. 'That's quite a cynical observation to make. What dark recesses have you dragged that from? Is it something from your own experience?'

Jay hid his anger behind a smile. 'No,' he lied. 'I've been quite fortunate in that respect. I was only making an observation.'

Mich smoothed her finger around the rim of the glass. 'Sure, if you say so, although I sensed a touch of agitation in your voice.' She regarded him for a moment. 'I'm susceptible to those kinds of things. When you mentioned some women "like to manipulate," it felt like you were referring to me.'

Jay picked up his drink. 'Nah, you're mistaken. Perhaps you've got a guilty conscience.'

'*Nah,*' Mich said, mimicking his voice. 'Whereabouts did you get that accent?'

'Up North.'

'That's a little vague. Liverpool, perhaps? There's more than a hint of scouse there.'

'Spot on. I live near Birkenhead.'

Mich clicked her fingers. 'I knew it; it must have faded over the years. Birkenhead accents are a lot stronger.'

'I've been around, haven't been back there for years now.'

'Is that right? Years you say. Wow. You must have left when you were very young, couldn't have been little more than a kid.'

'Yeah, that's about right. Never had any time for school. Left home when I was sixteen.'

Mich took out her pack of cigarettes, placing a cigarette in her mouth as Jay leaned forward with his lighter. Her face glowed against the yellow flame that flickered in her eyes and emphasised their darkness. She thanked him with a look, taking a deep drag of her cigarette before engulfing them in smoke. Jay waved the smoke away with his hand, quickly noticing a change in her. He remembered that look from when he was a kid. She'd worn it that hot summer's day in the woods, outside that dilapidated old house, when she'd shot Nash with his own gun. It was hard to believe someone so beautiful could do such a thing. But the coldness in her eyes confirmed it, and Jay knew the real woman behind the mask.

She took another drag of her cigarette, releasing the smoke as she said, 'And what did you do after that?'

'Took various crappy jobs, saved a little, then hitchhiked my way south.'

'That must have been scary for a naive sixteen-year-old? This place is full of animals at the best of times. Everyone trying to take advantage of you.'

'I wasn't so green.' Jay tapped the side of his head. 'Somebody taught me from an early age *that a man needs to use his loaf.*'

Mich let the cigarette drop from her mouth; a fearful look of recognition flashed in her eyes. 'I once knew some-body who used to say that.'

Jay grabbed her forearm as Mich tried to stand, gripping it tighter when she tried pulling away and forcing her back down in her seat.

'Get your hand off me, Jay,' she said through gritted teeth. 'Let me go, I said, or I'll scream the place down.'

Jay released her arm, getting himself ready if she made a run for it. Much to his relief, Mich decided to stay put. She smoothed a hand across the table and retrieved her cigarette. She popped it back in her mouth, dragging on it until it was fully lit. 'Birkenhead,' she said, raising her eyes. 'For a second, you had me fooled there, kid.' She regarded him for a moment, the intensity in her eyes forcing him to look away. 'Still shy,' she said with a grin. 'I remember you being cute. But I never thought you'd turn out as good-looking as this.'

'I couldn't have been that cute as a kid; otherwise, you wouldn't have abandoned me.'

'I didn't abandon you.'

'You left me with Shane, for Christ's sake.'

Mich shrugged. 'So?'

'He beat my mother half to death and tried to murder me.'

'How was I to know he'd freak out?'

Jay shook his head in disbelief. 'Getting him to bury Nash in the woods, pretending to be in love with him? I think they're pretty big clues, don't you?'

'How was I to know he was so weak?'

'Of course, you knew. Nash sussed him from the start, then used you to lure him in.'

'I'm glad we agree that it was all Nash's fault. Just like you, Jay, I was also a victim.'

'*Victim,*' Jay said with exaggerated surprise. 'That's the most ridiculous thing I've heard in ages. Victim,' he said again. 'I wonder, if he was still alive, what that Pete fella would have to say about that?'

Mich stubbed out her cigarette and took out another. She pointed at it, Jay. 'Shane killed Pete; I read about it in the papers.'

Jay leaned forward and gave her a light. 'Shane wasn't capable at the time. *You* killed him, Mich.'

'What makes you so sure?'

'I've had a long time to think about it.'

'Well, you shouldn't. Life's too short, especially for someone so young. You'll get nowhere by dwelling on the past.' She glanced over to the bar. 'If you're going to keep me talking, then the least you can do is get me another drink.'

Jay conceded with a shrug, keeping an eye on her as he moved away from the table. He didn't expect her to stay. Knowing Mich, she would run for it once his back was turned. Jay watched her reflection in the bar mirror. She stared straight at him, brazen and aloof, while the waitress, observing them throughout, poured the drink.

12

Jay walked back to the booth and placed Mich's large glass of white wine on the table.

Mich took a big sip, then, with fake interest, asked, 'You're not joining me?'

'No, I've had my fill for today. I need to keep a clear head.'

Mich held the glass in her hand. 'Sounds serious.' She raised it to her mouth, paused, then said, 'Why did you follow me here anyway? I take it you tracked me down. Or were you just passing, and it was all a coincidence?'

'No, it wasn't. I went out of my way to find you.'

'I must say, I'm flattered after all these years.'

'You shouldn't be. Ill feeling was my prime motivator and a big helping of desperation.'

Mich drank her wine. 'Well, I've nothing to offer you unless you want to fulfil some boyhood fantasy and take revenge on me.'

Jay smiled. 'There was a time, many years ago, when that was all I thought about.' He gave her a good, long look. 'You and that prick, Shane, broke my mother's heart. He beat her half to death, you know.'

'Renee was born heartbroken,' Mich said with a snarl. 'Some women just like being taken advantage of.'

'Perhaps,' Jay said, 'and some women are just born cruel; they fix upon people like a curse, bleed them like a leech, then toss them aside when they've no use for them.'

Mich forced a smile. 'You know, you were a lovely little boy, shy and cute, but in many ways an individual. It's a shame you lost all that.'

'What do you mean?'

Mich sipped her wine. 'Your hair, your clothes; you look like a young man trying so hard to be someone else.'

Jay sighed. 'And who might that be?'

'Nash, of course, as if you had to ask. I thought of him the moment I clapped eyes on you.'

'I had a feeling you'd say that. But there again, you've always been predictable.'

'Maybe,' Mich said with a shrug. 'I don't pretend to be something I'm not. You're not too far away from being that scared little boy. Believe me, you'll never be like Nash. You don't have the stomach for it.' She finished her wine and slammed her glass down on the table. 'Now hurry up and make your point. What the hell do you want from me?'

'I thought it was obvious after all this time. I'm here to collect what you owe me.'

'I don't owe you squat.' She motioned to stand, remaining in her seat as Jay grabbed her arm. 'Get off me,' she said, loud enough to turn heads.

Jay lowered his voice. 'Stop making a scene.'

'Don't tell me what to do, following me around, making demands; you're just a bit of a kid.' She looked over at the barmaid. 'What the hell are you gawping at?' The young woman said nothing in reply; all she did was blush and walk away. She returned moments later, accompanied by a lanky young man with a greasy mullet streaked with ash blonde highlights. His face was spotty and pale, the wisps of hair above his top lip trying desperately to look like a moustache.

'Can I ask you to leave, please, madam,' he said with a thin, shaky voice.

Mich feigned a look of surprise. 'May I ask why?'

'You're disturbing the other guests, and we won't tolerate customers who abuse our staff.'

Mich glanced at the barmaid standing at his side. 'How do you know I don't feel abused? I was having a private conversation. This young lady needs to mind her own business.' She looked at the manager's crotch. 'You need to do up your flies. Plus, there's a piss stain on your trousers.' Mich stepped out from the booth. 'If you're going to insult paying guests, then you need to raise your standards.'

She looked over her shoulder at Jay. 'It was nice to bump into you after all these years. Let's not make a habit of it.'

Jay got up and followed her outside, walking alongside her while she hurried down the street. She maintained a fast pace, never stopping for breath, and it was impressive that after all these years of drinking, she'd managed to stay fit. Jay tapped her arm. 'Slow down, for God's sake.'

'No, I won't,' Mich said without looking at him. 'I've told you to stop bothering me. Now back off, or I'll scream for the police.'

'That'll save me the effort, I suppose.'

She paused. 'What's that supposed to mean?'

'You shooting Nash, Pete's body. They would be very interested to hear you're responsible for two deaths.'

'Whatever,' she scoffed. 'I've got some stories of my own. All that money you stole. The way Renee helped you. Do you really want to drag your precious mother through all this?'

Jay guided her towards an alleyway and, lowering his voice, said, 'Fair enough. Neither of us is going to the police. But you need to give me something.'

'Like what? If it's money you're after, I spent it years ago.'

Jay nodded. 'I figured that would be the case.' He rested one arm against the wall and leaned into it. 'You still owe me, regardless of what you might think. I'm sure you know lots of people, Mich. Introduce me to folk; you need to give me something.'

She gave him an incredulous look. 'What the hell do you mean by *Something*?'

'People of influence; point me in the right direction.'

'Towards *what*?'

'I don't know, a job, someone working a con.'

She let out a loud laugh. 'God, you're naive. Do you really think that's how it works? That I'm an agent for some secret grifter employment exchange?' She gave him a sweeping glance, her pale blue eyes staring into his. 'You're so desperate to be him, aren't you?' She laughed again, then stifled it with her hand. 'Go back to the sticks, kid.' Mich shook her head in disbelief. '*Working a con*. What the hell would *you* know about that?'

Jay opened his mouth to respond, but Mich spoke over him before he could reply.

'Oh, my word,' she said. 'The ghosts keep coming out of the woodwork today.' She placed her hand over her mouth, '*Degsy Dempster*,' then laughed.

'You found her then,' Degsy said to Jay with a frown. 'Sometimes you need to be careful what you wish for because it's often a disappointment.'

Mich's eyes widened with surprise. 'You guys know each

other? How the hell? Don't tell me. My guess is that you hooked up at the *Losers' Convention*.'

Degsy looked at her and sighed. 'It's good to see all those years spent in charm school never went to waste. Why don't you humour us for an hour over a drink? Grace us with that smart mouth of yours.'

13

It was called Maggie's Bar, and by the state of the place, the owners, and those who frequented it, seemed oblivious that the 1970s had long passed and it was currently the mid-eighties. Jay scanned the room with a disapproving eye. Basement bars weren't his scene. Admittedly, it was larger than most, with private booths on either side and the floor elevated to three levels, each around a foot higher than the last. The brightest spot was near the bar, the light diminishing the more you stepped away from it until, having retreated to the back tables, you were in almost total darkness.

Jay sat with his back to the wall. Degsy sat beside him while Mich, with her back to the bar, sat in front of them, the outline of her hair tinted with a pale glow of nicotine-coloured light. She reminisced about old times, the music booming through the wall speakers barely rising above her laughter.

'Degsy Dempster and little Jay Ellis,' she kept saying. 'I feel like that grumpy old guy from that soppy Christmas book who gets haunted by the ghosts from his past.'

'That guy reforms in the end,' Jay said with a flat smile. 'But no spirits could ever change you; you're incorrigible.'

'Incorr what?' Mich said, her voice slurred. She scraped her chair closer to Degsy. 'Did you know Jay used to be a little bookworm, Degs? Before becoming a bigshot conman, Jay spent all his time in the local library.' Mich emptied her glass. 'He should have stayed there because the closest he'll ever get to running a con is reading about it in a book.'

'Maybe,' Jay said with a grin. 'But it won't be any book you'll ever write.'

'I wouldn't be so sure about that. I've been mulling over a con for a few days now. Wine helps me shape my ideas. You better be nice to me if you want in on it.'

Jay shrugged her comment off. 'Wine helps with many things, but it isn't your friend in this instance.'

'Your loss,' she said. 'Not that you'd be up to it.'

Jay opened his mouth to respond, but before he got a chance to retaliate, Degsy spoke over him.

'What con?' Degsy said, an expression of eager desperation plastered across his face.

Jay sighed. 'Don't humour her, for God's sake. It's the drink talking.'

Degsy shot him an annoyed look. 'Who I humour and who I don't is my business. Mich has a lot more experience than you. Let the lady have her say.'

Mich smiled. 'Thanks, Degsy. You always were a gentleman.' She glanced at her empty glass. 'Little Jay's right. Perhaps it's a foolish idea.'

Degsy scowled at Jay. 'Don't listen to him.'

'Okay,' Mich said with a shrug, 'but only because you insist.'

She took a deep breath, releasing it with a deeper sigh. 'And don't either of you say a word until I've finished. My proposal might sound a bit extreme at first. But trust me, it'll make sense, providing you hear me out.'

Mich paused, then nodded as though satisfied by the ensuing silence. 'I don't think I was made for marriage,' she said, focusing on Degsy. 'But when Henry Earlston kept asking me, I finally gave in. My prospects weren't too good at the time. So I thought, why not give it a try.'

She reached across the table and took one of Degsy's cigarettes. Jay offered her a light, but Mich, striking one of Degsy's matches, ignored him.

Mich lit the cigarette with one puff and blew the smoke into Jay's face. She flashed Degsy a smile. 'I guess it was a safe bet that things wouldn't work out. No matter how hard I tried, I kept hearing that mocking voice asking me who I was trying to kid? I tired of it in the end. Earlston couldn't do enough for me at first. But my attractions know their limits. Earlston dotes on his daughter. The bastard even confided in her about my so-called overspending. That's no position to be in for any wife. There's no way to win when you're always second best.'

Mich regarded them both while she smoked her cigarette. As Degsy tried to say something, she gave him a stern look. 'Hear me out first, I said. You can ask your questions in a bit.' She caught the attention of the waitress. 'A large white, please, darling, and the same again for these two.' She tapped the waitress's arm. 'Oh, and if Clate's around, tell him Mich is asking for him.'

Mich looked at Degsy through narrowed eyes. 'Where was I? I've lost my chain of thought now.'

'You were giving us a sob story about your failed marriage,' Jay said. 'Divorce is the easier answer. Save you a lot of trouble by the sounds of it; it might even cut short what's turning out to be a long story.'

Mich motioned to stand, remaining in her seat, when Degsy grabbed her arm. 'Ignore him. Carry on, Mich, it's getting interesting.'

Mich scraped the ashtray towards her and put down her cigarette. 'If only it was that simple. Stupidly, I signed some pre-nuptials before the wedding and didn't pay it much attention at the time.' She sighed. 'Divorce would leave me with nothing, and I can't afford that.' She fell silent while the waitress placed her drink on the table. The girl looked at Mich and smiled. 'Clate said these are on the house. He's busy with a few things now, but he'll be right over as soon as he's free.'

'I'll look forward to it,' Mich said, lifting up her drink. She sat quietly with the wine glass in her hand, watching until the waitress returned to the bar, then took a deep sip. 'That's enough back story; let's get to the crux of it. Earlston thinks the world of his *precious* daughter. He'd crumble if anything happened to her. He'd willingly pay a small fortune for her safe return if anyone were to abduct her.'

Mich appeared to gloat over the shocked look in Degsy's eyes. 'It won't be a real kidnapping, of course. It'll seem that way to Earlston. As far as his daughter's concerned, she'll think she's just spending some time away with me. A big payout where no one gets hurt. We'll just run it like any other con.'

Jay shook his head in disbelief. 'Kidnapping. You're really scraping the barrel this time, Mich. You can get twelve years for that.'

'It's not kidnapping,' Mich said through gritted teeth. 'We're running it as a *con*, which no longer concerns you, as you're not up to it.'

Jay pushed his drink away. 'A con that's got disaster written all over it.' He caught the look of fascination in

Degsy's eyes. 'Hey, old man. Don't tell me you're interested. You're just as crazy as she is.'

Degsy finished his drink then, using the back of his hand, wiped the residue from his lips. 'Granted, it sounds crazy from a layman's point of view. But you'd see the potential in Mich's idea if you had more experience.'

Jay sighed. 'Oh, I've got experience, all right. Mich has a habit of running cons that involve gullible kids.'

Mich drank her wine and then slammed the empty glass on the table. 'Earlston's daughter is sixteen. And you hiding stolen money and keeping it for yourself were hardly the actions of a gullible kid.'

'Maybe,' Jay said with a shrug. 'But things only turned nasty when you decided to run a con on me.'

'That was your precious Nash's idea. To be honest, I felt guilty at the time. But staring at the self-righteous look on your face, I don't feel too bad about it now.'

Degsy pushed out his hands. 'That's enough. You've said your piece, Jay. Grifters can't afford to be too sensitive. If you want to make a name for yourself in this game, I'd sleep on it if I were you.'

Degsy was hardly in the position to give advice, but Jay didn't respond, partly because there was some truth to it. But mostly, it was to let Degsy have his moment. Every old dog was entitled to shine for a day.

Degsy smiled. 'Sounds interesting, Mich. I couldn't commit without hearing the details.'

Mich took her cigarette from the ashtray. 'I haven't finalised everything yet. I'll answer any questions if I can. What do you need to know?'

Degsy nodded. 'Let's start with the big one. How much money can we make out of this?'

'A lot,' Mich said. 'Nothing less than fifty grand each. More if we're clever about it.'

'Phew! Things just got more interesting.' Degsy reached for the pack of cigarettes. 'Where are you going to keep–,' he broke off in mid-sentence as both he and Mich looked up at the tall, broad handsome guy standing behind her. The guy rested his hands on Mich's shoulders. 'Long time no see, beautiful.' He nodded at Degsy. 'What the hell are you doing hanging around with this old loser. I hope he isn't bothering you with his little schemes?'

Mich covered the guy's hand with her own, which looked childlike on top of his. 'He's fine, Clate. If anyone's doing any bothering, it's me.'

'Interesting,' Clate said with a grin. 'What about?'

'Nothing,' said Degsy before Mich could reply. 'She's not bothering us at all. Take no notice of her. She's a bright star amongst all this darkness.'

Clate stared at him, his eyes wary and unconvinced, then gestured towards Jay and asked, 'Who's this young pup?'

'He's nobody,' Mich said. 'Nobody at all. In fact, he was just leaving.'

PART II

LIFE OF CRIME

1

J ay had left Maggie's bar without responding to Mich's sarcasm. Their laughter had chased him to the exit, and, glancing over his shoulder, he'd caught the smug look on Degsy's face. The image lingered in his mind, which bothered him slightly. Two days had passed since they last spoke. The con was going ahead. Jay had bought into the idea, and, on the surface, they'd reconciled their differences.

Yet something didn't feel right. Pre-con nerves, perhaps. From cardsharp to pseudo-kidnapper was a giant leap. It was only natural to have doubts. For some reason, their words nettled him. What if the old reprobates saw something Jay couldn't see? He tried casting such notions from his mind, knowing his faith remained firm in his abilities regardless of what they thought about him.

There were also these constant jibes about him trying to be someone he wasn't. Jay never denied Nash's influence. But Jay was his own man, with his own ideas, and was beginning to grow tired of it. He needed to take control. A challenge that grew less feasible now Mich had pulled Clate into their little scheme.

Jay hadn't spent much time in Clate's company. Just that one occasion in Maggie's bar when Clate had referred to him as a *young pup*. It was barely a fleeting glance. But enough to sense that something much darker lurked behind his big, handsome smile.

Of the three, Degsy seemed the most perturbed by Clate's involvement, although he never dared to voice his objections.

'Clate's a pro,' is all Degsy ever said. 'Just don't get on the wrong side of him.'

Jay tried fishing for more, but Degsy responded with a disgruntled silence whenever he asked why. Although intrigued, Jay chose to leave it alone for the time being, having learned from an early age that, given enough time, the ugliness in folk always revealed itself.

Regardless of any misgivings, Clate's apartment off Harrow Road lent itself nicely to Mich's plan. The con wouldn't have worked without it. Degsy's place was a dump, and it would have proved challenging to remain inconspicuous by confining the girl to a hotel. One of Jay's concerns was the place wouldn't be lavish enough. Mich had spoken a lot about Jenny Earlston in the last two days. The girl sounded clever and headstrong. *A chip off the old block,* to use Mich's words, and by Jay's reckoning, a girl who shared and had a solid understanding of her father's high standards.

Mich reassured him the place was fine, and Degsy, to confirm that said, 'Clate bought that place in his heyday. It's more Maida Vale than Harrow Road. Three-story town-house in its own little mews. Very plush by all accounts.'

Jay glanced at his watch; it was almost noon, and twenty minutes from now, he and Degsy were due to meet. He got up from the bed, walked over to the sink, and rinsed his face with cold water. He studied his reflection in the mirror. For some reason, the tiredness in his eyes reminded him of home. He hadn't called his mother for days, but a feeling in his stomach told him she was all right.

Jay resolved to speak with his mother soon, the thought quickly fading from his mind while he made his way to the cafe at the end of the street. Degsy watched him from his usual table. The old grifter had probably been sitting there all morning.

'Coffee, no milk,' Degsy said as Jay approached the counter. Jay looked at the waitress and smiled. 'A tea with no sugar, please. Best get old misery guts a black coffee, I suppose. Put a drop of arsenic in it if you have any.'

The waitress laughed. 'We've run out, I'm afraid. Sit down, love. I'll bring them over to you.'

Jay strolled over to the table and slumped into his seat. He snatched the cigarette from Degsy's mouth and stubbed it in the ashtray.

'Hey,' Degsy protested. 'What the hell do you think you're doing?'

'Protecting our health. I don't want you flaking out on me until this job's over. I'm getting tired of your smoking.'

'It's the only pleasure I've got left.'

Jay grinned. 'Yeah, that and your moaning.'

'You've changed your tune. A few nights ago, you were certain Mich's scheme was headed for disaster.'

'That was before I bought in. You were right about what you said. This could be an easy earner if we play it right.'

Degsy sat quietly as the waitress placed their drinks on the table.

Jay smiled at her. 'Thanks.'

Degsy stirred his coffee, staring intently at Jay. 'That's a good attitude. Let's hope you keep it in mind when you play your part.'

Jay looked at him and frowned. 'Why shouldn't I? All I'll be doing is making a few phone calls.'

Degsy shook his head. 'Nah, that's Clate's job. You and I will be babysitting should things turn nasty.'

Jay frowned. 'I don't think that's a good idea, do you?'

Degsy sipped his coffee and shrugged. 'There's no point dwelling on it. That's the way it is.'

'How can you be so casual about it? This wasn't the plan.'

'Plans don't always run smooth. Sometimes you need to be flexible.'

Jay clenched his hand into a fist. 'This has nothing to do with flexibility, Degsy. It's just stupid. It's a poor deal for you and me.'

Degsy smiled. 'If you're having second thoughts, kid, leave now while you have the chance. There's no shame in being scared. You're still young; you've got many opportunities ahead of you.'

'It's not a case of being scared. This was supposed to be an easy con. The girl isn't supposed to be aware she's being kidnapped, for God's sake.'

Degsy drank his coffee. 'Who said that's changed? That's still the case from what I can see.'

Jay shook his head in disbelief. 'The plan was for Mich and Jenny Earlston to spend *quality time* together. The girl will freak out when she claps her eyes on you and me. Even Mich's mouth isn't smart enough to explain her way out of that one.'

'She won't have to,' Degsy said with a grin. 'We'll be on the lower floor. Clate's place is split into two apartments.'

Degsy laughed. 'If only you could see the look on your face. I had you rattled there for a bit.'

Jay regarded him for a moment. 'I suppose you think you're clever.'

A look of triumph flashed in Degsy's eyes. 'You bet I am, kid. Cleverer than you'll ever be.'

2

—————

Mich watched the sunrise over the city for the first time in years. She sat by the upper floor window, drinking copious amounts of coffee, basking in a wedge of warm light. She felt younger with the sun in her hair. That old empty feeling settled in the pit of her stomach, offering anxiety and hope in the quiet hours of the morning. Earlston was attending a conference. So today had to be *the day*. Otherwise, they would miss the opportunity. Mich had thought about nothing else for days, dropping little hints to Earlston and repeating the story until even she started to believe it.

A *girly couple* of days was how she pitched it. Earlston was hooked from the start. All the man wanted was an easy life, and the prospect of a troublesome wife bonding with his precious daughter proved enough to reel him in.

That's if Jenny wants to go, of course, Mich had added slyly. *We haven't got along these last few weeks. I'm afraid she's going to say no.*

Earlston responded as expected, giving his wife a hug, a

rare note of authority in his voice as he proclaimed, *You leave Jenny to me.*

To Mich's surprise, Jenny agreed without a fight. The girl rarely went against her father's wishes and showed no hint of disapproval. At first, Mich thought it was too good to be true, but Jenny's enthusiasm never waned; she even wrote an itinerary. Museums and art galleries had never been Mich's thing, and as much as she loathed such places, it saddened her slightly that she and Jenny would never get the chance to share them. In a feigned attempt to make amends, Mich cast the emotion aside and began fixing the girl some breakfast.

She went all out: sausage, eggs, bacon, black pudding, and brown toast, with a pot of coffee and orange juice to wash it down. She carried the breakfast tray to Jenny's room, tapping the door gently before walking in. Unsurprisingly, the girl was still asleep. 'It's awfully dark in here,' complained Mich. 'Let some light in, for heaven's sake. These curtains have been drawn for days now.'

When the girl didn't respond, Mich slammed the tray onto the dressing table to wake her up. Jenny turned on her side, breathing heavily with her eyes closed, her face locked in sleep.

'Rise and shine,' Mich said softly until her voice grew louder, forcing Jenny to suddenly sit up.

Jenny pushed the hair from her face and gave Mich a startled look. 'Jesus, Mich. What on earth do you think you're doing? Get out of my room, shouting like a madwoman. It's early morning, for God's sake.'

Mich flashed Jenny her widest smile. 'A morning person, you're definitely not.' She drew back the curtains, smiling as Jenny squinted against the sudden blast of daylight. 'Eat your breakfast before it goes cold. You can't start the day on an empty stomach, especially when we're going on a trip.'

Jenny fell back onto the pillows. 'I just agreed to that to keep Daddy quiet. A *girly trip*. I never imagined you to be so naive. You do realise I've no intention of going anywhere?'

Mich took a deep breath, waiting for her anger to subside, and held it for as long as possible. She exhaled deeply. 'Now that is disappointing. What do you think your father will have to say about this?'

Jenny shrugged. 'Who knows, but seeing as he's away until tomorrow, we'll have to wait and ask him when he gets back.'

Mich answered with a smile. 'We don't need to wait at all.' She delighted in the surprised look on Jenny's face. 'Your dad's flight isn't until ten-twenty. He'll be in his office for the next hour, so let's call him.' Mich walked out of the bedroom and casually made her way to the phone. She picked up the receiver, cradling it against her shoulder as she keyed in the number. She'd barely heard the line click before Jenny snatched the receiver away and hung up. The girl, tousle-haired and red-faced, gave her a fierce look. 'Fine,' she said, her arms folded across her chest. 'Let's go on your *stupid* trip.'

'It's not a trip as such. We'll just go shopping, a health spar, then visit some of those galleries you like.'

Jenny rolled her eyes. '*You,* in a gallery. Look, Mich, you can drop the act. I'll say nothing to Daddy. As far as he's concerned, we had a lovely time. Deep down, I know you feel the same. Let's stop all this nonsense and do our own thing. Neither of us needs to suffer; there's no need to go through with this.'

For a moment, Mich was inclined to agree. The girl might have been a pain, but she certainly had good instincts. Perhaps this was Mich's chance to opt out, forget about her little scheme and take her chances on something else. Clate's words sounded in her head. *Are you sure about this, Mich?* he'd kept asking *because once that girl's in my place, and I've made that call, there's no going back*. He hadn't needed to spell it out. Mich had lived on the periphery for years. She'd grassed on Benny Bray, for God's sake, and managed to keep it a secret. Anyone who had tried blackmailing her was dead. A fake kidnap was nothing compared to what she had been through. She must be getting soft in her old age. Such thoughts strengthened her resolve. There was more to gain than lose; she'd taken bigger risks than this.

'There's every need,' Mich said with a smile. 'You and I need to patch things up and get along better; besides all that, I promised your father.'

'Since when did you ever keep a promise?'

'Since now.'

Jenny narrowed her eyes. 'What are you up to, Mich?'

'I'm sorry?'

'You heard. What's behind all this?'

Mich could feel her heart pounding against her chest but managed to compose herself. 'You always have to think the worst,' she said calmly. 'There's no ulterior motive. Things need to change. We need to start getting along, that's all.'

Jenny looked unconvinced but didn't say anything. She turned towards her room. 'Fine. I suppose I best eat that breakfast, then we can get a move on.'

3

While traipsing through those brightly lit shops, Jenny spoke as little as possible. Mich's fake excitement grated on her nerves, and the only way to cope was to remain unresponsive. Mich remained undeterred, pestering Jenny about buying new clothes, then wittering on about any item that caught her eye. The farce continued for over an hour until Mich's suggestion they grab a coffee became a welcomed respite.

A nearby cafe would have suited Jenny just fine, but Mich insisted on a bar. Jenny agreed without a fuss. City pubs had an olde-worlde feel about them. She liked the scuffed oak tables and the green leather seats, relishing the noontide solitude while basking in the dull half-light.

Jenny sipped her coffee, the small white mug looking drab against the elegance of Mich's wine glass. Mich shot Jenny a smile. 'You look like you're enjoying that. We're having fun, right?'

Jenny shrugged. 'Sure, I guess.'

Mich drank her wine. 'Well, that didn't sound very convincing.'

'Sorry, but that's the best you'll get.'

Mich regarded her for a moment. 'There's no arguing against that. So I might as well make the most of it.'

Jenny returned Mich's smile with her own. Mich was giving it her best shot, working too hard, in fact. Yet Jenny was convinced something was amiss. She could sense when Mich was lying and felt compelled to put her newfound enthusiasm to the test. 'How long are we staying here, Mich?'

Mich gave her a casual shrug. 'Another hour?'

'An *hour*? I thought we were going to the national gallery?'

Mich rolled her eyes. 'There's plenty of time for that. Trafalgar Square will be chock-a-block at this time of day. Don't look like that, Jen. We'll go. I promise. But I want to give you a surprise first.'

'What surprise?'

Mich finished her drink and stood up. 'You'll have to wait and see. It won't be a surprise if I tell you, will it?'

Jenny sighed. 'I've never liked surprises.' She finished her coffee and started to put on her coat, pausing when Mich touched her arm.

'Okay,' Mich said with a sigh, 'half an hour then.'

Jenny pulled away. 'No, Mich, I'm going back home. All this was your idea. You asked me, remember? If you're not going to stick to what we agreed, there's no point in this. I'd much prefer to spend my time alone.'

'I'm sorry. You're right. I had such a good time that I thought a quick drink would be a good idea. But, as always, I got carried away.'

Jenny stood and began buttoning up her coat. 'That's fine. I was starting to get tired, anyway. We gave it a go, Mich, but it's probably best we call it a day.'

Mich's eyes widened with surprise, and, for a moment, she was the palest Jenny had ever seen her. 'No, let's not,' she said, a hint of desperation in her voice. 'I want to make this work. Please, Jen. To hell with that other drink. Let's go to that gallery. Time for you to educate me. Please, give me one last chance.'

～

THEY TOOK the Northern line from Charing Cross to Leicester Square. Then walked the rest of the way, Mich complaining about her heels hurting as Jenny led them through the crowded street. Eventually, they arrived at Trafalgar Square, ascending the wide concrete steps that led to the gallery, the pigeons scattering in their wake. When she stepped inside, Jenny felt different, enchanted by the marble columns, the scent of magnolias, and the mosaic flooring in the main hall.

'Let's start at the bottom and work our way up,' Jenny said, conscious of her over-enthusiasm. 'The early medieval works are my favourites, but you'll probably like the Italian Renaissance.'

Mich followed her through the door. 'If you say so. What makes you so certain?'

Jenny flashed Mich a grin. 'You're not the only one with surprises. You'll just have to wait and see.'

Jenny caught Mich rolling her eyes, and to make their time here as bearable as possible, she bypassed her interests and led them straight to *Diana and Actaeon*.

Mich stood silently in front of the painting for a good ten minutes. 'I'm supposed to like this?'

Jenny nodded. 'I thought it would be your kind of thing.'

'Why, because it's a little raunchy?'

Jenny blushed. 'There is that. But I thought you'd be more interested in its story.'

Mich frowned. 'What story? All I see is a guy in an orange dress perving over some naked women by a pool.'

Jenny laughed. 'There's a bit more to it than that.' She pointed at the painting. 'That guy is Acteon, the hunter, and he comes across the sacred pool of Diana, the goddess of the hunt, something no man should ever do.'

'Which one's Diana?'

'The woman on the right, wearing a crown with a crescent moon.'

Mich nodded approval. 'Thought so. She's looking pretty pissed off to me.'

'She's giving him the death glare, which turns him into a stag where he's eaten by his own hounds.'

'Charming,' Mich said. 'But it was his own fault, right?'

'What makes you say that?'

Mich shrugged. 'You said he saw things he shouldn't see; there's always a price to pay for that.' A faraway look settled in Mich's eyes; she fell silent for a moment and then said, 'likewise, being seen also has its consequences.'

After that, she became quieter, following Jenny through the gallery, linking her arm with her own. Jenny felt uncomfortable at first. They had been arguing for months and adjusting to their newfound peace was strange. Her father's words ran through her mind: *Mich is trying hard here. Why not give her the benefit of the doubt?*

4

_____

With the same effort he used to ignore Degsy's relentless smoking, Jay tried banishing those niggling thoughts from his mind. They refused to let him be, plagued him with negative feelings, rooting in the pit of his stomach, designed to ruin his day. He kept telling himself to move on. Mich and Clate were running things; he was a new face here and needed to prove himself.

Jay wandered from room to room, and although he loathed to admit it, the apartment was modern and clean and exceeded his expectations. On the surface, it looked like Clate had it made: his own club, a small apartment block in a mews; why would he want to get involved in this? Jay headed back to the lounge, wondering if Degsy had any answers?

The old man sat slumped on the red leather sofa. A cigarette smouldered from the corner of his mouth. The holes in his brogues stared brazenly like a black eye as he rested his feet on the table. Jay stepped over Degsy's legs and sat in the chair opposite. They stared at each other in silence until Degsy leaned forward, flicked the ash from his cigarette, and said, 'What's wrong?'

Jay shook his head. 'Nothing; why do you ask?'

'You've got that look about you.'

'What look?'

'Pensive, moody. That face you pull when you're thinking.'

'Any faces I pull are the only ones you're meant to see. So don't kid yourself; you can't read me like a book.'

Degsy shot him a wry smile. 'If you say so, but there's something on your mind.'

'Clate,' Jay said with a sigh.

'What about him?'

'It seems odd, don't you think, for someone doing so well to be part of this?'

Degsy nodded. 'I have a theory about that.'

'Go on.'

'You share something with me first. Quid pro quo, as they say.'

'What do you want to know?'

Degsy stubbed out his cigarette and lit another one immediately after. 'What happened all those years ago with you and Mich? I can piece most of it together, but a few things still bother me.'

Jay leaned forward. 'You can piece most of it together, huh? Well, I'm interested to hear your version of it.'

'Well,' Degsy said, 'I know you took that money belonging to Bowen and Nash. Incidentally, how did you acquire it?'

'I found it in the woods after watching Bowen fall to his death.'

'Phew. That's pretty cold and calculating for a kid; how old were you?'

'Thirteen, and it wasn't calculating. I saw an opportunity, that's all. And *cold* was something I definitely wasn't. I was the complete opposite, in fact.'

'The sensitive type, huh?'

'Yeah, something like that.'

Degsy nodded. 'So you took Nash's money, and he came looking for it. Listening to you and Mich going on at each other, as far as I can tell, he befriended you?'

'Yeah,' Jay said with a sigh. 'Mich and Nash pretended to be a married couple. Nash was the fatherly role model, and Mich, the wayward wife; she had an affair with my mother's boyfriend.'

'That didn't end well by all accounts?'

'The idiot thought they were in love until she ran out on him.'

'He got hit by a car, right? That's a brutal way to go.'

'He was a bully and a coward; he beat my mother half to death and tried to kill me too. Trust me, he deserved it.'

Degsy regarded Jay while he smoked his cigarette. 'How did Nash die? As far as I recall, the newspapers didn't go into much detail. A blow to the head by all accounts?'

'Internal haemorrhage.'

'From your mother's boyfriend?'

'Nope, Mich shot him. She missed his body but still managed to send a bullet scraping across his head.'

Degsy took his feet off the table and leaned forward. 'Mich and Nash go back years. They were close. Ran lots of cons together. I find it hard to believe.'

Jay shrugged. 'I can't see why.'

Degsy shook his head. 'What would drive her to do something like that?'

'Lots of things. Greed. Spite. Who knows? Mich is full of surprises as Jenny Earlston is about to find out.'

'I know, but she's no killer. She must have been desperate to–'

Jay cut Degsy short with a deep, exasperated sigh. 'Your concern is very moving. I answered your questions. Let's move on; we've talked enough about her. I want to talk about Clate now.'

'From one mystery to another, huh,' Degsy said with a smile. 'Anybody with any sense would keep their nose out of Clate's business. Our current predicament suggests we're not as smart as we'd like to think, and seeing as I'm also intrigued, I'll tell you the little I know.'

Jay waved the smoke away from his face. 'Good; any chance you could do it without a cigarette?'

Degsy gave him a disgruntled look. An expression he held while he stubbed out his cigarette. He put his hands behind his head and leant back. 'I also approached Clate with a business deal.'

'When?'

'A few weeks ago.'

'I take it he wasn't interested.'

'He said it was a crazy idea, laughed in my face.' Degsy lowered his arms and slipped a cigarette from his pocket, dropping it on the table as Jay gave him a stern look. Degsy slapped his hands onto his lap. 'He had me believing him for a while until Mich brought him into this.'

'Why the change of mind?'

Degsy leaned forward. 'My scheme was a good solid con. Far less risky than this little caper.' Degsy glanced down at his cigarette and licked his lips. 'I wanted Clate to invest. I never asked him for any capital. All he had to do was provide the venue.'

'So what's your point?' Jay asked.

'My guess is the club's no longer his; he used it to pay off his gambling debts; all he is now is a frontman; he needed permission first before he could run with my con.' Degsy regarded the room. 'As for this place, I reckon it's all show. Any bigmouth with a deposit can get a mortgage.' He snatched the cigarette from the table and popped it in the corner of his mouth. 'Thanks,' he said after Jay gave him a light. 'It's just a theory, of course, and if Clate ever got wind of it, I would deny everything.'

A door slammed upstairs, and at the sound of someone walking above them, Jay and Degsy exchanged glances. 'Sounds like they're back,' said Degsy with a lowered voice.

Jay shook his head and smiled. 'It's a good job you're here. Columbo's got nothing on you.'

Degsy frowned, drew on his cigarette and blew the smoke at Jay. 'You've got to hand it to Mich. From how she described Earlston's daughter, I thought she would struggle to convince the girl to come here.'

Jay looked up at the ceiling. 'I never doubted it for a second. Mich can be very persuasive.'

5

The apartment wasn't as modern as Jenny hoped, but still better than she thought it would be. It was minimalist to the extreme: beige walls and carpet with the smell of recently assembled MFI flatpack furniture. Its best feature was the cream-coloured leather sofa. Two Swiss Cheese plants, each with its own beige pot, were placed on either side of it. Everything stood facing the window, petrified in their bland confinement, basking in the evening light.

Jenny struggled to convince herself this was her father's idea. Rented apartments weren't his thing. He enjoyed fine dining, swimming pools and room service. If he wanted them to have a great time, surely he would have insisted on booking them into a first-class hotel. During the taxi ride here, Jenny suggested this to Mich, who shrugged off the notion saying, 'Your dad left the decision to me. Apartments are more intimate, don't you think? Plus, I got us an excellent deal on this.'

No would have been Jenny's typical curt reply. But they had shared something at the gallery, although she wasn't sure what. A hint of something, an understanding perhaps, had passed between them. She found herself less inclined to retaliate, which, aided by their afternoon Spa, softened her approach. Even now, she opted for a restrained silence. Nodding and smiling as Mich sat beside her and sold her the merits of the apartment.

'I've spent enough time in hotels,' Mich sighed. 'Nine-teen-eighty-six, and most of them still don't have air condi-tioning. I've never had a good night's rest in a hotel; the air's stifling.' She glanced around the room. 'At least you can breathe here.'

Jenny didn't have to try too hard to imagine what Mich had been up to in those hotels, but, for now, at least, she stopped herself from asking. Instead, she reached for the remote and switched on the TV.

'What time is it?' Mich asked.

Jenny glanced at her watch. 'Almost six-thirty.'

'Why don't you watch that quiz program you like.'

Jenny pulled a face. 'Nah, I can't relax when I'm hungry. I thought we could go out somewhere.'

Mich regarded her for a moment. 'No, let's not. It's been a long day for you. I'll get us a takeaway.'

Jenny motioned to stand up. 'I'll come with you.'

'There's no need. You stretch on the sofa and relax.'

Jenny tried explaining she needed the walk, but Mich insisted she stayed put. Mich put on her coat. 'I'll be back in no time; just watch the TV.'

Mich walked briskly into the hall, then out through the front door, the clip-clop of her heels echoing down the steps. Jenny rushed to the window, waiting for Mich to cross the courtyard. A few minutes passed, and still no sign of her. On hearing the mumble of voices coming from the ground floor, Jenny switched off the TV. It sounded like a woman and two men, and on recognising Mich's voice, Jenny hurried into the hall. She tried opening the front door, pushing down on the handle, growing more frantic when realising it was locked.

Jenny thumped the door with her fist. 'Mich,' she shouted. 'Mich, are you still there? The door won't budge.' She waited for a response, stepping back from the door when she heard somebody walking up the steps.

A key turned in the lock, and Jenny watched as Mich pushed open the door. 'Are you okay?' Mich said. 'What's all the shouting about?'

'The door wouldn't budge. I couldn't get out.'

'Where were you going?'

'I wanted to see who you were talking to.'

'Why?'

Jenny shrugged. 'Just curious, I suppose.' She regarded Mich for a moment. 'Did you lock the door from the outside?'

Mich nodded.

'Why would you do that?'

'Habit, I suppose. Plus, your dad made me promise to keep you safe.'

'Safe from what?'

'God knows. Relax, Jen. What's wrong? What's all the panic about?'

'I just wanted to see who you were talking to, and when the door wouldn't open, it stressed me out.'

Mich closed the door and took her coat off, holding it over her arm while Jenny followed her into the lounge. She rested it on the chair, 'it's quiet in here,' then switched on the TV.

Jenny regarded her with a frown. 'I thought you were going for a takeaway?'

'I was,' Mich said with a smile. 'But the old gentleman in the downstairs apartment kindly offered to go for me.'

Bewildered by what she was hearing, Jenny shook her head in disbelief. 'Why would a total stranger do that?'

'Good-natured, I guess. I got talking to him and his son in the foyer. I asked if they could recommend anywhere, which they did, although it's a good thirty-minute walk; luckily, they were on their way.'

'And you just handed over your money?'

'No, actually. I told them what to order, and they said to pay them when they returned.'

Jenny forced a smile. 'Wow. What a fortunate coincidence.'

Mich scowled. 'Don't say it like that.'

'Like what?'

'Like there's something sinister about it. You always see the worst in things. This city still has some good people, you know.'

'That's hard to take coming from you, Mich, seeing as you're the master of cynicism. I just think it's a little strange, that's all.'

'Coincidences often are.' She walked towards the kitchen, tripping slightly over the telephone line. 'Blasted thing.' She followed the line to its source.

'What are you doing?' Jenny asked.

'Moving this phone to the other room where it's safe. I almost broke my bloody neck. That damn cable is a death trap.'

Chance would be a fine thing, Jenny almost said. She closed her eyes, took a deep breath, and then slumped down onto the sofa. She stared aimlessly at the wall, studying the poor finish of the paintwork, becoming increasingly aware of every line and crack.

6

Degsy felt embarrassed by Mich's mistakes, especially after boasting about their profession-alism for weeks. To make matters worse, the kid pointed it out, a look of satisfaction in his young eyes, each condescending word settling like a foul taste in the mouth.

'So you've left her on her own,' he'd said, shaking his head. 'The apartment has a phone, right?'

Degsy pictured the brief yet unmistakable, panicked look on Mich's face. 'Yes,' she'd said dismissively, 'but I doubt she would use it.'

Jay answered her with a nod. 'But you can't be certain of that.' He'd looked at Degsy and grinned. 'Surely that's a rookie mistake. It surprises me you guys haven't got these things covered, considering all your years of experience.'

Mich didn't say a word, and as Degsy trudged up the Kilburn High Road, he wasn't sure what bothered him most: the look of triumph in Jay's eyes or being sent out like some lowly errand boy to buy a takeaway?

Degsy turned up his collar to ward off the cold; he stopped to catch his breath, his bones aching; he was too old to walk the streets. The cars passed him in a flurry of polished steel. He watched them racing into the distance, tapering off to a thin line of shimmering headlights. He reached into his trouser pocket; the twenty-pound note Mich gave him smoothed warmly across his fingers. Degsy considered it with a smile, picturing Jay's face when Mich said, 'I'll tell them our neighbours downstairs offered to go for the food.'

Even Degsy had laughed, more so when Jay said, 'Genius. A pair of kindly strangers going out of their way to help. Jenny Earlston's really going to buy that one.'

'What else am I supposed to say,' Mich said in her defence.

Jay answered with a shrug. 'You shouldn't have to be saying anything. Putting yourself into an awkward position. I thought you were a pro?'

'The girl's hungry.'

'Fine. Then it would have been easier for the two of you to go out. And as for you, Degsy, I don't know what you're looking so smug about; you're the one going for the takeaway.'

'I'm an old man,' Degsy had protested.

Jay answered with a shrug. 'Things are what they are. There's nothing I can do about that.'

Degsy wasn't sure what bothered him most: Jay using his own words against him or the cards falling back into the kid's hands just when Degsy was starting to get a grip. He relinquished the thought with a sigh, his pace almost slowing to a crawl as he trudged his way up the hill. He had half a mind to spend the money on booze. Years had passed since he'd frequented *The Old Bell*. Irish pubs were always the best crack, and the phantom smell of Guinness haunted his senses. He gripped the twenty in his hand, keeping it firmly in his pocket while holding onto it.

Every pub he passed enticed him to go in; that old unquenchable thirst took hold of him, forcing his hand to shake. Degsy remained steadfast, fixing his gaze on the brilliant golden lights from the sign above *The Great Wall* takeaway. At least it was warm inside; his stomach rumbled against the aroma of roast duck and fried rice; meat sizzled from the kitchen as saliva flooded his mouth. Much to his relief, it didn't take long to place the order; the only downside was that he had a twenty-five-minute wait. Degsy took the news with a smile. 'I'll be back later,' he said and headed to the pub.

The Old Bell was busier than he expected. He remembered it as an old man's pub, a refuge for outcasts and hardened drinkers. Tonight, groups of young people filled the place; they seized every table, loud and unapologetic, pushing the regulars to the outskirts of dark solitary spaces.

Degsy weaved through the crowd and joined the queue at the bar, keeping his head down to avoid eye contact. He still bore the bruises from that time in the alleyway, and the last thing he needed was unsavoury attention. Eventually, he found a gap, quickly ordering a whisky and a lager chaser.

After retreating to the far side of the bar, Degsy rested his weight against the wall, nursing his lager while staring through the window. The music's boom battled against the cacophony of voices, and Degsy could barely hear himself think. He rested his drink on the windowsill and tried calming himself by lighting a cigarette. A thin tear trickled down his cheek; his tired eyes burned while every deep exhale thickened the low grey cloud of smoke.

Degsy glanced around, his heart thumping against his

chest when he saw him. Even among the mass of faces, Nick Bryant stood out. His slicked-back hair glinted beneath the amber-coloured lights. Clean-shaven and dressed for a night on the town, a sky-blue flexed jacket had replaced his ill-fitting suit. Bryant looked so sure of himself, chatting confidently with the two teenage girls standing on either side of him.

Degsy lowered his head, keeping his eyes fixed on the floor, wondering if he'd been spotted, never daring to look up. With shaking hands, he finished his drink, emptying his glass with three desperate gulps. Degsy shouldered his way through the crowd, pushed open the door and stepped outside.

Hurrying back to the takeaway, he half-expected Bryant to call out his name. Degsy quickened his pace, conscious of somebody behind him, expecting that familiar clammy hand to land heavily upon his shoulder. *What the hell was he doing around this way?* Degsy mumbled, the anguished look on his face turning into a grimace as Bryant's sickly grin lingered in his mind's eye.

He shoved open the takeaway door and strode to the counter. 'Order for Dempster,' he said, ignoring the disgruntled sighs from behind him.

'There's a queue here,' a woman shouted.

Degsy turned to face her. 'I joined it half an hour ago. This is a pickup; I'm here to pay, love.'

A look of self-righteous indignation melted from the woman's face. Degsy waited for another comment, but the woman didn't say anything else. The lad behind the counter brought Degsy's food, reading out the order while Degsy tapped his foot with impatience. 'Aye, that's mine. How much do I owe you?'

'Seven-fifty, please.'

Degsy handed him a tenner, never bothering to wait for his change and hurried out. With his head bowed, he hurried down the Kilburn High Road. He was confident he'd left the pub unseen, although that doubting inner voice tried convincing him otherwise.

7

Jenny was happy to take the box room, but Mich insisted on giving her the ensuite. It was kind of her the more she thought about it. However, there was something off about Mich's persistence. As Jenny lay snug beneath the quilt, languishing in the rays of morning sunlight, she concluded there was something odd about the entire night. It started with Mich locking the door, followed by the strangers downstairs offering to go for the takeaway.

Jenny wanted to thank the elderly gentleman for bringing their food, but Mich, eager to get shut of him, refused to invite him in. Jenny didn't let the incident pass unnoticed, but Mich tried shrugging it off when she challenged her.

'He didn't seem keen to hang around,' Mich said in her defence.

Jenny remained unconvinced. 'I'm not surprised after you snatched the food from his hands. You barely gave him a smile, didn't even say *Thank you*.'

'Sorry. I guess I'm just tired and hungry. I'll apologise in the morning.'

'Shouldn't you go there now? Were you expecting our food for free?'

'I paid him before he went.'

The answer caught Jenny by surprise. She regarded Mich for a moment. 'Really? Because you told me he said to pay him when he returned.'

Mich shook her head and frowned. 'I think you're confused, darling. Honestly, I swear I never said that.'

Jenny played the scene repeatedly in her mind. The aroma of last night's sweet and sour lingered uncomfortably like Mich's blatant lie. She threw off the quilt, sat up, and rested her feet on the carpet. This soulless room strengthened her resolve to go home. The strained truce between her and Mich had outstayed its welcome. She stretched her arms, yawned, and then trudged to the bathroom.

Jenny brushed her teeth in a daze, frowning at her reflection as she wiped the toothpaste from her lips. After slipping off her t-shirt and pants, she turned on the shower, standing naked outside the cubicle until the water got hot. Shivering, Jenny placed a hand on her stomach and smoothed it across the goosebumps over her skin. Water gushed from the shower, its heat giving her an instant buzz as she stood beneath it. Jenny closed her eyes and sighed. This entire trip had been a big mistake. She didn't believe a word Mich said. Last night's behaviour confirmed her suspicions. She needed to talk it through with her father. What the hell was this awful woman up to?

Like a malign spirit summoned by ill thoughts, Mich waltzed into Jenny's bedroom. 'I'm turning on the extractor fan,' she shouted. 'There's too much steam in here.'

Jenny folded her arms across her chest. 'Do you mind? Don't barge in here like that. I'm having a shower.'

Mich waved the protest away with her hand. 'I came in to pass you a towel. When I heard the shower going, I realised you didn't have any.' Turning her back to Jenny, Mich stood facing the door. 'You've got nothing I haven't seen; there's nothing special about you.'

'I never said there was. But don't you think I'm entitled to a bit of privacy?'

'I guess,' Mich said with a sigh. 'Let's forget it. I was only trying to help. Let's not argue. What do you fancy doing today?'

Jenny closed her eyes and massaged the shampoo into her hair. 'Thanks for all your efforts, Mich. I've had a nice time and everything, but without wanting to sound ungrateful, I'm exhausted. So I'm going to head home today and give our little excursion a miss.'

She waited for Mich to try talking her out of it, but the only response was silence. Jenny rinsed the shampoo from her hair, surprised to discover Mich was no longer standing there. 'Don't be like that,' she shouted. 'Mich, Mich,' again, there was no answer. She heard a loud thud as Mich slammed the bedroom door shut.

Jenny dried herself with haste. There was little point in continuing this pretence. It was a shame things hadn't worked out. Undoubtedly, Mich would sulk for a few days then things would return to normal. At least Jenny had learned something: being cooped up in that apartment for days did nobody any good. She felt revived after visiting the Gallery and was determined to start going out more. She dressed with equal vigour, making her bed and packing her things while listening to the Peter Powell show on the radio.

The charts weren't really her thing. She liked *The Smiths*, and *the Bunnymen*, anything more indie.

Jenny grabbed her things and strolled over to the door. She pressed down on the handle and tried pulling it towards her, using more strength when the blasted thing wouldn't open. Jenny tried again, her heart pounding in her chest as she frantically pulled on the handle. 'Mich,' she cried. 'Mich,' and banged the door with her fist.

'Calm down,' was Mich's harsh response. 'You're like a crazy person. Stop all the hysterics, for God's sake.'

'I can't open the door.'

There was a momentary pause, then, with a coldness of tone that was all too familiar, Mich said, 'That's because it's locked.'

Jenny kicked the door. 'All this because I'm going home? You're taking this too far. Open the door, you crazy bitch.'

'Calm down first.'

'I will as soon as you let me out.'

Mich gave an exasperated sigh. 'Later, perhaps, once you've calmed down, but at the moment, I can't do that.'

8

Henry Earlston was no stranger to loneliness. After the death of his first wife, he threw himself into his work. For a time at least, long hours of obsessive toil helped quieten those insatiable feelings of grief. Meeting Mich offered hope, and for a while, he saw her as his saviour. Today's call changed that. The fear and desperation in Mich's voice told him she was as weak as anybody else. That unrelenting feistiness, unmistakably hers, was nothing but false bravado.

Initially, the man's tone had been light; for a moment, Earlston registered it as a prank call, somebody's sick idea of a joke. The notion quickly passed as the man's dark intentions settled as a grim realisation. His message was short and to the point, 'Two hundred thousand in used notes, Earlston. You've got two days. Don't talk to the police or authorities, or you'll never see your wife or daughter again.'

'Who is this?' Earlston stammered. 'This is insane. No, you listen to me; how do I know they're safe?'

Then Mich came to the phone, her voice thick with emotion, her words barely comprehensible. 'Just do as they say, Henry. Pay them what they ask. Trust me, they're serious.'

'Are you hurt? What about Jen? I'm doing nothing until I'm certain she's all right.'

Mich broke into tears. 'She's okay. Very frightened–'

'Let me speak with her,' Earlston had insisted.

'I'm sorry, Henry. But they won't let her come to the phone right now.'

Earlston tried to say something, falling silent when the stranger spoke over him. 'She'll be fine, providing you do as you're told. Just get that money together and keep your mouth shut. I'll call you at noon tomorrow to check in.'

Earlston had spent the last thirty minutes slouched on the floor with his head in his hands, his back resting against the radiator. His mood blackened while he tried to make sense of it. The throbbing pain in his head intensified as he grappled with every wild scenario. Over the years, he'd stepped on a few toes. All businesses brought their share of fallouts. Admittedly, not all his deals had been legit. Yet he'd been careful not to make too many enemies and could recall nothing that would provoke a reaction as extreme as this.

To prevent himself from sobbing, Earlston bit into his fist. The picture of his daughter lingered in his mind's eye, forcing him to get up. He paced the room. Jenny's suffering must be ten times worse than his. 'Come on,' he shouted to himself. 'For God's sake, man, get a grip.'

Something inside him, panic perhaps, urged him to call the police. The notion vanished as he shook his head. *No authorities* was the one strict instruction. It might prove fatal to do otherwise. He needed to follow their orders, for now, at least. Sunlight splintered through the blinds, casting a cage of shadow across the wall. Earlston hurried into his study, sat at his desk, and pulled open the top drawer. With trembling hands, he took out his leather-bound ledger and began flicking through the pages. The number he was searching for stared at him brazenly in red ink. Earlston reached for his phone and dialled the number, wiping his clammy hand on his shirt while waiting for a response.

The line rang, and it felt like an age before someone answered. 'Hello, 01-353-8421,' said a woman's voice.

'Is Charles there?'

'Can I ask who's calling, please?'

'It's Henry.' Earlston cleared his throat. 'Henry Earlston.'

'Oh, hello, Henry. I didn't recognise your voice.' She paused for a second. 'I'll see if he's still here. I think he might have gone out.'

Earlston recognised the ploy: Charles Hoffman lounging in his favourite chair while his wife notified him of the call, checking if it was somebody he wanted to talk to. Fortunately, it was. 'Henry,' said Hoffman's deep voice. 'To what do I owe the honour?'

'Sorry to call you at home.'

'Not a problem. How can I help you? Everything, all right?'

'Yes,' Earlston lied, but Hoffman was no fool. Being a successful financial advisor required the ability to read people, and he undoubtedly recognised Earlston's sense of urgency.

Again, Earlston cleared his throat. 'The Bradbook shares, I'm looking to sell; wondered if you could get me a good price?'

'They've fallen flat lately.' Hoffman went silent for a moment. 'Crayburns are a better option, especially if you're after raising more capital.'

'Timescales?'

'Oh, a good few weeks, a month even.'

'That's too long.'

'It's pretty quick, to be fair, considering all the tie-ins. I–'

'No,' Earlston interrupted. 'I need something in the next few days.'

'A *few days*. That's a tad optimistic. Even with the most enthusiastic buyer, it'll take a week.'

Earlston placed his hand over the mouthpiece and sighed into it. He removed his hand and smoothed it across his sweating brow. The momentary silence rang in his ears. 'No. No. That's too long. Can't you help to push it through?'

'I'll try,' Hoffman said after a long pause. 'Is everything all right, Henry?'

Even though it was said with suspicious hesitancy, Hoffman's concern sounded genuine. Earlston tried lightening his tone. 'Of course, just trying to raise some funds, that's all.'

'Might I ask why?'

'A pet project of mine. It's all a bit hush-hush.'

'I didn't mean to pry.'

'I know that. I've a new place in mind. Something to surprise the family.'

'You're moving?'

'No, this is more of a holiday home, an extra property.'

'Interesting,' said Hoffman after a brief pause. 'Expensive?'

'Why do you ask?'

'Just wondered if you could draw the money from the bank. You can get something nice for forty to fifty K. Cashing in the Bradbook shares now would only give you three to four times that. Why not wait a few years. Surely someone with your experience knows that's a wiser investment.'

Earlston took a deep breath, tempted to slam the phone

down. 'I appreciate the sound advice, Charles; however, that being said, I'd appreciate it more if we could move forward with this.'

'Absolutely,' Hoffman said with strained reciprocation, 'I'll get back to you ASAP,' then hung up before Earlston could reply.

Earlston snapped the ledger shut and placed it face down on the desk. He reached into another drawer, rummaging through the pile of recent junk mail and utility bills until fishing out his chequebook.

An old photograph of Jenny stared up at him. The girl looked so sweet and innocent. How old was she in that captured moment? She couldn't have been no older than ten. The day flashed clearly in Earlston's mind: that cloudless blue sky, the sun beating down on them while they walked idly across the Margate sands. *Poor Jenny, Sweet Jenny,* he whispered as an insatiable feeling of loss consumed him. But you have a wife too, the guilt-ridden voice in his head eagerly reminded him.

Forcing himself to think of Mich, he tried picturing their first encounter, a romantic rendezvous, a kiss. Nothing presented itself from his memory, as though their time together never existed. Earlston picked up the chequebook, slapping it across the back of his hand. It wasn't the time for sentimentality. Like a drunken man suddenly awakened by the cold wash of morning light, the sobering thought of visiting the bank quickly brought him to his senses.

9

Clate hated the smell of the kitchen, the grease under his fingernails, and that constant oily film across his skin. He loathed the bar too, hated the false smiles and the endless whining from those hopeless ash-grey faces. Most of them had opinions about everything, the rising unemployment, the Wapping dispute, and even that Scouse comedian who ate someone's hamster.

The place had brought him nothing but pain. A pain, on paper at least, that wasn't even his. '*We'll let you stay on for a bit*,' one of Bray's lackeys had said. Both they and Clate knew it was meant as an insult. Acting manager was no position for a man of his standing. Losing the place in a card game was indeed a fall from grace.

'I've got some business to attend to,' Clate said to the doorman. He threw the man a set of keys. 'I want this place empty by twelve. Pay the girls from the petty cash, then lock up.'

The doorman nodded. 'Oh, Clate,' he said as though something had suddenly sprung to mind. 'Clate,' he said again.

Clate didn't turn around and walked through the door without answering. He stood on the corner of Old Crompton Street for at least ten minutes before he could hail a taxi. 'The bottom of Kilburn High Road,' he said as he climbed into the back and slammed the passenger door shut.

The taxi edged forward along the busy road. 'Who do you fancy for the cup?' the driver said. 'Dalgliesh's boys should nail it, I reckon.'

Clate was in no mood for small talk. 'Football's not my thing,' he said and silenced the driver with a sigh.

Clate sat as if he was in a daze, the busy street passing him by unnoticed while the noise of the oncoming traffic engulfed him. His conversation with Earlston lingered in his thoughts, and he felt confident the man would not run to the police. Clate didn't know what angered him more: the man's eagerness to please or the desperation in his voice. Men like Earlston had the good life handed to them on a plate, but that was about to change. Not only would he learn how to beg, but for the rest of his days, he would know what fear was.

The taxi abruptly stopped, the engine rattling as the driver said, 'That's two-eighty, mate.'

Clate handed him a fiver. 'Keep the change,' he mumbled, then got out.

With his hands in his pockets, Clate hurried down Kilburn Park Road, then took a right into the Cedar Mews courtyard. At the main entrance, Clate looked up at the top-floor apartment. He could hear the noise from outside: a faint hammering, a hysterical scream, each brief spell of silence broken by sporadic shouting. Clate went inside, ran upstairs, and banged the door with his fist.

Mich let him in, frowning as he fanned away the cigarette smoke.

'Jeez, Mich, the air in my club is cleaner than this; open a window at least.'

'I would if I could.' She nodded towards the bedroom door. 'But little lady Fauntleroy won't stop screaming.'

Clate followed her into the lounge, gesturing for Degsy to remain seated as he motioned to stand up. Clate shook his head at Degsy and sat in the chair opposite. He looked up at Mich. 'A nice easy con, you said. Take the money and run *"the girl won't even know she's been kidnapped."*'

Mich rolled her eyes. 'Sarcasm won't help. What was I supposed to do? She insisted on going home. All I could think to do was to lock her in her room. All she's done since is try to get out.'

'So I can hear,' Clate said as the screaming and banging resumed. He threw Degsy a look. 'Where's the pretty boy?'

Degsy shrugged. 'Who knows? Gone out somewhere, said it was important business.'

Clate shook his head. 'I told you both to stay put, to sort things out if we encountered a *situation.*' He snatched the cigarette from Degsy's mouth. 'You should have checked in with me first. *Important Business.* I'll let you know what's important and what isn't. At the moment, you guys don't get to decide that.'

A high-pitched scream resonated up the beige walls, and the relentless thud sounded like the girl was trying to kick the door in. Clate slapped his hands onto his lap and stood up. 'You and pretty boy should have sorted this.' He let out a defeated sigh. 'But it seems I have to sort out all the nastiness myself.'

Clate held out his open hand and looked at Mich, 'Key,'

he demanded. She placed it on his palm, watching him while he closed his hand into a fist.

Feeling the cold metal against his skin, Clate stormed out of the lounge, stopping when he reached the bedroom door, unlocking it with a swift turn of his wrist. He shoved open the door, 'Hey, what's all the noise about?'

The girl's eyes widened with surprise; she looked at him for a second. Then something in her face changed. 'You better let me–'

'Shut your mouth,' Clate said, knocking her to the floor with a hard, resounding slap. 'You stay quiet now; staying quiet is your only way through this.'

10

Jay had no business to attend to; he just needed to be out of that apartment and get away from Degsy. The old man got on his nerves and seemed to take pleasure in it. There was no malice behind his words. Each small victory gave him strength. Degsy's best days were long behind him. The con, siding with Mich and Clate, gave him something to cling onto. If only they were as bright as they made out. No wonder neither of them had made it big. At best, they looked like amateurs, and Jay cringed at every blatant mistake.

Ever since Jay was a boy, walking helped him think. The vast, open fields of his youth were out of reach, but with the sun bright in the clear sky, he made do with the London streets. He wandered through Maida Vale, side-tracking into Abercorn Place, Hall Road, and then back into Sutherland Avenue. The white, pillared stucco houses of Warrington Crescent were things of dreams. He yearned for a touch, a glimpse, wanting this and more. The home he'd always dreamed of. This life, the things he'd always strived for.

Jay took a deep breath, wandering aimlessly towards

Warwick Avenue until he found a telephone box. He pulled open the door, grimacing at the smell of stale urine as the door closed slowly behind him. Jay dug into his pocket for change and placed a fistful of ten-pence pieces on the counter. Cradling the phone between his neck and shoulder, he dialled the number, slotting in three coins when he heard the pips.

'Hello?' said a tired voice.

'Desmond, it's Jay.'

'Hello?'

'It's Jay, Desmond. Have you gone deaf?'

There was a momentary pause that felt like a long silence. 'Jay,' Desmond said with a sigh. 'Are you all right?'

'I'm fine.'

There was a rustling sound, and then Renee's unmistakable voice said, 'Where the hell have you been, Jay? We've been worried sick.'

'Sorry,' Jay said. 'I've been meaning to call. Just lost track of time. I'm in–'

'Don't tell me where you are, as long as you're all right?'

Jay felt the worry in his mother's voice. 'I'm fine. What's wrong?'

'Some people came to the house.'

'What people?'

'Scary people, with scouse accents. People, I'm sure you know.'

Jay momentarily closed his eyes and sighed. 'I'm so sorry, Mam. Are you okay?'

'Shaken up a bit, but I'll live.'

'Did they hurt you?'

'No. The bastards barged their way in. They pushed Desmond around a little.' She went silent for a moment.

'They slapped Desmond across the face, across the face, Jay, in his own bloody house.'

'I'm coming back. I'll be–'

'No, Jay, don't. You stay where you are. They're done asking their questions.'

'What questions?'

'If I knew where you were. Thankfully, I'm a poor liar. So, they didn't need much convincing when I told them I didn't know.'

'I'm sorry, Mam. I'm so–'

'It's a bit late for sorry. I warned you, Jay. I told you to get those stupid ideas out of your head. Nash was no good. Trying to be like him is a big mistake. Look where it's led you.'

Jay didn't answer and slotted in more coins when he heard the pips. 'I'll come home. I'll–'

'No,' Renee insisted. 'No, Jay. It'll just make things worse. They're probably watching the house. You stay away for a while until all this mess goes away.'

'At least let me leave a number–'

'No. It's best that I don't know where you are. If they call again, ignorance is the only way to protect you.'

'How will I know you're both safe?'

'Isn't it a bit late for that?' Renee let out a heavy sigh. 'We'll be fine. Don't worry. Call back in a few weeks. You watch what you're doing, Jay. You take care of yourself.'

Jay tried to apologise again, but Renee hung up before he could say a word. He pushed open the telephone box door and stepped outside, welcoming the fresh air falling coolly across his skin. The sky had clouded over, and the grey hues it cast across the city heightened the lingering emptiness inside him. Jay continued along Warwick Avenue, took a left down Blomfield Road, nipped down the footpath signposted *Little Venice* and ambled along the canal.

London's hidden beauty never failed to surprise him. Moored canal boats formed an endless line along the narrow stretch of water. The leafy walkway gave the illusion of foreign lands. It was the same feeling he often had as a kid, a mixture of sadness and delight, where the elated grandeur of being detached neared the borders of loneliness.

Jay recalled Renee's words and pictured Jackmond's thugs barging into Desmond's house. His heart told him to go home, but Renee was right; it would only make things worse. Trouble awaited him at both ends. For the time being, staying put made more sense. At least he could make some money out of it. Either way, Jay didn't have much choice. It felt like a fool's errand, no matter how he looked at it. He couldn't go back with nothing. Capital and reputation were the keys. Only money helped men like Jackmond to find forgiveness.

11

J ay had barely walked through the door when Degsy said, 'Clate's here; he's not happy; he wants to speak with you.'

A look of expectancy lingered in the old man's eyes. A look Jay had seen so many times before, at the boxing matches, where countless faces waited hungrily for the fight. Jay glanced up at the ceiling. 'I take it he's upstairs?'

Degsy nodded.

'How come you're down here?'

'Clate told me to wait for you.'

Jay grinned. '*Told*? That's interesting. I assumed you were a partner in all this, although it seems Clate's running things now.'

Degsy frowned. 'A word of advice, you hold your tongue when you speak with Clate. I know you're quick with your hands. But Clate's not Bryant. You probably haven't come across the likes of him before. So try your best not to be a smart mouth, or it won't end well for you.'

'So you keep reminding me,' Jay said as he walked out the door and took the stairs to the upper apartment.

Mich answered after one knock. 'Look who it is. The prodigal son returns.'

Jay followed her inside, grimacing at the strong smell of booze on her breath. She sat on the arm of Clate's chair and pointed at the chair opposite. 'Sit.'

Jay did as she asked, scanning Clate with one glance while the big man sat staring at him. Clate wore black slacks and a white cotton shirt with the sleeves rolled up at the cuffs. A gold medallion nestled against his hairy chest. It glinted when it caught the sun, as did the sovereign rings on his fingers. Clate puffed on his cigar, the smoke curling through his hand as he plucked it from his mouth. 'Where've you been?'

'Out.'

'You've no business going out. You should have been here keeping an eye on things. We've had ourselves a *situation*.'

'What situation?'

Clate glanced towards the hall. 'The girl tried to get out; she got a bit agitated.'

Jay glanced at the smear of dried blood on Clate's hand. 'Looks to me you've already sorted it.'

Clate leaned forward. 'I did what needed to be done. None of this is pleasant. Perhaps things could have been handled differently if you'd been here.'

Jay leaned back into the chair, resting his hands behind his head. 'Things shouldn't have needed handling in the first place.' He threw Mich a glance. '*A nice easy con where the girl wouldn't even know*. That was the plan the last I heard.'

Clate rose from his chair. 'Stand.'

'What?'

Clate licked his forefinger and thumb, then pressed them against the tip of his cigar. 'Stand.' Clate raised his voice. 'Stand. Get up, I said.'

Jay slowly stood up, pushing back his chair to give more space. He took his hands from his pockets, catching sight of Degsy watching them from the doorway.

'Apologise,' Clate said.

Jay, watching Clate's every move, said, 'For what?'

'Not doing as you're told and screwing up.'

Jay took a deep breath. 'Firstly, you don't get to tell me what to do.' He looked at Mich as she sat up, undecided about what sickened him most, the gloating look in her eyes or the smug smile across her face. 'As for screwing up, these two are managing that without my help.'

As Clate jerked forward, Jay moved his left foot slightly, partly extending his left arm with his right held close to his body and his fist near his chin.

'Nice stance,' Clate said through a fit of laughter. 'Looks like Scouse knows how to defend himself.' Clate smiled. 'Sit down, Sugar Ray. I only wanted to see if you had any balls. Sit down, for God's sake. There's been enough commotion for today.'

Clate slumped back into his chair, holding his grin, while Jay sat opposite. Clate gave Mich a shove. 'Go get us something to drink.'

Mich answered him with a glare. 'What did your last slave die of?'

Clate laughed and rested his big hand on her shoulder. 'Asking too many questions. Now fetch us some of that wine you've been hoarding.'

Mich rolled her eyes and sighed. 'I'll get you and Degsy a glass.' She threw Jay a fierce look. 'Sugar Ray doesn't touch the stuff.'

Clate slapped her behind as she stood up. 'Is that so?' he said, looking at Jay. He shook his head with exaggerated disbelief. 'Teetotallers are the ones to watch. Degsy. Degsy, get yourself over here. Why the hell are we partnering with a man who doesn't drink?'

Degsy mooched into the room and sat down on the sofa. 'He doesn't smoke either,' Degsy said and lit another cigarette.

Clate sighed into his hands and then slapped them down upon his lap. 'He's right in what he says, though. This isn't an easy con; it's a frigging mess.'

Jay nodded in agreement. 'How was your call with Earlston?'

Clate wiped the tiredness from his eyes. 'As expected, I suppose. He was obliging, frightened, but there was something in his voice.'

'Like what?' Mich asked as she handed Clate a glass.

Clate sipped his wine. 'I'm not sure. I just sensed a bit of hesitancy.'

Mich passed Degsy his glass. 'Hesitant about what?'

Clate released an irritated sigh. 'I don't know, about contacting the police, I suppose.'

Mich laughed. 'He hasn't the nerve, trust me.'

Jay regarded her for a moment. 'We trusted you about this being an easy con and look where that got us.'

'You shut your mouth,' Mich said, 'You shut your big–' pausing when Clate held out his hand.

'Enough,' Clate said. He looked at Mich and sighed. 'The kid has a point, though.'

Mich shrugged. 'A point that serves no use. It is what it is. Let the girl go if you're getting nervous.'

Clate finished his drink and, holding the stem between his forefinger and thumb, twirled the empty glass. 'Letting her go would be the end for us.' He gave Mich a fierce look. 'I warned you there'd be no going back once we crossed that line. We've come too far now.' He stretched out his arm and offered Mich the empty glass. 'So do something useful and fill this up.'

'Fill it yourself.'

'I said fill it up.'

Mich snatched the glass from his hand and went to the kitchen, cursing them all under her breath. Degsy, who had sat quietly through it all, asked, 'How long did you give him to pay?'

'Two days, like we agreed.' Clate raked his fingers through his hair. 'It'll be a long two days the way things are going. I can't be around here all the time. I've got a club to run. Do you understand?'

Jay nodded, feeling the dark intensity of Clate's eyes bore into him.

Clate gave him a flat smile. 'Good. That's why I need you here. Someone smart and level-headed to take care of things.'

12

In this partially lit room, Jenny could hear their voices. They travelled faintly across the hall, the stern, deep tones interspersed with sudden bouts of laughter. She lay on her side, peering through her tousled hair, her skirt raised partially over her blouse, the concrete floor cold beneath the cheap thin carpet.

Initially, the slap had knocked her out. Afterwards, Jenny drifted in and out of consciousness. No one had ever struck her like that, and she cried until she could cry no more, until the run of dry tears dirtied her face. Pushing the tip of her tongue across her newly chipped tooth, a relentless pain throbbed inside her mouth. She felt useless and weak, but her fear revolted her more and filled her with self-disgust.

Jenny pushed the hair from her face and slowly sat up, trying to make sense of it. Who was the stranger? An intruder? No, Mich had locked her in. Her lover, then. Jenny suppressed a scream. Mich had gone crazy. Was all this just to teach her a lesson? If it was, she had taken things too far.

The crazy drunken bitch, Jenny almost cried. What on earth was she thinking?

Jenny stood and hugged herself against the cold. The feeling was a sharp contrast to her morning shower, the only similarity being the goosebumps across her skin. She edged closer to the door, listening attentively, pausing whenever the mumble of voices became louder. When they grew quieter, Jenny pushed down on the handle, surprised to find the door unlocked. She took a deep breath and opened the door, standing motionless, her body caught between shadow and a dullish yellow light. Jenny pulled the door wider, breathing heavier now, and stepped out into the hallway.

Treading softly along the carpet, the sound of broken glass stopped her in her tracks. 'Jesus, Degsy,' a man shouted. 'Watch what you're doing. I haven't long decorated this place.'

There was a mumbled response; the voice sounded tired, much older.

'*Degsy*,' the man said. 'Come on, get off your arse and clean it up.' A brief silence followed, 'Clean it up, I said,' and Jenny ran down the hall at the sound of heavy steps trudging across the carpet. The sprint lasted only seconds, but the space between her and the front door felt miles away. She pressed down on the latch, feeling a cold hand clasp her forearm when she tried pulling the door open.

'She's trying to get out,' the man standing behind her hollered. Jenny turned to face him, undecided what repulsed her more, the red veins across his bulbous nose or the stale smokiness of his breath?

When she tried pulling free, the old man tightened his grip. 'It's the girl, I said; she's trying to get out. Are you all deaf?'

Like a hungry pack answering a distress call, they hurried towards her. Mich was out front with a younger guy, who Jenny hadn't seen before, close behind her. The brute who had struck her stood at the back. He stretched his long, muscular arm and pointed at them with his glass. 'What's all the fuss about. The foyer door's locked. Just get her back in her room.'

'That's what we're trying to do,' Mich shouted over her shoulder. 'She wouldn't be here if you'd locked the door after you.'

The old man released her arm. 'You best go back to your room, love. Makes no sense to make things worse now.'

Mich shoved the old man aside. 'Go and clear up that glass, Degsy. Let me handle this.' The old man shrugged and walked away. Mich gave the younger man a fierce look. 'Same goes for you, Jay.'

The younger man shook his head. 'I'll stay here if that's okay with you, seeing as she knows all our names now.'

Mich answered him with a sigh, turned to face Jenny, and held out her hand. 'Come on, Jen. Let's go back to your room. There's no reason you should suffer anymore because of this.'

Jenny pushed away from her hand. 'There's no reason I should suffer at all.' She banged her fist against the door. 'Now, let me out of this place.'

Mich shook her head. 'I can't do that, honey. Your father owes these men money. They won't release us until he pays up.'

'*Us*,' Jenny shouted. 'It was you who locked me in. You're part of this.'

Mich shook her head. 'Believe me, I had no choice.' Tears welled in her eyes. 'They threatened to hurt me. I locked you in the room to keep you safe.'

'Bullshit,' Jenny said. 'You must think I'm stupid. The trip, the apartment, the takeaway. It's all part of your pathetic little plan.'

'Not my plan, Jen. Theirs. Believe me, I had no choice. God knows what would have happened if I refused to go along with it.'

'You could have gone to the police.'

'It's not as easy as that. I know these people from old. I know what they're capable of.'

'From old? Yeah, I thought you all seemed a bit friendly.'

Mich sighed. 'My chequered past. It's not something I'm proud of.'

Mich touched Jenny's arm, scowling when Jenny shrugged away. Mich's lies made Jenny want to scream and continue screaming until she had howled her lungs out. She managed to suppress it, silenced partly by fear and bewilderment from Mich's involvement.

'Let me out,' Jenny said, her voice almost a whisper as though suddenly conscious of the futility of her request. She slumped down onto the carpet, her back resting against the door. The big man, who had struck her previously, stepped back into the hall. 'Is that damn brat still not in her room?' His speech sounded more slurred than before, and he swayed slightly, a stance he quickly corrected by leaning his weight against the wall.

'Go back inside, Clate,' the younger guy said. 'You too, Mich.'

At first, Mich refused to budge. Then something changed her mind, Jenny's scowl perhaps. Whatever it was, it drew her towards Clate as he motioned her forward with his hand. 'Come on, Mich. Let young Jay handle this.'

The young man called Jay strolled towards her; standing less than a foot away, he rested on his haunches. The softness in his eyes could easily have been mistaken for tenderness should a girl not know any different. A smile lit up his face. A face that Jenny would have thought of as goodlooking in better circumstances.

He pointed at her lip. 'That looks pretty swollen. I can get you something from the freezer to put on that.'

Jenny shook her head. 'You'd be helping me more, yourself too, if you just let me go.'

Jay regarded her for a moment and, for a second at least, appeared to consider it. He smiled. 'I would if I could. The best thing I can offer is to ensure you stay safe through all this.'

She regarded him for a moment. 'What if Daddy doesn't pay?'

'He loves you, right?'

She nodded her head, the quickness of her response making her feel childlike.

'Exactly,' Jay said. 'He thinks the world of his girl; he'll do whatever it takes.'

'And if he doesn't?'

'Keep those thoughts out of your head. Let's hope it never comes to that.'

13

Jay persuaded the girl to follow him to the kitchen and offered her a hot drink. She sat on a breakfast bar stool, her shoulders hunched, her hands clasped around a mug, her pale arms resting on the counter. She kept her gaze fixed ahead, rarely looking in his direction, even when answering him. Jay had searched the freezer to help with her lip; unsurprisingly, he found it empty with no trace of ice. He searched through the cupboards and drawers, feeling pleased when he came across a bottle of Co-codamol. Eventually, he convinced her to take two; then, he sat opposite her with his tea.

For a while, neither of them spoke, then, with a flash of fearful realisation in her eyes, she said, 'How long have those tablets been here?'

Jay shrugged, watching while the girl drew the bottle towards her. Jenny held the bottle to her face, her lips trembling slightly while reading the small print on the label. 'Seems legit. I remember these tablets being smaller.'

Jay nodded. 'Maybe the last time you took one, you were a kid.'

She placed the bottle on the counter. 'I'm not a kid anymore. Those tablets could have been anything for all I know.'

Jay nodded, thinking how vulnerable she looked. She was still a kid, regardless of how she saw herself. Not that he was much older. But the seven years between them was a great distance. He sensed her eyes follow him as he picked up his cup. A rumbling noise sounded from her stomach. 'You must be starving,' Jay said.

Jenny shook her head.

'Course you are. I don't think you've eaten all day. I'll fix us something to–'

'No,' she said when he motioned to get up. 'There's nothing here. Anyway, I'm not hungry. I ate before. One of your bosses, the old man, got another takeaway.'

Jay stifled a laugh. 'He's not my boss.'

'Oh, I just assumed. You're a bit young to be in charge.'

'I never said I was in charge.'

She hesitated momentarily, a look of curiosity in her eyes, seemingly dumbstruck by a heap of questions. She settled for only one. 'When will you let me go?'

'Soon.'

'When?'

'As soon as your dad pays.'

'When will that be?'

'A day or two from now.'

While she studied him, Jay concluded she would make a poor card player. There were too many telltale signs, the slight narrowing of the eyes, the small raising of an eyebrow. Every minute twitch told the world what she was thinking. 'How much does he owe you?'

Jay almost told her he didn't owe them squat but had the

good sense to keep his mouth shut, quickly recalling Mich's lie. 'Enough,' he said.

Jenny sat up. 'Must be to go this far.' She looked down at the counter, 'It's a shame you have to split it four ways. Daddy would reward you if you fetched me home,' then casually glanced up.

Mich was right when she said the girl was sharp. Unfortunately for Jenny, she'd read Jay wrong, mistaking kindness for weakness, labelling him as a soft touch. He could see it in her sad eyes, thinking she was playing him for a fool. Jay was steps ahead of her. He knew all too well what it was like to give adults the run-around.

It was hard not to be impressed. Such insight and cunning took Jay back to that long scorching summer ten years ago. He hid the knowingness from his eyes, pretending to give Jenny's proposition some thought, and played along with it. 'Reward, you say. How much?'

The girl gave a slow smile, then quickly concealed it. 'There's no reason it shouldn't be the same amount he owes you.'

Jay felt dismayed by the flash of expectancy in her eyes and saw glimpses of his younger self in the girl's sad desperation. 'That's something to think about,' he lied, not intending to deceive but to lessen the girl's misery.

From her facial expression, his words offered hope. 'Why think about it? Daddy always says hesitation is the enemy of good fortune.'

A door opened from the direction of the lounge, and as the slow sound of footsteps approached them, Jay and the girl exchanged glances. Like the harbinger of sad news, Degsy broke the silence with his tired old face. 'Clate said the girl needs to go to her room. You've spent enough time talking.'

Jay shot Degsy a fierce look. 'Talking calmed things down.'

Degsy shrugged. 'Don't shoot the messenger. I'm just telling you what he said.'

Jay nodded. 'Fine, go back to the lounge and tell him we're going now.'

Like a dog with its tail between its legs, Degsy did as he was told. An immediate silence hung among the evening shadows, broken only by the intermittent thrum of the refrigerator and the old man's faint grumbling.

Jay gestured towards the bedrooms. 'You best do as Clate says.'

The girl sighed. 'What if I don't want to?'

'I don't think *want* has anything to do with it. There's little point in aggravating Clate any further, especially when he's been drinking.'

The girl touched her lip. 'That pig slapped my face.' Tears welled in her eyes. 'What else is he going to do?'

'Nothing,' Jay said, more wishful thinking than a factual statement. 'Just do as you're told, and no harm will come to you.' He watched while the girl slumped off the stool, then followed her down the hall. She was taller than most girls her age, and her black polka dot skirt and paisley blouse showed she had a good figure. Not that he looked at her in that way. She was just a child and, behind her scheming and false bravado, a very frightened one too.

When she entered the bedroom, Jay stood in the doorway. She sat on the edge of the bed, the epitome of obedience, with her clasped hands resting on her lap. She shivered slightly.

'Did you bring any other clothes?' Jay asked.

'A jumper and some jeans. Why?'

'The heating isn't great in these apartments. I'd get changed if I were you. It gets cold in here.'

'I'll change once you've gone.'

Jay blushed. 'Of course, silly. I didn't mean anything by that.' Struck by a sudden awkwardness, Jay placed his hands in his pockets. 'Mich said you like to read.'

The girl nodded.

'Me too; what kind of books do you like?'

'Fiction,' she said with a shrug.

'Dickens?'

She shook her head. 'No, mostly contemporary.'

'I can bring you something to read if you like?'

'I brought my own,' she glanced at the battered *John Irving* paperback resting face down on the bedside table.

Jay acknowledged it with a nod. 'Looks like you're almost finished.'

'It'll last me a couple of days. I'll be home by then, right?'

14

During his early morning appointment at the bank, Henry Earlston did his utmost to project an image of composure. He spoke with a casual air and calm confidence that, for years, had been unmistakably his. On the surface, everything looked fine, but his sweating palms, the palpitations, and the tight feeling in his stomach told another story. Yet the illusion remained unspoiled, and except for wiping his palm after their initial handshake, the branch manager, Mason Davenport, seemed none the wiser. In fact, he complimented Earlston on his appearance, referring to his black and pink paisley tie.

Davenport was equally well-dressed, sporting a three-piece tweed pinstripe suit, fitting attire for a man of his standing. As usual, Davenport was straight to the point. 'It's always good to see you, of course. But you could have saved yourself a journey and discussed this over the telephone.'

'Indeed,' Earlston said. 'However, this particular request is a little more sensitive.'

Davenport narrowed his eyes. 'Sounds serious; please continue.'

Earlston shifted in his chair. 'I need to extend my overdraft. Only as a temporary measure. I'll have the funds to clear it by the end of the week.'

'Why not wait until you have the funds? Save us all the paperwork.'

Earlston forced a smile. 'I'm afraid it's a bit more urgent than that.'

Davenport nodded. 'Fine. What do you need, one, two thousand?'

'Fifty, in fact.'

Davenport jerked his head back. 'Fifty K. Overdrafts don't stretch that far.'

Earlston rubbed the back of his neck. 'A loan then.'

'Neither would a personal loan cover it. You'd need a business loan for that.'

Earlston took a deep breath and slapped his hands down on the table. 'Whatever it takes. It's only temporary. No more than a week. Surely, you know I'm good for it. I'll pay it back.'

Davenport removed his glasses and rubbed his eyes. 'I've no doubt you will. But it's not as easy as that. Business loans for that amount of money require joint approval. Also, Henry, you don't even have a business plan. You haven't even come here with a proposal.'

Earlston sighed into his hands. 'Can't we work around that?'

Davenport put his glasses on and leaned back into his chair. 'Given enough time, yes. We need a business plan and the corresponding paperwork, and that, my friend, can't be done in a week.' He flashed Earlston a sad smile. 'Is everything all right?'

'Yes, of course.'

'So, why the rush?'

'I need it for an investment. It's an excellent opportunity I don't want to miss.'

Davenport looked unconvinced. 'If you don't mind me saying, this all seems a bit spur of the moment. From what I can see, you've always had good business sense.' He glanced up to the left. 'In fact, I recall you saying one should always take a step back when it came to investments.'

Earlston sensed his ears burning and the sweat beading across his forehead. He tried looking nonchalant with a shrug. 'Sound advice in most cases, but sometimes you must change your approach depending on the circumstances.'

'Perhaps,' Davenport said. 'It still doesn't change anything.' He gave him a long stare. 'While you're here, I have other questions about your finances.'

Earlston rubbed his sweaty palms down his trousers. 'Such as?'

'Your monthly salary barely covers your outgoings. You've extended your overdraft a few times these last few months; however, you remain increasingly in the red.'

Earlston cleared his throat and, with a weakened voice, said, 'It's only temporary. It'll soon be sorted.'

Davenport pursed his lips. 'I sincerely hope so. Perhaps it's time to start curbing some of your expenses. Nip them in the bud, so to speak. From my experience, these are early signs of someone struggling to manage their finances.'

'It's only a few months in the red,' said Earlston raising his voice. 'It hardly makes me destitute.'

'I meant no offence,' Davenport was quick to add. 'I wouldn't be doing my job if I didn't offer such advice.'

Earlston took a deep breath. 'Yes, I know. I'm sorry. And no doubt they'd be more heeded in better circumstances.'

'Circumstances?'

'My investment, I mean, and the pressure of securing a loan.'

'Yes. That is what it is, I'm afraid.' He hesitated. 'You still want me to press ahead with that?'

Earlston smoothed his hand across his forehead. 'I guess. What's the earliest we can make progress?'

'I'll see what I can do. I'll try my best, Henry. I'll fax you what I need and point you in the direction of a consultant. With some nudging on my end, we might have something by the end of next week.'

'That's almost a fortnight.'

'Still very good, considering. Do you still want to go ahead?'

Earlston sighed. 'I suppose if it's the best we can–'

'Fine, give me a few hours, and I'll get things rolling.' He glanced up at the clock. 'If there's nothing else, I'll let you get on.'

In a moment of madness, Earlston considered telling him the truth. The notion quickly passed. Now, hours later, Earlston still winced at his foolishness, more so when he pictured the self-righteous look on Davenport's face. In better times, he wouldn't have tolerated the man's presence, let alone allowed him to lecture him on his finances.

Earlston leaned forward in his chair and stared at the telephone. Hoffman said he would contact him today. The minutes felt like hours, the hours days, and it took all his resolve not to call him.

Jenny's face haunted his mind's eye. The demons in his head goaded him to imagine the worse. The girl was pretty and young. Earlston pressed his fist against his lips. God knows what they might have done to her. His wife too, and stricken with guilt, Earlston forced himself to think of Mich.

Earlston stood and hurried over to the telephone, his hand-shaking while dialling Hoffman's number.

Hoffman answered after three rings.

'Did you sort it, Charles?' said Earlston, dispensing with the formalities.

Silence lingered on the other end of the line until Hoffman released an irritated sigh. 'I'm fine, Henry. Thanks for asking.'

'Sorry, Charles, sorry. I'm not myself. That's very rude of me.'

'That's all right,' said Hoffman in an aggrieved tone. 'Yes, it's sorted. I managed to shift the Crayburns stock and the Bradbook shares too.'

'Well done, Charles. Well done.'

'It's not all good news, I'm afraid.'

'Go on.'

'They took advantage of the rush, used it to negotiate on the price.'

'How much?'

'With the two combined, it comes to just over two hundred K. Listen, you can get three times that if you hang on for–'

'It's fine. Can we transfer the funds tomorrow?'

'Friday at the earliest.'

'But I said two days.'

'I did warn you that was a foolish hope. Friday's the best you'll get. Take it or leave it.'

'I'll take it, of course.'

'Fine,' Hoffman said with a sigh. 'I'll finalise arrange-ments with you in the morning.'

Earlston wanted to confirm a time, but before he could ask, Hoffman hung up.

15

Clate woke with a thumping head, the bed quilt barely covering him, while Mich's naked body lay face down beside him. He swallowed against the stale taste in his mouth, repeatedly blinking until his eyes adjusted to the sunlight. Choosing only to drink the good stuff, he rarely suffered hangovers. But Mich had a fondness for cheap wine, and alongside the economical pricing, feeling like hell the next day was part of the guarantee.

Clate stretched his arms and yawned. Mich didn't move, remaining dead to the world, even when he sat up. He gave her a shove, prodding her lightly with his finger until she grunted a response.

Clate laughed. 'Today's the day of reckoning. I thought you'd be on pins. How the hell can you sleep through that?'

Mich released a frustrated sigh and turned over onto her back. She squinted towards the blinds and then covered her eyes with her hand. 'What time is it?' she said in a hoarse voice.

Clate glanced at his watch. 'Almost eleven.'

'For God's sake, Clate. What are you doing, waking me up this early?'

'*Early*? Most people are a good few hours through their day.'

Mich turned on her side. 'Good luck to them. Now leave me alone to sleep.'

Clate shuffled over to the side of the bed and rested his feet on the carpet. Glancing around the room, he sighed. Up until last year, he'd had big plans for the place. With the mortgage proving too much, Clate knew the bailiffs would knock at the door within weeks. Not that he cared. The Costa del Sol was only a few days away. Sun-drenched images filled him with a sense of yearning, and he pictured cocktails and topless blondes on the beach. Clate gave the room one last scan, impatience and the promise of better times forcing him to his feet.

Giving the girl the ensuite made sense, although it didn't stop him from cursing the short, cold walk to the bathroom. Pausing outside the girl's room, Clate pushed down on the handle, repeating the action to reassure himself it was locked. He pressed his ear against the door, only removing it when he heard the faint sound of her breathing. Naked but for a pair of boxer shorts, his large muscular frame moved heavily down the hall. The bathroom door shuddered open with a mighty shove. Clate slipped off his boxers, turned on the shower then stepped into it.

Sleep was a distant memory, the sudden surge of freezing water bringing him to his senses. Clate hollered against the cold, his dramatics easing as it grew warmer. He lathered his head and body in soap, relishing the hot water falling across his skin. A sudden stinging caused him to wince, and, trying to ease the pain, he smoothed his thumb over the small cut on his finger. The girl needed a slap to calm her down and show her this was serious. Clate did what was required. He treated everyone the same, applying the same philosophy to both sexes. It was easy to follow; watch your mouth and toe the line. By all means, feel free to do as you please but be prepared to face the consequences.

After standing beneath the shower for fifteen minutes, Clate stepped into the steamy bathroom. He dried himself in a rush; that feeling of freshness was short-lived as his head throbbed beneath the wet towel, and his body succumbed to tiredness. It had been a long time since he felt this rough. He dressed with less haste and, with a sense of anticipation burgeoning inside him, checked in on Mich before he left.

The woman remained dead to the world. She lay on her back, her face an expression of serene contentment, the wall clock ticking in unison to the rise and fall of her chest. Annoyed by her lack of concern, Clate leaned over and tugged her pillow. She woke with a start, mumbled incomprehensibly, then, on recognising the man standing before her, slammed her head down on the pillow. 'Are you still here, Clate. I thought you went hours ago.'

He grimaced at the staleness of her breath and drew his head away from it. 'I've only been gone thirty minutes. I've only just finished showering.'

She answered without opening her eyes. 'Go if you're going. Why the big song and dance about it?'

Clate stared down at her, almost tempted to lift her by the arms and knock her teeth out. 'Today's the deadline. I'm calling your husband later, or have you forgotten about him?'

She slapped her hand on top of her forehead and sighed. 'I try my best to, but some people won't let me do that.' As though sensing his stare, she opened her eyes. 'What?'

'You're a cold-hearted bitch.'

Mich dropped her arms to her sides. 'You shouldn't drink if you're going to have a hangover. What the hell are you starting on me for?'

'No one's starting on you. I think you should be a bit more concerned, that's all.'

'About what?'

'About that husband of yours. I told you I sensed a hesitancy. What if he decides not to pay?'

'He'll pay, don't you worry. Hesitancy is what he does. The man can't take a piss without debating it.'

Clate laughed. 'I truly hope so, for all our sakes.' He regarded her for a moment. 'Because if he doesn't, well–'

'Well, what?'

Clate sucked the air in through his teeth. 'The girl's seen every one of us. We'll have to make some nasty choices if things go wrong.'

His words forced Mich to sit up. 'What nasty choices?'

'I thought that was obvious.' He registered the alarm in Mich's eyes. 'That girl can identify every one of us. I'm not doing time if this goes tits up. If things go wrong, I won't be leaving any witnesses.'

'Don't talk like that, Clate. Even the thought of such things upsets me.'

'So it should. Perhaps it'll help you to take this more seriously.'

'Who said I wasn't?'

'You did; by the way you're lazing in bed until God knows when. Your husband might be trying to con us, and you don't seem to care either way.'

'Of course, I care.'

'Well, act like it then,' Clate said through gritted teeth.

A hint of brazenness settled in Mich's eyes, quickly fading when Clate gave her a fierce stare. He was tempted to slap her in the mouth, knock some sense into her, although he feared he wouldn't stop at that.

Mich lowered her eyes. 'Why are you looking at me like that, Clate? You're scaring me.'

'Good. You keep that feeling to hand; it'll help you to focus.' Clate strolled out of the room with a smile, happy to leave her with that thought; why should he carry all the burden?

16

C late got a taxi to Maggie's bar; ignoring the driver's attempt at conversation, he pretended to read the paper. None of it was good news. The only headline that caught his interest was a story about a showbiz impresario kidnapping and torturing his former business partner. The journalists described it as brutal and cold. Clate wondered how they would describe *him*. All he was doing was running a con. You couldn't compare him to this sick fool, and he took comfort in that thought, concluding his motivations were a million miles away.

When he walked into the club, the cleaner was just finishing up. 'I've been extra thorough today,' the woman said, raising her voice over the Hoover's raucous din. 'Must have been a busy night.'

Clate scanned the bar. Her efforts seemed in vain. Except for the empty ashtrays and the track marks on the carpet, he noticed little difference. He motioned for her to stop, relishing the silence as she switched the Hoover off. 'You done the toilets?'

The woman answered with a defensive nod.

Clate gave her a flat smile. 'If that's the case, why don't you knock off.'

'I haven't done the kitchen.'

'We don't do food tonight. So, it should be all right.'

She looked at him and shrugged. 'Suit yourself. It's your money. I'll see you tomorrow.'

Clate watched while she put everything away and helped her with her coat. He walked her to the door, watched until she was out of sight, and slammed it shut.

It always felt good having the place to himself. The girls didn't start their shift until after two, which gave him a few hours of peace. After lighting a cigar, Clate breathed the smoke out with a sigh. He patted his pockets, checking for his keys, then slipped through the side door and strolled to the telephone box at the end of the street. Thankfully, it was free. Clate stepped inside, drawing on his cigar before he dialled. Clate dug in his pocket for change as the booth filled with smoke, pushing in the coins when he heard the pips.

'Earlston?' Clate said, growing more agitated when a weak voice answered, 'Yes.'

Clate drew hard on his cigar and blew the smoke into the receiver. 'You know what today is, right. It's time for you to pay up.'

Earlston didn't answer, and Clate listened to the man breathing in the ensuing silence. 'Earlston? Earlston? Are you still there? I'm surprised the cat's got your tongue, considering what day it is.'

'I know what day it is.'

'Good. You got the money?'

Earlston cleared his throat. 'Yes and no.'

'What the hell's that supposed to mean?'

'I can get the money,' he paused, 'but it's complicated.'

Clate closed his eyes and sighed. 'What do you mean complicated? I hope you're not playing for time. You sound like a man working with the police. That young daughter of yours wouldn't fare well from that.'

'Is Jenny all right?'

'She was.'

'What do you mean?'

'She's safe and well, waiting to come home. But your little antics have just put an end to that.'

'I'd never mess you around, not when Jenny's involved. I promise. I'd never do that.'

'Let's hope so.' Clate took a drag on his cigar. 'So, tell me about these *complications*.'

Earlston breathed deeply. 'That amount of money is a big ask. It takes time to get it together, especially when it's cash.'

'How long do you need?'

'Until the end of the week.'

'That makes it Good Friday. That's Easter. A bank holiday. How–'

'That doesn't affect us,' interrupted Earlston. 'The money's good for Friday; I swear to it; this is a private transaction.'

Clate listened to the panic in Earlston's voice. He'd long been familiar with the sound of fear. The weakness of other men often surrounded him, and he used this momentary pause to savour it. 'How about tomorrow?'

'Friday's the best I can do; trust me, I've tried. Normally, for that amount of money, it takes weeks.'

Clate grinned. It was a quicker turnaround than he'd hoped. He hadn't expected anything until the end of next week. An insight he kept to himself.

He made Earlston wait, relishing the man's pain in the

silence. 'Friday then,' he said with a sigh. 'We'll speak soon regarding the details.'

'Can I speak with Jenny?'

Clate smiled, undecided what tickled him more, the desperation in the man's voice or that he hadn't asked about Mich. 'We'll see.'

'And she's all right?'

'Yes, for now. But if Friday never comes. Things will get nasty.'

'What does that mean?'

Clate sighed. 'You know what it means. Friday, and nothing less,' then slammed down the receiver when he heard the pips.

When he pulled open the telephone box door, an elderly woman wearing a headscarf and a green mac, followed by a bald man in his forties, had formed a small queue. The woman grimaced as she sniffed the air and, waving her hand in front of her, said, 'this box is a public service. It's bad enough with people urinating, never mind filling it with cigar smoke.'

Clate dug his hand into his pocket and pulled out a fistful of coins. Opening his hand, he offered them to the woman. 'It's a filthy habit, I agree. Take these as a form of compensation.'

The woman scowled, 'I don't want your money,' and pushed past him. Clate laughed, then stared at the bald man, holding it there until the man looked away.

Again, Clate laughed and felt more than pleased with himself while walking back to the bar. Sadly, the feeling was short-lived. He'd been inside less than ten minutes when someone started banging at the main door, calling for him to let them in. Clate checked his watch; the girls weren't expected for another hour.

To drown out the incessant banging, Clate turned on the radio. Sam Cooke's soulful voice floated rhythmically through the bar. Jazz was more his thing, but at least it was a tune he knew. Whoever was at the door seemed adamant about being let in. *What a wonderful world*, Clate sang at the top of his voice and then turned the volume to full blast.

Clate endured it for under twenty minutes, opting for silence when the thumping inside his head became unbearable. He poured himself a double whisky, its sweet fragrance almost making him retch. *Hair of the Dog*, he said aloud and, with his hand trembling, drew the glass to his mouth. Clate glanced at his watch and strolled towards the main doors, knowing the girls would arrive soon. Mary was usually the first, full of attitude and complaint; her loud voice was always on the cusp of shouting.

The doors swung open with a shove, and Clate stood outside, relishing the warm air and squinting against the sudden blast of daylight. The traffic rumbled in droves, an endless stretch of steel tapering off into the distance. Clate scowled as he sniffed the petrol-tainted air. Homesickness was an infliction for the weak. Clate would never suffer from that. He couldn't wait to leave, knowing he would never give a second thought about this place.

Clate turned to face the doors, looking over his shoulder when someone said, 'You're Clate, right?'

Clate turned around, assessing the stranger with a glance: mid to late twenties, kind of oily looking, from his ill-fitting suit to his scuffed shoes, everything about him said cheap.

'I might be,' Clate said, 'who's asking?'

The kid offered Clate his hand. 'The name's Nick Bryant. I'm part of Benny Bray's lot.'

'Benny sent you here?'

Bryant shook his head. 'Nah, I was in the area. I thought I'd pop in and say hello.'

'That's very friendly of you; why on earth would you do that?'

Bryant gave a hesitant shrug. 'I drink here from time to time, thought it would be nice to finally talk to you.'

'Well, you've just done that, so now it's time to be on your way.'

Bryant's face creased into a smile. 'Don't be like that. I'm only trying to be friendly. Anyway, I heard Benny kind of owns this place now.'

Bryant's words took Clate by surprise. 'Kind of; he's what you'd call a silent partner.'

'Best type.'

Without answering, Clate motioned towards the door. 'I've lots to do today. Tell one of the girls Clate said to give you a free bar.'

Bryant stepped forward, 'That's very kind,' pausing when Clate blocked his way. Clate gave him a long, icy stare. 'Where the hell are you going?'

'I just thought–'

'Well, you thought wrong. This is just to let the girls in; we're not open yet.'

'Don't be like that, Clate. I've been waiting around for hours.'

Clate narrowed his eyes. 'Was that you banging before?'

Bryant nodded.

'You're a persistent little tyke; I'll give you that.'

Bryant clenched his jaw. 'I heard music, just assumed you were open.'

'*Assume,* makes an ass out of you and me.'

'What?'

Clate sighed. 'Never mind. Listen, I best crack on. Thanks for calling by to say hello.'

Bryant didn't move. 'Come on, Clate, don't be like that. I've gone out of my way to say hello. I'd hate to go back to Mr Bray and inform him you were unfriendly.'

Clate shook his head in defeat. 'Indeed, come on, you best come in.'

17

Degsy had been playing babysitter since noon. To be fair, Jay had been good with the girl, not that Clate had any need to strike her like that. Last night, in a moment of drunken sincerity, Clate claimed it was all done for effect. Degsy remained unconvinced. Clate had always been free with his hands, and a string of ex-girl-friends and former waitresses bore witness to it.

Clate wasn't that bad, concluded Degsy while slipping off his shoes and resting his aching feet on the table. In fact, he'd started showing Degsy some respect. Even a man as brutal as Clate possessed a sense of decency. Jay was all right too, more intelligent than most, that's for sure, and for all his ribbing, Degsy couldn't help but like him. As for Mich, she remained a thorn in all their sides. Thankfully, she left Degsy alone, directing all her anger at Jay.

Degsy released a sigh, clasped his hands, and rested them on his gut. This was one of the easiest cons he'd done. Granted, it came with more risk. All they needed to do was to sit tight. Earlston was bound to pay up, and now Jay could handle the girl Degsy failed to understand why Clate was so stressed. The answer came to him in a vision, in the form of Mich, robed and bedraggled, standing before him. Her sleepy eyes cast him a scathing glance and, with a gravelly voice, said, 'What the hell are you looking so pleased about?'

Degsy shrugged. 'That's hard to decide, your ageless beauty or charming demeanour.'

Mich shot him a look of reproach, then sat in the chair opposite. 'I thought you were keeping an eye on Jenny?'

'I am.'

She glared at him in disgust. 'Sure, it looks like, and get your smelly feet off the table.'

Degsy didn't move. 'I'm leaving her alone while she's quiet.'

A hint of worry settled in Mich's eyes. 'She's too quiet if you ask me. When did you last check on her?'

'I haven't.'

'You *what*?'

Degsy unclasped his hands and placed them on his lap. 'Simmer down, for heaven's sake. Jay checked on her before he left.'

'When was that?'

'When you were still dead to the world a few hours ago.'

Mich pushed Degsy's feet off the table.

Degsy sat up. 'What the hell do you think you're doing?'

'Go and check on her, you old fool. You lazy old fool. She could have done something to herself, for all you know.'

Degsy slipped on his shoes. 'If you're that concerned, why don't you check on her yourself. You're supposed to be her stepmother, for God's sake.'

Mich sighed. 'I'd probably make things worse. Anyway, I don't have the head for it now.'

Degsy stood. 'Whose fault is that? You're supposed to be a professional, not stay up drinking half the night.'

'That's good coming from you. You're the biggest alky I know.'

'Takes one to know one, I guess,' Degsy said and strolled towards the girl's bedroom, pausing when Mich threw a cushion at his back. 'Very mature,' he said without turning around, fumbling in his pocket for the key.

Degsy unlocked the bedroom door as quietly as he could, filled with an unexpected nervousness while he inched it open. He peered at the girl through the gap, her body partly covered by the quilt, unable to tell if she was breathing. Degsy whispered her name. 'Jenny? Jenny? Are you all right now?'

The girl didn't reply. 'Jenny,' he said again, growing more anxious. He sensed Mich standing close behind him. 'Is she all right, Degsy?' Mich whispered, the smell of perfume and cigarettes surrounding him as her breath breezed warmly across his neck.

Degsy shrugged. 'Don't know.'

'What do you mean, you don't know?'

'I can see her shape in the bed. But she's not responding.'

Mich poked his ribs. 'Go and check.'

Degsy released a deep breath, pulled the door wider, and tiptoed inside. The girl lay on her back, her eyes closed, her skin smooth and pale and seeing her there, looking so innocent, it suddenly dawned on him how young she was.

'Jenny? Jenny, are you all right?' When the girl didn't respond, Degsy inched closer, stopping when he saw the empty tablet bottle on the bedside table. He dashed over to the bed, grabbed the girl's shoulder and gave her a shove. 'Jenny, Jenny, wake up.' He looked over his shoulder towards the door. 'I think the girl's overdosed; she needs to be taken to the hospital.'

Mich rushed into the room. 'What? Where the hell did she–' Mich went silent as Jenny opened her eyes and, pointing at the tablet bottle, said, 'How many of those did you take?'

Jenny frowned. 'Two, why?'

'What happened to the rest?' Degsy said.

Jenny sat up and covered herself with the quilt. 'There were only two in the bottle. Jay gave them to me.'

Degsy shook his head and smiled, his sense of relief captured by the expression on Mich's face.

'Did Daddy pay?' Jenny said. 'Is it time to go home now?'

Degsy shook his head. 'Not just yet, love.'

'When then? And how is he going to deliver the money? Are you taking me with you when you go to collect it?'

Degsy rubbed his hand across the back of his neck, 'You'll know soon enough,' realising even he didn't have an answer to those questions.

The girl recoiled. 'Then what do you want?'

Degsy tried reassuring her with a smile. 'There's no need to be frightened. I was just checking in on you, that's all.'

Mich stepped closer and sat on the edge of the bed. 'I asked him to, Jen. I wanted to make sure you were all right.' The girl's eyes traced over Mich's shape, quickly turning from a look of initial surprise to a mix of disappointment and disgust. 'You sleeping with them now?' Jenny said. 'Why are you walking around dressed like that?'

Mich tightened the chord on her robe and folded her arms across her chest. 'There doesn't seem to be much wrong with you.'

The girl let the quilt slip from her hands. 'Let me go,

Mich. Please.' Tears welled in her eyes. 'I'll explain to Daddy you had no choice. He loves you. I'm sure after time he can forgive this.'

'And you?'

The girl regarded her for a moment. 'You acted under duress.'

Mich smiled. 'That's the truth, honey, although I know you don't believe that.'

'Tell them to let me go, Mich,' Jenny said, raising her voice.

Mich silenced her with a *Shush*. 'Keep your voice down, Jen. Clate's in the other room. He's in a foul mood. God knows what might happen if you wake him.'

The girl's demeanour changed at the mention of Clate's name. She now looked passive and afraid, and the fiery spirit that ordered Mich to set her free had deserted her. Degsy looked at Mich then, catching the triumphant look in her eyes, averted his gaze in shame. Fixing on the girl, Degsy tried expressing kindness through a smile. 'Do you want something to eat?'

The girl shook her head.

'A hot drink then?'

Once again, the girl shook her head.

Degsy sighed. 'I can't believe you're not hungry. You haven't eaten since yesterday.'

Mich got up and started walking out of the room, pausing at the doorway. She glanced at Degsy over her shoulder. 'We'll get her something anyway; it's up to her then; she can take it or leave it.'

Degsy nodded and followed Mich into the hall, locking the bedroom door behind him. He strolled with her to the kitchen, plopped down on the cold breakfast stool and watched quietly while Mich took two mugs from the draining board. Mich filled the kettle with water and rested her weight against the counter. 'I'm dying for a smoke,' she said, catching the pack with both hands when Degsy threw over her cigarettes. She popped one into her mouth, shuffling over to Degsy as he offered her a light. Mich drew her face closer, drawing on her cigarette, her eyes reflecting the yellow flame. She pulled back her head, releasing the smoke with an exaggerated breath.

Mich handed Degsy the pack.

'Thanks,' he said, taking one out. He looked at Mich and smiled. 'Nice thinking, by the way, lying about Clate like that.'

Mich shrugged. 'It seemed the only way to shut her up.' She drew on her cigarette. 'It wasn't really a lie. Clate seems a little jumpy. God knows how he would have reacted if he'd been in.'

Degsy nodded in agreement and lit a cigarette. 'She's a smart kid–'

'Too smart if you ask me.'

Degsy laughed. 'She raised some valid questions, though.'

Mich opened her mouth to reply, pausing when she heard the kettle click. She walked over to the counter and, with her back turned, asked, 'Tea or Coffee?'

'Coffee, white.'

'Sugar?'

'Four, please.'

Mich shook her head and laughed. 'Jesus, Degsy, it's no wonder you've got false teeth.' She strolled over with the drinks and slowly placed them on the counter. Mich grimaced as she took a sip. 'Which questions?'

'The ones about payment and how we exchange her on collection day. Nobody's discussed that.'

Mich tried dismissing it with a shrug. But Degsy saw the worry in her eyes. He recognised it from his own. Even after all these years, suspicion never failed to take root. Nobody was beyond mistrust, especially when they could take everything from you. Mich pointed at him with her cigarette. 'I'm sure I remember talking about it from day one. Clate and I will do that.'

'*You*?'

Mich glared at him. 'I'm part of the exchange, right.'

'You were, but now the girl knows you're inv–'

'Coerced. I'll convince her I was coerced.'

Degsy sighed. 'If you say so.'

'I do.' Mich took a drag of her cigarette. 'Anyway, Earlston thinks I'm a victim, and until he sees me, he'll keep believing that.'

Degsy didn't reply. Instead, he drank his coffee and glanced down at the counter. He drew hard on his cigarette and flicked the ash into his cup. 'And on the day of reckoning?'

'I'll take my share from Clate.'

'Then you'll just walk away?'

'Of course, that's what I do.' Mich laughed. 'Surely, you don't expect him to take me back?'

Degsy shook his head. 'Nope.' He regarded her for a moment. 'This discussion we had, which I don't seem to recall, where did Jay and I fit into all this?'

'You stay here, I suppose. Clate will give you both your share once he gets back.'

Degsy dropped his cigarette into his cup. 'Now that's the part I don't like.'

Mich dragged Degsy's cup towards her and used it as an ashtray. 'You need to discuss that with Clate.' She shot him a cheeky smile. 'But in the meantime, we promised Jenny some food. There's money in my purse. Even kidnappers need to eat.'

18

Clate's unmistakable voice hollered from the street before he staggered into the Mews. It sounded like singing, but the familiarity of the words, not the tuneless rendition, enabled Degsy to recognise the song. As Clate drew closer, the volume of the din increased. Degsy checked his watch. Nine in the evening was early for Clate. He'd probably been drinking all day, and after his antics proved too much, one of the girls had shipped him home in a taxi.

The driver had definitely earned his money tonight, and Degsy listened to the incoherent mumble of the man's voice helping Clate up the stairway. A key turned in the lock, and the front door shuddered open.

'Here we go,' Mich said at the sound of Clate's footsteps moving sluggishly down the hallway. He popped his drunken head around the door, scowled, then, in a slurred voice, said, 'Hell Mich, you look like crap. I can't believe you're not even dressed yet.'

Mich stood, 'I was just going for a shower,' and quickly made her exit.

Clate swaggered into the room and gave Degsy a fierce look; it wasn't the loathing in Clate's eyes that forced Degsy to sit up but the man following behind him. Clate slumped into a chair and, pointing at Mich's vacant seat, said, 'Don't just stand there, Bryant, take a pew.'

Bryant flashed him a sickly smile, 'I'll sit next to my buddy here if that's okay,' and sat next to Degsy on the sofa.

Clate rubbed his chin. 'You two know each other? Now isn't that a coincidence?'

Bryant rested his clammy hand on Degsy's shoulder. 'It sure is. Degsy and I go back a long way. I was starting to wonder where he'd disappeared to. I've been looking out for him for days.'

Clate's face creased into a smile. 'Is that so? The day just gets stranger and stranger. There's nothing better than old friends being reunited.' He clapped his hands. 'Let's have a drink; this calls for a celebration.' Clate pressed his hands into the arms of his chair, relaxing them when Degsy stood up.

Degsy stepped over the big man's feet. 'You stay put, Clate. I got some whisky in while you were out. Let me get this.'

Bryant motioned to stand, 'Let me help you,' remaining seated when Clate shook his head.

'Stay put; Degsy's fine.' Clate slapped a hand down onto his stomach. 'I don't know about you two, but I'm clemmed. Any chance of any scran?'

Degsy paused and glanced over his shoulder. 'We got a takeaway, saved you a few ribs.'

'Something for your friend too.'

Degsy looked away and trudged into the kitchen without answering.

Beneath the cold glare of the halogen lights, Degsy

pressed his fingers into the counter's edge and, standing in front of the window, stared out into the darkness. He felt hollow inside, as though someone had just gutted him with a knife.

Closing his eyes, Degsy took a deep breath, releasing it through a defeated sigh. Bryant was like a curse, and there seemed no way to escape him. Degsy turned to his left, unscrewed the lid from the bottle of whisky, picked it up, and poured some into his mouth. He grimaced at the taste, then turned his head towards the strong smell of perfume.

'Yuck,' Mich said. 'You better clean that tip; people need to drink from that.'

'I didn't put it in my mouth.'

Mich frowned. 'No, but you breathed all over it.'

Degsy shifted over to the sink and rinsed a cloth under the tap. He wiped it over the tip and, glaring at Mich, screwed on the lid.

She responded with a mocking laugh. 'Don't look so hurt; what the hell's wrong with you?'

'Nothing,' Degsy mumbled and stood by the leftover cartons from the evening's takeaway with the bottle still in his hand. He nodded at the tray of ribs. 'Do us a favour and take these in for Clate.'

'Can't you do it yourself?'

'I could,' Degsy said with a sigh. 'But I need to take in some glasses.'

Mich grabbed a plate from the draining board and tipped the ribs onto it. 'Who's his friend?'

'A lowlife called Bryant.'

'Yeah, he looks a little creepy.' She gave him an inquisitive smile. 'I take it you don't like him?'

'No, and neither should you.'

'What do you think Clate's told him?'

Degsy grabbed some glasses with his free hand. 'Hopefully not too much.'

When they entered the lounge, Clate smoked a cigar while Bryant fiddled with the stereo. Clate watched Degsy from his chair, his eyes unblinking, while Degsy placed the whisky and glasses on the table. 'Pour me a large one, Degs, and for Bryant too.'

Mich offered Clate the food, shaking her head as he snatched the plate. He ate like a ravenous dog, pausing between mouthfuls to lick the barbecue sauce off his fingers. 'Bryant,' he said, 'Bryant, grab some food before I demolish this.'

'Fill your boots,' Bryant said with a laugh and remained crouched in front of the stereo. 'How come you've got no records? This is a waste of a good system, Clate.' He fell silent as if waiting for a response, then, with a shrug, said, 'I guess we'll have to settle for the radio.'

Bryant kept turning the dial, surfing through the channels, until stopping on one he liked. He danced over to his seat. 'Do you like this one, Degs?'

Degsy shrugged. 'Never heard of it; they all sound the same to me.'

Bryant gave him an incredulous look. 'You mean to say you've never heard *A Kind of Magic*? Where the hell have you been these last few weeks?'

As his body tensed, Degsy felt himself blush. 'Avoiding people, keeping out of harm's way.'

Bryant gave him a knowing smile. 'Very good, Degsy, very good. You keep doing that now.' He focused his attention on Mich, but somebody hammered on the front door before he got a chance to speak. He threw Clate a glance. 'Neighbours complaining about the noise?'

Clate shook his head and laughed. 'Nah, another guest

joining the party.' He pointed at Degsy. 'Come on, Degs, get up; you need to let your little friend in.'

Degsy pushed himself up from the sofa and went to answer the door, cursing every one of them while he trudged begrudgingly down the hall. *Bryant's here,* he mouthed while Jay stood staring at him in the doorway. Jay didn't say a word. Not that he had to. Everything Degsy felt and thought was written all over the kid's face.

When Degsy and Jay walked into the lounge, Bryant stood up. 'Wonder boy's here too.' He slapped Jay on the back. 'I would have worn my Tux's if I knew you were coming.' Shaking his head with exaggerated surprise, Bryant pointed towards the hall. 'Toilets down there?'

'Yeah,' Clate said through a mouthful of food. 'Third door on your left.'

Bryant grinned. 'I need to empty my bladder. All these coincidences call for a celebration.'

They all watched while Bryant made his exit, and the moment he was out of sight, it was Mich who broke the silence. 'Who the hell's that creep? Why did you bring him here? Answer me, Clate. We can't have him here while all this is going on. He just adds more risk. I can't believe you brought him here. You've been telling everyone to act smart. What the hell were you thinking? I–'

Clate interrupted her with a sigh. 'Be quiet, woman, for God's sake. Do you think I brought him here out of choice? I don't want him here any more than you do.' Clate sighed as he wiped the residue of sauce from his lips. 'It's not as easy as that.'

Mich shook her head and frowned. 'Only because you're drunk. Normally you wouldn't give these creeps the time of day. Why on earth would you humour him like that?'

Something in Clate's nod appeared to recognise Mich's

frustration. 'It's complicated. He's one of Benny Bray's crew. Sending him on his way would be like giving Benny a slap across the face, and, for the time being, we can't afford to do that.'

Mich didn't say a word; she turned a little pale. Not that Degsy could blame her. Benny Bray had that effect on you. The mention of Bray's name was enough to silence most people.

19

The music boomed, each monotonous song blending into the next. Whenever Degsy requested peace and quiet, Bryant grinned and turned up the radio. Once the wine kicked in, Mich abandoned her concerns. She was an incorrigible drunk, working her way through the lounge, pestering each of them to dance. Only Bryant obliged, swaying with her from side to side, his clammy hands wandering too far, the expectation in his eyes matching the smug expression on his face.

Clate looked unaffected. If he and Mich were an item, no one would have guessed it. He tapped his hand discordantly with the music's beat, peering through piggy eyes as he battled against sleep.

Only Jay appeared to share Degsy's concern. The kid sat quiet and alert, watching Bryant throughout, expressing his annoyance whenever he and Degsy exchanged glances.

Jay stood up and motioned towards the hall, pausing when Bryant, raising his voice over the music, called out to him. Jay cupped his hand to his ear. 'What?' he mouthed, then turned to the stereo and lowered the volume.

Bryant flashed him an aggrieved look. 'Hey, party pooper. Why did you do that?'

'I couldn't make out what you were saying. Also, I could barely hear myself think.'

Bryant slipped his hands from Mich's waist. 'I was asking what you're up to?'

'Why?'

Bryant shrugged. 'Just curious, that's all. You keep slipping out every ten minutes or so. Either you've got a weak bladder, or you're checking on something.'

Jay shook his head. 'Not that it's any of your business.'

Degsy rubbed the back of his neck. Bryant was no fool; he read people pretty well, not that it took any effort to see Jay's defensive answer was clearly hiding something.

Bryant narrowed his eyes. 'You've got me curious now. I need to look for myself.'

Jay grabbed Bryant's arm. 'Stay and enjoy the music. There's nothing to see, and you've got no business there even if there was.'

Bryant pulled his arm free. 'Get your hands off me.' He tilted his head slightly. 'Nothing to see, huh? So how come one of the rooms is locked?'

Degsy tried to interject, but Bryant spoke over him.

'I put my ear to the door,' Bryant said with a smile. 'Sounded like a girl crying to me.'

Clate appeared to be sleeping off the drink for the last ten minutes until Bryant's curiosity quickly sobered him up. Clate stared at Bryant through tired eyes. 'It's my niece. She likes the door locked; she's feeling unwell.'

Bryant pressed his lips to a fine line. 'Niece, huh? What's her name?'

'Jenny.'

'Nice name. I knew a Jenny once. How old is she?'

'Sixteen.'

Something sparked in Bryant's eyes. 'That's no age to be locked in your room. Get her out here.'

'Leave her be; she's fine.'

'She didn't sound fine. Let's bring her out so she can enjoy the party.'

'She's fine.'

'But–'

Clate slammed his hands down onto his chair. 'She's fine. Now leave her alone, I said.'

Bryant answered with a wary nod, the menace in Clate's voice holding him silent. He motioned towards Mich to resume their dance, retreating to the sofa when she turned her back on him.

Degsy barely managed to contain his smile, but somehow he did, lowering his eyes while he filled Bryant's glass. Bryant sipped his wine, occasionally looking over at Clate like a scolded puppy trying to win his master's favour. 'Thanks for your hospitality today, Clate. It's very kind. Benny's going to be impressed when I tell him about that.'

Clate answered Bryant with a grunt, scowling at Jay when he shook his head. Jay responded with a smile, 'Benny Bray,' he said. 'He sounds like somebody worth knowing. I keep hearing his name all over the place. I think I'll introduce myself.'

Bryant turned his attention back to Jay. 'It's a name you need to know in our line of business.'

Mich let out a sarcastic laugh. 'And what business might that be?'

Bryant ignored the dig and, looking at Jay, said, 'Benny isn't someone you go looking for. He'll find you if he's interested. You need to start at the bottom. The last thing you need to do is poke your nose into all his shit.'

Jay regarded him for a moment. 'Thanks for the good advice. So what about you?'

Bryant shrugged. 'Me?'

'Yeah, where do you fit in the hierarchy.'

Bryant frowned. 'Hierarchy?'

Clate sighed. 'Yes, *hierarchy*, you moron. He means what role do you play in Benny's organisation?'

Bryant's eyes widened with surprise. 'Oh, I see. Then why the hell didn't he say that.' He regarded Jay with a smug smile. 'I'm a collector.'

'Collecting what?' Jay asked.

'Money mostly, but it can be anything that aims to pay off a debt.'

Clate slowly sat up. 'I thought Corey Brown dealt with all that?'

Bryant paused for a second. 'Nah, Corey's more out East these days. He was spreading himself too thin, so Benny asked me to concentrate on the North-West.' He attempted to elaborate further, but Mich interrupted him.

'I think we've said enough about Benny Bray, don't you?' She looked over at the Stereo. 'I'm going to turn that up if we can't talk about anything else.'

Degsy conceded with a sigh and stood up. 'Mich is right.' He stifled a yawn. 'I'm going to call it a night.'

Bryant glanced at his watch. 'Yeah, it's getting late for me too. If you're heading back to Queensway, I'll share a cab with you.'

Degsy and Clate exchanged glances. Clate wiped the tiredness from his eyes. 'Degsy's my guest for a while; he's staying in the downstairs apartment.'

For a few seconds, Bryant stared at them open-mouthed. 'Wow, Degsy, last time we spoke, you were smoking roll-ups in your flea-bitten flat. You've certainly come up in the world since then.' He regarded Degsy for a moment. 'I have to say I'm impressed.' Bryant slapped Degsy on the back. 'Come on then, old-timer, I'll walk out with you. At least you can point me towards a taxi.'

'Jay's your best bet for that.'

Jay nodded. 'Sure, it's about time I made a move.'

Jay motioned to stand, remaining in his chair when Clate said, 'Let Degsy do it. I need you to stay here for a bit.'

With a defeated sigh, Degsy made his way to the hall, with Bryant following closely behind him. He opened the front door and gestured for Bryant to pass. 'No, you go first,' Bryant said. 'Age before beauty and all that.'

Degsy shook his head and stepped out into the foyer, glancing over his shoulder when Bryant slammed the door behind him. They trotted down the steps, Degsy leading the way as they stepped out into the courtyard. Degsy turned up his collar and dug his hands into his pockets, his breath frosting in the amber-lit darkness.

'Jesus,' Bryant said, vigorously rubbing his hands while shivering beside him. He looked towards the Mews entrance, pointing beyond it at the grey-lighted street. 'I take a left down there, right?'

Degsy nodded. 'Yeah. That'll bring you onto the Kilburn High Road.'

'Walk with me.'

Degsy grimaced. 'Nah, I best get inside.'

'Walk with me, I said. That wasn't a request.'

Degsy glanced up at the apartment and saw Mich watching them from the window. He held her gaze, turning his head when Bryant laughed and stepped away. 'She's not bad for her age, Degs. I think I'm in with a chance. Did you see her coming on to me?'

Degsy didn't reply. Instead, he quickened his pace and started walking alongside him.

The city dozed, the shop signs flickering in a desperate hope to attract while the sporadic flow of traffic trailed off into the distance. Degsy hated the city at night; he loathed the vacant loneliness of it all, the stench of petrol, the faint aggressive shouts, and their impending threat of violence.

When they reached the crossroads, Degsy stopped. 'You normally get taxis running through here, but it's a safer bet walking further into Kilburn, especially at this time of night.' He turned his back on the road, facing the direction of the mews.

Bryant grabbed his arm. 'Where the hell do you think you're going?'

'I did what you asked. I'm tired, and it's cold, and if it's okay with you, I'm going to head back. They'll come looking for me if I'm gone too long.'

Bryant gripped his arm tighter and led him to the side building on their left. 'No one's going to miss you, Degs. I'd prefer you to wait with me if that's all right. We need to have a little chat.'

'Fine,' Degsy said with a shrug. 'What do you want to talk about?'

Bryant released Degsy's arm, slipped his hand into his jacket pocket and pulled out a packet of cigarettes. He offered one to Degsy, then took one for himself, cupping his hands around the flame as Degsy gave him a light. Bryant took a deep drag and blew the smoke at Degsy. 'What's going on?'

Degsy shrugged. 'Nothing.'

'What's going on, Degsy?'

Degsy drew on his cigarette. 'Nothing, honest. I don't have a clue what you're talking about.'

'What the hell are you and Wonder Boy doing with Clate and Mich?'

'I've known them a long time.'

'Bullshit. You've never mentioned it to me. In fact, you've never bothered with anyone for as long as I've known you. You were the same old lonely little loser until a week ago.'

'I ain't no loser; don't you talk to me like that.'

'Fine,' Bryant said with a grin, 'tell me what's going on then. Your little rendezvous has con job written all over it.'

A yellow taxi sign came slowly into view. Bryant ignored it, quietly smoking his cigarette as it drove past. He gave Degsy a cold, hard stare. 'I saw you, you know, that night, up at the Old Bell.' Bryant laughed. 'Don't look so surprised. I've got eyes at the back of my head. Not that I need them with you. You're easy to find; you're like this city, an unmistakable foul smell.' He shook his head and laughed before drawing hard on his cigarette. 'I know your little gang think I'm stupid, but you know me better than that.' He flashed Degsy that creepy grin. 'I've been watching you for a while. Jesus, Degsy, did you really think me showing up at Clate's club was just a coincidence?'

Degsy raised his trembling hand to his mouth and drew hard on his cigarette. He did this several times, almost smoking it down to the stub. 'I guess not,' he said, flicking the ash onto the pavement.

Bryant narrowed his eyes. 'Good, so stop taking me for a fool and tell me what's happening. I want to know everything about Clate and Mich's involvement and who was crying in that locked room.'

20

J ay longed for his bed; instead, because Clate insisted he stayed to keep an eye on things, he settled for the sofa. Thankfully, they'd all gone to bed, leaving Jay to enjoy the room's stillness and listen to Brian Matthew's *Round Midnight* show on the radio. He'd heard Degsy return and wanted to ask him about Bryant. But he was comfortable now, the night sounds washing over him, his eyes adjusting to the darkness as he stared at the elongated shadows.

Jay thought about Jenny. They had mostly ignored her today, and when checking in on her, he found her curled up in a ball, the quilt draped over her legs, her face marred by a run of dry tears as if she'd cried herself to sleep. He'd watched her for a while to confirm she was still breathing. This was no experience for a girl her age. Cooped up here in this room, she was no better than a wild animal.

Jay cast away the notion with a sigh. *Stop trying to be something you're not*, his mother often said. Maybe she was right. All he needed to do was keep his head down, find a nice girl, and get a steady job; then, he wouldn't have found himself in this situation and, more importantly, put his mother and Des in danger. Mich would have been nothing but a bad memory, and Degsy another faceless name in a book.

Jay slipped his hand into his pocket and pulled out Nash's old diary. He held it close, gaining comfort from flicking through the pages. Nash would have easily managed Clate and taken control from the start. Jay tapped his head and smiled, then whispered *because a man needs to use his loaf*. Everyone kept saying how desperate he was to be like Nash. Jay never gave it much thought. Yet, lying alone in the early morning hours, he couldn't help but wonder what his old friend would make of him. He would tell him to wise up for a start, stop feeling sorry for himself and assess the situation.

Jay nodded in agreement and proceeded to flick through the diary. He scanned through the names and, for some reason, settled on the one that said *Mich*. Her name was circled in red ink with *Benny Bray* written alongside it. Jay had seen it countless times, never taking any notice until tonight.

When Clate mentioned Benny Bray, Jay noticed a sudden change in Mich's demeanour. A look of discomfort settled on her face, which also turned pale now that Jay recalled it. She had shifted uncomfortably in her chair and threatened to turn up the Stereo, seeming desperate to change the subject. The more he pondered it, Jay grew keener to know why. Clearly, Mich and Benny Bray had history. The question that remained was, What? Perhaps old Degsy could shed some light on it?

Holding on to that thought, Jay closed his eyes. He turned on his side, then lay on his back. No position offered respite. Now the mystery of Mich and Bray had taken root;

sleep was beyond him. Unanswerable questions badgered his mind, forcing him to sit up. Who could he ask? Degsy held his cards close to his chest, and Clate would only warn him off. Mich was definitely off-limits. The only option was to speak with Bray himself.

Approaching Bray seemed an impossible task. To begin with, Jay didn't know where to find him but, more importantly, didn't know what the man looked like. The solution only pointed one way, and, as much as he hated the idea, his only hope lay with Degsy. Luckily, the old man didn't rate Jay one bit. Opportunity hid behind the disguise of a fool. Degsy would tell him what he needed to know. These days the old man was ridiculed and ignored. Degsy believed it was his God-given right to shine. All you needed to do was pander to his ego, and there would be no shutting the old boy up.

At the thought of Degsy, Jay smiled. The expression was short-lived. The image of Bryant suddenly plagued his thoughts and wiped it cleanly from his face. Bryant was hiding something. That momentary pause, the slight stammer, when Clate questioned him. What was he doing here, anyway? Jay understood why Clate didn't want to offend Benny Bray. Jay remained unconvinced by Bryant's professional curiosity, growing in the conviction that Bryant turning up at Clate's club was more than an unfortunate coincidence.

Jay strolled over to the window, looking out over the courtyard. The city was at rest, and he felt unsettled by the night's silence. It always made him feel this way, the optimism of tomorrow's promise sullied by a growing feeling of anticipation. Jay opened a window and took in the night air, relishing its coldness inside his chest. Then he released it through an exaggerated breath.

'That's a deep sigh,' said the voice behind him.

Jay let out a gasp and quickly turned around. 'Jesus, Mich, what the hell are you playing at, sneaking up on people like that?'

'I couldn't sleep.' She flashed him a sly smile. 'I didn't mean to scare you; I forgot you were so sensitive.'

Jay frowned. 'What do you want?'

She responded with a mock pout. 'That's not very nice. I came to ask if you wanted a hot drink?'

Jay nodded. 'Sure, I'll help you make it.'

He followed her to the kitchen, pausing outside Jenny's door as they passed. Mich turned on the kitchen lights. 'Don't worry about Jen. She's tougher than you think.'

'She's only sixteen, for heaven's sake. She's just a kid.'

Again, she gave him that sly smile. 'A kid who's taken a shine to you.'

'How can you say that? This situation is sick enough without you making a joke about it.'

Mich flicked on the kettle and began rinsing out two cups. 'No need to jump down my throat; I was just saying.'

'Well, don't.' He gave Mich a long look. 'Clate's got that girl frightened out of her wits. You should be looking out for her.'

Mich glared at him. 'Who said I wasn't? I keep checking in on her, making her drinks; it's not my fault if the girl won't speak to me.'

Jay forced a laugh. '*Not your fault.* It was your idea to kidnap her, for God's sake.'

'You're only talking like this because you're *scared.*'

Jay gave her an incredulous look. 'Of course, I'm scared, and so should you be.'

Mich turned around at the sound of the kettle's click. She dropped a teabag in each cup, filled them with boiling water then added the milk. She gave them both a stir and then handed Jay a cup. 'I'm trying my best with Jenny; it's not my fault if the girl refuses to eat.'

Jay drew the tea bag from his cup with a spoon. 'Well, you need to try harder. You're the one who dragged her into all this mess. The girl needs more space; it's not healthy being cooped up like that.'

Mich gave a nonchalant shrug. 'You need to speak with Clate. That's the way he wants it.'

'What Clate wants and what's right are two separate things.' Jay sipped his tea. 'Clate needs to clear his head because he's making too many poor decisions at the moment.'

Mich flashed him that annoying smile. 'I know; what the hell was he thinking inviting that Bryant creep?'

Jay shrugged. 'Bryant invited himself. This Benny Bray seems to be the one to worry about.'

Jay studied her face for a response, but Mich immediately looked away; cradling her cup in both hands, she left the room without answering.

21

J ay only managed a few hours of sleep. That groggy feeling seemed a fair price to pay to be awake before Degsy. The old man was a creature of habit, waking every morning at six o'clock. He claimed to have learned the discipline from when he was a kid. Jay remained unconvinced, attributing old age to why Degsy only needed five hours of sleep. Not that any extra hours would help. Degsy could hibernate for the winter, and the cynical old curmudgeon would be no different. That was usually the case, but Jay noticed something off about him today. He was quiet for a start. No matter how hard Jay tried, he struggled to get the old man talking.

Jay pointed at Degsy's plate. 'You haven't touched that food. I've been frying that up since five-thirty this morning.'

Degsy prodded the egg with his fork, letting the yolk ooze onto a slice of bacon. He broke off a piece of white, paused, and then dropped the fork onto the plate.

Jay frowned. 'Something wrong with it?'

Degsy shook his head. 'Nah, I just don't have much of an appetite.'

'That's not like you.'

'Yeah, well, it is today.'

'Okay, no need to bite my head off.' Jay regarded him for a moment. 'What did Bryant say to you last night?'

'Nothing. Why do you ask?'

'Curiosity. It seemed odd, don't you think, him showing up like that?'

Degsy tried shrugging it off. 'Not really. The kid's a leech, an opportunist. Clate has a lot of dealings with Benny; he and Bryant were bound to cross paths, eventually.'

Jay seized his chance. 'I keep hearing that name. How well do you know Bray?'

'Well enough.'

'What's that supposed to mean?'

'It means well enough to leave him alone. Bryant was right for the first time in his life. Don't go poking your nose in.'

'I couldn't even if I wanted to; I don't even know what he looks like.'

'Good. My advice is to leave it like that.'

'You sound like Mich. She freezes up whenever you mention him.'

'Many girls do, especially those who used to work for him.'

'Don't talk stupid; she never worked for Bray.'

'Don't call me stupid; she was a waitress at the Indigo in the late sixties.'

'Belgravia?'

'Wardour Street, you dope. She was–' Degsy shook his head. 'Very clever. Very clever indeed. I fell for that hook, line, and sinker.'

Jay smiled. 'I don't have a clue what you're talking about.'

'Sure, you don't,' Degsy said and lit a cigarette.

Jay leaned back in his chair, watching him in silence, raising his hand occasionally to wave away the smoke. Degsy remained quiet, never uttering a word until he'd smoked his cigarette down to a stub.

Jay grimaced at the plate. 'That's a waste of decent food. You were supposed to eat that, not use it as an ashtray.' He scraped back his chair and stood. 'I'm going to shower and then go out for a bit.'

'How long?'

'A good few hours.'

'What shall I tell, Clate?'

'Tell him I needed some air. I'll keep an eye on the girl when I get back.'

Degsy sucked the air in through his teeth. 'He's not going to like that.'

'Well, he'll have to; he's not the only one who needs space.'

'Where shall I tell him you went?'

'Here and there.'

Degsy crossed his arms. 'Here and there wouldn't be near Soho by any chance?'

Jay shook his head. 'No.'

Degsy's eyes remained unconvinced. 'I'd give it a miss if you want my advice.'

'But I don't.'

'Fine,' said Degsy as he stood up. 'I know you think you're being clever, but trust me, no good will come of it.'

'Don't worry, I'll be fine.'

Degsy sighed. 'If you say so, kid. Don't say I never warned you.'

~

THE SHOWER PERKED Jay up for a while, although navigating the tube for the last forty minutes quickly lessened its effect. Twice he'd taken the wrong exit and hurried back on himself, the sweat seeping through his shirt as he braved the crowds at Piccadilly circus. The number of people took him by surprise. Locked away in that stifling apartment, he'd forgotten about the Easter Holidays. Perhaps he'd shut them out, a subconscious denial that beyond his own suffering were people with everyday lives happily enjoying themselves.

Jay pushed such thoughts aside. He needed a clear head. Getting a meeting with Benny Bray seemed impossible enough without being hindered by his own frustration. He stopped abruptly in the busy street, watchful among the crowd, waiting for a friendly face so he could ask for directions. Most passed him by with a shrug. Others didn't bother to speak. Finally, somebody did, a tanned, dark-haired girl carrying a heavy rucksack.

She pointed back down the street. 'You are walking the wrong way, yes. You need to turn back. Go straight for a few minutes, turn left onto Shaftesbury Avenue, then left again onto Wardour Street.'

Jay mirrored her bright smile, holding it as he turned around and followed her directions. He pictured her face in his mind's eye, undecided about what amused him more, a tourist being the only person to come to his aid or her French accent. London seemed to be a gathering of transients. Even Degsy, who had lived here all his life, constantly maintained he was passing through. Jay was starting to understand why. The city possessed an undeniable buzz. But the theatre signs' bright glow, the traffic flow, and the Chinese restaurants' enticing aromas were imbued with a sense of loneliness. The kind of loneliness that found its way under your skin, scarring you with a profound feeling of solitude, which, if you allowed it, intensified beneath this vast, grey sky.

Jay found his surroundings surprisingly familiar, considering his only exposure to Wardour Street was through photographs and TV. He likened it to revisiting a dream. The peep shows, and strip bars were vivid and real when previously they had been vague memories, fragments of his imagination.

Huddled brazenly between a renovated shop and a bureau de change, the Indigo nightclub's blue and violet hues reflected in the wet pavement. Jay hesitated by the door, then pressed it with his hand, surprised and a little troubled when it swung open. He stepped into its murky foyer, the sickly scent of massage oil and stale cigarettes growing stronger as he crept down the red-carpeted stairway.

The soft light cast by the table lamps rescued the room from total darkness. It was larger than Jay expected, its wide, deserted stage looking out onto the rows of vacant, ebony tables. The bar on the left ran the room's length. With their backs turned, three suited men sat at the far corner. They chatted, oblivious to Jay's presence, their laughter loud and unapologetic. Their broad shoulders were hunched, and their closely cropped heads haloed beneath the optics frosted glow.

'Hey,' Jay said, standing still when each of them glanced over their shoulder. They all turned around, stepping off their stools, when the guy at the end said, 'Who the hell let you in?'

Jay offered out his hands, palms up. 'Sorry, the door was unlocked. I thought you were open.'

The guy standing in the middle glanced at his watch. 'It's

not even noon. You need to come back after eight.'

Jay nodded and smiled. He gave them a quick scan. They looked so similar with their gelled-back hair and taupe double-breasted suits. On studying them closer, he began to see a remarkable difference. The one who had spoken was taller for a start. He was older, too, in his early to mid-forties, his pock-marked skin spoiling his good looks.

'On your way then, son,' he said with accustomed authority.

Jay remained where he was. 'Apologies for the intrusion. I was hoping to speak with Mr Bray.'

The men looked at each other and laughed. Then the younger looking one, with the freckles and auburn shine in his hair, said, 'Remind me, who are you again?'

'Jay Ellis.'

He relaxed his shoulders and, with exaggerated ease, said, 'Of course, that's right. The famous Jay Ellis. I'll fetch Benny now. He told us he was expecting you.' He turned as if to walk away, then, holding his position, said, 'You've got some nerve; I'll give you that.' He clapped his hands. 'Now scoot before you get hurt. I'd keep off the Coke if I were you. I don't want to see you here again. You cocky little prick. Go, I said. Go on, on your way.'

Jay didn't flinch even when the guy swaggered towards him. Slipping his hand behind his back, the guy took out a cosh. He held it to his chest, pausing when the older guy said, 'Relax, Chad, just hold fire for now.'

Chad's face broke into a smile. 'I am relaxed, Roy, just sending this Dipstick on his way.'

Roy slapped Chad on the back. 'I'm glad to see you doing what you get paid for. Be patient, you can curb his misguided confidence in a minute, but first, I want to hear what he has to say.'

Chad acknowledged the command with a sigh. He pointed at Jay with the cosh. 'Speak up, *Jay Ellis*, don't keep Roy and me waiting.'

Jay glanced quickly towards the stairs. A part of him regretted it now and wondered if heeding Degsy's words and making a run for it might be the wiser option. The choice was quickly removed as the third guy, who still hadn't spoken, walked casually up the stairs, ensuring the entrance was locked.

Roy flashed him a smile. 'We don't want any more waifs and strays wandering in. I thought you'd be pleased now you have our attention.'

'I need to speak with Mr Bray,' Jay said.

Roy shook his head. 'Not without an appointment.'

'Then let me make one.'

'Nah,' Roy said.

Jay glanced over his shoulder towards the stairs. 'I'll come back later tonight.'

Roy slipped his hands into his pockets and stepped forward. 'That might have been an option five minutes ago, but you no longer get to decide.'

Jay shrugged. 'Fine. What do you want from me?'

'I want to know why you came here and if it's worth Benny's time.'

Jay sighed. 'I wanted to talk about a friend of yours and a theory of mine.'

Roy narrowed his eyes. 'A *theory*?'

'Yeah, just a notion I had about something that hurt Mr Bray a long time ago.'

Roy turned to Chad. 'Get young Jay here a drink.' He pointed at a table, 'Let's sit down,' and reading Jay's hesitation, said, 'You came here to talk, right? So come on, sit down. I'm listening.'

22

Refusing to eat seemed the only form of protest. Hunger couldn't be controlled on a whim. It plagued her body and soul and consumed her every thought until she finally succumbed and devoured the takeaway like a pale ravenous animal. She hated herself for displaying such weakness, even more so during the act. She loathed each bite of meat slithering down her throat, the congealed layer of grease across her lips and the dried barbecue sauce crusting her fingers. Martyrdom was something she read about in books. It was best left there. Her plight was real. The swelling on her lip and the ache in her stomach confirmed that. To survive, she needed to build her strength. Her father would want her to dig deep. Foolish emotion was the catalyst of weakness.

Jenny thought of her father while she lay on the bed. She wondered what he was doing now, sitting by the phone or pacing the room. Picturing his warm smile and the creases around his eyes, she longed for him to remain strong. Good hearts seldomly fared well under duress. A kind soul came with more than its share of weaknesses.

Tears welled in her eyes, forcing her to take a deep breath and stifle them with a sigh. She pushed her hair away from her face, listening attentively, waiting for the familiar chatter of voices. They'd been quieter today, but now, as though reading her thoughts, she heard the distinctive sound of Mich's voice. 'Jenny, Jenny?' it said softly, and although it forced her to sit up, the girl refused to answer.

She watched the handle turn and the door gradually ease open. For a moment, Mich seemed more apparition than flesh. Her blonde peroxide hair and pale skin gave her the appearance of a ghost, the haunted look in her eyes adding to the illusion.

Mich glanced down at the floor. 'I'm glad to see you finally decided to eat.'

Jenny held her stare with her own. 'This nightmare's bad enough; there's no point going hungry.'

Mich nodded. 'Indeed, perhaps we can help each other through this.'

'You can start by setting me free.'

Mich lowered her eyes. 'I'm so sorry, Jen. But I can't do that.'

'No, I didn't think you would.' Jenny studied her with an icy glare. 'How long before I can go home?'

'Soon.'

'How soon?'

'Clate reckons it's only a few days now.'

Jenny touched the swelling on her lip. 'Have you spoken to Daddy?'

Mich shook her head. 'Clate has, though.'

'How was he?'

'As you'd expect, frightened, concerned.'

'And he's going to pay?'

'Of course, he is. You needn't worry about that. He wants you home and safe; he'll do whatever it takes.'

Jenny felt a surge of disappointment and relief, desperate to remain expressionless while struggling to contain the emotion. She calmed herself with a deep breath. 'And what about you, Mich?'

'What about me?'

'What are you going to do afterwards? You played a part in this–'

'Under duress.'

Jenny forced a laugh. 'Are you still sticking to that story? How stupid do you think I am?'

'It's not a story; it's complicated.'

'Yeah, right. You just can't help yourself, can you? It's one lie after another.' Jenny regarded her for a moment. 'Do you honestly expect me to believe that?'

'You can believe what you like; your daddy will understand; it won't be the first time I've begged for his forgiveness.'

'*Forgiveness*. This isn't some stupid row. It's kidnapping and extortion; if this nightmare ever ends, you've no way back from this; you're out of our lives for good.'

Mich stepped closer, her long, ringed fingers tightening into fists. 'You'd like that, wouldn't you?'

Jenny gave her a cold smile. 'Second to getting out of this place, it's all I've ever wanted.'

Mich retreated slowly into the hall and closed the door without answering. Jenny heard the turn of the lock, undecided about what sickened her more, Mich's blatant deceit or the lingering scent of her perfume. Jenny noticed it during their time at the gallery, which felt like years now, although it was only days ago. At first, she'd found it pleasant. Its floral-like fragrance was a fitting accompaniment to the impressionist landscapes and their brightly painted gardens.

The fragrance held no attraction for her now; neither did their time together at the gallery the more she thought about it. Even the paintings she'd once held in high esteem were tainted by the experience. Their depictions of plague, beheadings and the crucifixion of Christ had more relevance now that she could place them against her own suffering. She pictured her predicament as a scene, a windowless, drab room where a tearful girl lay frightened and ashamed, the hint of defiance in her eyes sedated by the knowledge that her captors had the upper hand, where neither she nor her father could offer any resistance.

It made her want to weep. Somehow, she managed not to do that for the first time in days. She got up from the bed, walked to the ensuite bathroom and undressed. Having not washed for a while, she stood beneath the shower for over thirty minutes, relishing the sensation. Afterwards, she dried herself without haste, rubbing the coarse towel slowly across her skin. As she dressed, she felt a dull ache in her back, coupled with a new tiredness. Thankfully, she'd brought a box of Tampax, but she'd planned to be at home during this time, and her period was the last thing she needed in this madness.

Jenny strode over to the bed and began searching frantically through her rucksack. She knew the outcome from the start. Something inside her, blind hope perhaps, urged her to continue, making her believe that a pack of paracetamol lay hidden beneath her clothes and books. Eventually, she gave up, banged her fist against the door, and shouted, 'Mich, Mich, come here. I need to speak with you.'

Jenny banged the door again, pausing when she heard someone in the hall. They'd warned her to keep quiet, and now, in this brief silence, she suddenly considered the consequences. She gently stroked her lip, and as the door opened, all she thought about was Clate.

For once, Mich was a welcomed sight and having shed her mask of concern, she stood there looking tired and aggrieved with her hands resting on her hips. 'What's with all the banging, Jen? I thought you'd stopped all that.' Mich lowered her voice. 'Clate's in the other room. Please, Jen, don't make this any worse. Don't bring attention to yourself.'

Jenny raised her eyes. 'I'm not; it's my time of the month. I need some paracetamol.'

A hint of understanding flashed through Mich's eyes. 'I'll fetch you some now; wait here quietly.'

Jenny answered with a nod and, as Mich walked away, inched out into the hallway. The stifling, warm air reeked of cigarettes, and from the direction of the lounge, she heard the muffled voices from the TV. Jenny stepped forward and, without hesitation, ran down the hall. She never considered the risk; her only focus was to get out, to cry for help, and make her plight known in the cold, grey open street. When she got to the end of the hall, she grew anxious. Jenny reached out to the front door, then stood still, petrified, watching it slowly open.

They stared at each other, and Jenny, filled with shock and dismay, wondered who could have done that to Jay's face. She studied the large bruise across his cheek; his black eye, swollen shut, drew her gaze from his swollen lips.

'Are you all right?' she said, glancing over her shoulder to see Mich striding down the hallway.

23

J ay couldn't decide what bothered him more, Degsy's relentless stare or the smile that said, *I told you so*. He'd prepared for Degsy to gloat but hadn't expected, this soon at least, for the girl to see him like that. The fearful look on her face lingered in his mind's eye. He was tempted to go to her room to reassure her. Convince her she wasn't destined for the same fate. Instead, he let the notion pass. Not that Degsy would let him out of his sight. Feasting on Jay's predicament with gluttonous eyes, the old man seemed determined to have his say. Degsy pointed at the table. 'You look fit to drop; sit down, for God's sake.'

Jay eased himself onto a stool, wincing while he caressed his ribs.

Degsy mocked him with a grin. 'Who's the old man now? Takes it out of you, doesn't it? A good kicking like that.'

Jay ignored the remark and, with significant effort, rested his elbows on the counter. Slowly, he raised a hand and placed it on his chest, grimacing with every deep breath.

Degsy shook his head with fake concern. 'I'd give you some tablets, but the girl's taken the Co-codamol.'

Jay answered with a strained nod. 'She needs them more than me.'

'I very much doubt that.'

Jay sighed. 'My mam's painkillers are what I need, or something a bit stronger.'

Degsy laughed. 'Give you some whisky if you like? Or I can ask Bryant to give you some of that magic grass he smokes.'

Jay shook his head. 'Nah, whisky's fine. Why are you bothering with Bryant? I thought he would have been the last person you wanted to see?'

Degsy held his hands to his chest. 'He is, but somehow he's managed to get his hooks into Clate.'

Jay lowered his voice. 'Where is Clate?'

Degsy nodded towards the hall. 'In the lounge with Mich.'

'Clate needs to get rid of him; he should know better, especially with everything going on.'

Degsy strolled to the far counter and returned with two glasses and a bottle of whisky. He half-filled both glasses and pushed one towards Jay. 'It seems Clate's not alone.' He raised his glass and smiled. 'Here's to sharper minds.' Degsy downed his whisky in one. 'Speaking of which, how did your little trip to Soho go today?'

Jay held the whisky to his mouth, grimacing as he took a sip. 'Not the way I planned.'

Degsy burst into a cough, and Jay, barely able to raise his arm, slapped him lightly on the back; it was more an act of courtesy than a genuine attempt to stop the man from choking. 'I'm fine,' Degsy said with a hoarse voice. He wiped the tears from his eyes. 'Your little escapade today. What the hell were you thinking?'

Jay released a deep sigh. 'See who Benny was; introduce myself.'

'Didn't you think that was a stupid thing to do, given what's going on? I thought you were smart. Why take the risk?'

Jay lowered his eyes and gave a weak shrug. 'I never put any of us at risk. I just went to Benny's club–'

'To do what?'

'Find out a bit more about Bryant. Don't give me that look. I didn't ask about Bryant directly. I pretended I wanted a job.'

Degsy refilled his glass. 'So what did Benny say to you?'

Jay looked down at the table. 'I never got to see him. I had to talk to a guy called Roy first.'

Degsy gripped his glass. 'Roy Cullen,' he said as though the name was a bad taste in his mouth.

'You know him?'

Degsy sipped his whisky, then sighed. 'Yeah, I've had the pleasure of his company.'

Jay shifted slowly on the stool. 'That's not how I'd describe it.'

'Whose fault is that? I told you not to go poking your nose in.' He focused on Jay's swollen eye. 'I thought you worked at that Liverpool casino.'

'I did.'

'Then you should know the kind of people you're dealing with.'

'I just wanted to talk.'

Degsy laughed. 'The Indigo isn't the place for that. *I just wanted to talk*. Where did you think you were going, the Citizen's Advice Bureau?' Degsy swirled the whisky in the glass. 'What on earth did you say?'

'Nothing.'

'It must have been something. Look at the state of you.'

Jay picked up his glass, sniffed the whisky, and then placed it on the counter. 'I went to the Indigo, asked to speak to Benny Bray, said I was after a job and was told I needed to speak with Roy Cullen first. I said that was fine, went to sit down, then they started laying into me before I even got to the table.'

'And you never said anything out of term.'

'No.'

Degsy narrowed his eyes. 'Roy Cullen's as sharp as they come. He's Benny's righthand man. Are you sure you didn't mention anything else, provoke him in any way?'

Jay shook his head.

Degsy looked unconvinced. 'It doesn't sound like him. It's not something he'd do.'

Jay shifted slowly from the stool and, with excruciating effort, stood up. 'Perhaps he was encouraged by his friends. They seemed a bit restless.' Catching his reflection in the glass kitchen cabinet, Jay gently touched his eye. He grimaced at the sight of his face, turned to Degsy, and said, 'You ponder it for as long as you like because I didn't do this to myself.'

Degsy concurred with a sigh. 'I guess. God knows what Clate will have to say about this.' He took out his pack of cigarettes. 'He'll want you off the job, that's for sure.'

Jay frowned. 'Why?'

'I'm surprised you have to ask that since we're only days away.'

'What difference do a few cuts and bruises make.'

'None, if you're staying at your hotel, but while you're

here.' Degsy lit his cigarette. 'They might attract unnecessary attention.'

Jay motioned stiffly towards the door. 'What happened to the notion of us sticking together? You've been off since Bryant showed up. Now you're suddenly keen to keep your distance.'

Degsy drew hard on his cigarette. 'And whose fault is that? You can't say I never warned you.'

'Warned him about what?' boomed Clate, smoking his cigar in the doorway.

Degsy shrugged and flicked the ash from his cigarette. 'I'm not saying anything; you need to ask Jay about that.'

Clate stared at him, his face a mixture of amusement and disgust. 'No need. News travels fast. Bryant told me.'

'*Bryant*?' said Jay.

Clate puffed on his cigar and released the smoke with a sigh. 'Yeah, he came by the club today; the kid's like a bad cold; there's no shaking him.' He pointed at Degsy with his cigar. 'Did he say anything to you the other night?'

Degsy shook his head. 'No, nothing, just commented on the cold, then I pointed him towards a taxi.'

Clate stepped further into the kitchen. 'Well, he's sniffing around, that's for sure.'

Jay rested his weight against the wall. 'Just warn him off.'

'I told you before that's not an option,' said Clate. 'He's like a foxhound with a scent. He knows we're up to something. And you've widened his opportunity to go chasing after that.'

'*Me*?' Jay said.

Clate drew on his cigar, blowing the smoke into Jay's face. 'Yeah, *you*. Bryant said he kept shtum about you being my guest; now it seems we owe him a favour.'

'What kind of favour?'

Clate shrugged. 'God knows. He'll be here later. I've told Mich to get close to him; you be nice to him too; the best we can do now is humour him until this is all over.'

24

When he told her to get close to Bryant, Clate reminded Mich of Nash. She played the part so well, the wayward wife, the slut girlfriend, and Nash often cast her in that role all those years ago. It was nothing short of being a whore. Admittedly, the prize was bigger. All she did was sell strangers a fantasy, pamper their egos and sleep with them for a price. It wasn't a new revelation. She had known it for years, even during her time with Nash. Whoring was it all was, and she had long since stopped believing it was part of anything more sophisticated.

Sitting next to Bryant on the arm of his chair, Mich couldn't decide what irritated her more: the snide smile on his face or his nauseating odour of sweat and cheap after-shave. He wore the same yellow cotton shirt from when they had first met, and from the wine stains on his jacket, she concluded he only owned one suit. Whenever Bryant spoke, Mich felt his warm breath breeze foully across her skin; his clammy hand gripped her waist like the clutches of an immovable curse.

Mich laughed convincingly at his jokes, sharing his disdain while he sneered at Jay. She enjoyed that part, at least. It was good to see the kid brought down to size. She always found such confidence tiresome. What else did he possess except for good looks? Jay was nothing but a poor man's Nash; the bruises on his face bore testament to that, a never-has-been whose misguided confidence gave him no right to be sure of himself.

Bryant felt that too, his voice loaded with contempt as he said, 'I thought you were smart; what the hell were you thinking showing up at the Indigo?'

Jay's loosely clasped hands tightened. To his credit, he remained silent. Bryant would have to work harder because the kid clearly wasn't biting. Aided by a pest's resilience, Bryant remained undeterred. 'You were lucky; all you got was a slap. Folk have been dumped in the Thames for less than that.' He paused as Degsy sniggered. 'What's so amusing?'

Degsy shook his head and shrugged, his face growing redder the longer Bryant stared at him. Mich was also tired of the old man. How long had he been in this game? A world-weary old fool who still believed he had years. Clate would abandon him without giving it a second thought. So would she, providing she had the opportunity.

Bryant moved his gaze onto Jay. 'I can't figure out why you mouthed off like that?'

Jay looked at him and frowned. 'I only asked them for a job.'

'It's not what I heard.' He gripped Mich's waist tighter and pulled her onto his lap. 'You should be grateful I kept my mouth shut about knowing you.'

Jay flashed him a sarcastic smile. 'It's much appreciated.'

'It wasn't for you. I did it to help Clate. He's got enough

on his mind; it's best he remains unassociated. Hanging around with gobshites marks you like a dark shadow.' Bryant studied Jay for a second. An inquisitive look passed across his face as though Jay had been a passing stranger in a crowd, and this was the first time he'd truly noticed him. 'What I fail to understand is why you're still here?'

Jay leaned forward in his chair and sighed. Clate had ordered them to keep Bryant amused. But Mich could see the creep's presence slivered beneath Jay's skin. 'I'm staying as his guest, renting one of the apartments.' The words sounded strained the instant they left Jay's mouth. As for keeping Bryant amused, the conspiratorial glance he threw Mich's way acknowledged Jay was making a poor job of it.

Mich stroked Bryant's neck to distract him. He responded with a long kiss, and Mich, barely able to maintain the charade, almost squirmed when he rolled his tongue inside her mouth. They broke off to Degsy's sigh. 'Get a room, for God's sake,' the old man's face mirroring Mich's repulsion.

Bryant considered it with a smile. 'Speaking of rooms,' he hesitated and, turning to Mich, said, 'How's the girl?'

'The girl?'

'Clate's niece.'

'She's fine.'

'Where is she?'

'Resting.'

Bryant narrowed his eyes. '*Still*? Do you mean she's still in that room? That's a bit unhealthy, don't you think?'

Mich shook her head and smiled. 'No, not really.'

Bryant slapped his hand down on her thigh. 'Well, it does to me. A girl her age needs to be out and about. No wonder she's always sleeping cooped up in that room.'

'It's not what it seems. She's tired, that's all.'

'I bet she is. Let's get her out here; give her some daylight.' He gestured to get up, tilting back into his chair when Mich pressed him into his seat. 'Stay where you are; leave the girl alone.' She glanced towards the stereo. 'I'll find us some music. Last time you were here, we couldn't stop you dancing.'

Bryant rolled his eyes. 'That's because I was drunk.'

'Now that's an idea,' Mich said and stood up. Bryant grabbed her arm, clutching it tighter when she drew away from him. She gave him a fierce stare, ordering him to let her go. Bryant didn't comply, the determined look in his eyes growing stronger with each protest. Mich dug her nails into Bryant's hand. 'Come on, let me go. Let me go, I said. I want to get us a drink.' Mich relaxed her fingers when her nails started to draw blood. She raised her voice to a shout. 'Stop it, Bryant; it's gone beyond a joke now.'

Bryant loosened his grip. 'Bring the girl here, and I'll let you go.'

Mich managed to pull free. 'No. I've already told you she's resting.'

Bryant sank into his chair and sighed. For a moment, he appeared inclined to follow Mich's command. Then a defiant look passed over his face, and with a swift snap of his fingers said, 'Let's put it to the vote.'

Mich caught the surprise in Jay's eyes and shook her head with a look of bewilderment. She repeated Bryant's words as though they were some strange incantation, then, quickly coming to her senses, said, 'What on earth are you talking about?'

Bryant shot up from his chair. 'You keep saying leave the girl to rest. I say otherwise. But that's just you and me. I'm interested in Jay and Degsy's opinion.'

'No,' Mich said. 'Clate placed the girl in my charge. I get

to say what's good for her. *Their* and *your* opinion don't count.'

Jay stood up. 'Mich is right. Let's have a drink, Bryant. The girl's nothing to do with you; stop being a dick about this.'

Bryant wandered over to Jay and squared up to him. 'You're in no position to be calling someone a dick. So I'd keep your mouth shut if I were you.' He turned to Degsy and smiled. 'Well?'

Degsy frowned. 'Well, what?'

'Should we let the girl get some air? What are your thoughts on that?'

Degsy tried shrugging it off, but Bryant kept on at him. Eventually, the old man gave in and, looking down at the carpet, said, 'I suppose no harm could come of it.'

'*No harm*?' said Mich through gritted teeth; she glared at him until he looked up. Degsy struggled to hold her gaze, fidgeting like an embarrassed schoolboy, more so as the look in her eyes said, *What the hell are you thinking*? The old man reacted with an apologetic shrug, blushing as Mich and Jay stared at him.

Bryant leaned over Degsy and slapped him on the back. 'Good for you, Degs. That makes it a tie.'

Mich sighed. 'Drop it, Bryant; you've had your joke; it's gone too far now.'

Bryant held up his hands. 'Who said it was a joke. I'll hold off until the big boss gets back.'

Mich frowned. 'What do you mean?'

'It's a tied election now. Clate has the deciding vote.' He motioned towards the hall, stopping when Mich blocked his way. 'Where are you going, Bryant?'

'To get a drink, thought you wanted to party?'

'I'll get it,' she insisted, refusing to budge while Bryant tried to push past her.

'Understood,' Bryant said with a sigh. 'Now get out of my way; I need to piss, for God's sake.'

Grudgingly, Mich let him pass, watching him swagger down the hall, tempted to pick up the heaviest object she could find and chase after him. She was undecided about what she hated more, the way he touched her or that sickening smell of his.

25

J enny wanted to hammer against the door and scream, but her body remained weak. A crippling pain confined her to her bed while the warm dusty air, tainted by stale food, grew more malodorous. She pulled the quilt closer to her chest. After providing a temporary respite, the tablets started to wear off. Jenny wanted to rest, but the loud unrelenting chatter and the ravaged fleeting images of her father made it impossible in this place. Fear conspired with her constant feeling of dread. Every creaking floorboard and slamming door brought its own sense of foreboding.

Sluggishly, Jenny turned over onto her back, pressed her sweaty palms into the mattress and, battling against the pain, eased herself up. She gazed blankly at the drab beige walls, focusing on the wistful faces formed by the tiny crevices and cracks. Their grimaces turned to smiles while their eyes, devoid of pity, mockingly stared back. Averting her gaze to the door, Jenny watched the handle slowly turn. Her body stiffened, more so when the door eased open.

She expected to see Mich and felt ill-prepared for the

odd-looking young man standing before her. He looked oily and pale; mischief glinted in his sunken eyes while he placed his bony, nicotine-stained finger on his lips. Jenny tried to speak, but he silenced her with a 'shush.'

'Don't be frightened,' he said softly, and Jenny couldn't decide what alarmed her more, the way he crept towards her or the eeriness of each whisper. He sat beside her on the bed, and while he observed her through dark eyes, she felt her heart beat thickly inside her throat.

The cruel face creased slowly into a smile. 'You're Jen, right?'

Jenny answered with a nod.

He offered her his hand. 'Most people call me Bryant; I'd like you to call me Nick.'

Nick let his hand fall onto his lap, seemingly unaffected by her refusing it. 'I wanted them to let you out. There's no reason a pretty girl your age should be cooped up like this.'

Unsettled by his lingering glance, Jenny pushed her hair from her face. Somehow, she managed a smile. 'Thanks. What did they say when you asked them that?'

Nick's shoulders sagged as he sighed. 'They were furious to tell you the truth. Mich told me she was responsible for you. That you needed rest, and I should mind my own business.'

Jenny took a deep breath. 'You know that's not true.'

Nick placed his finger on his lips. 'Shush, keep your voice down.' He studied her with a frown. 'When you said it wasn't true? What did you mean?'

Jenny lowered her hands, letting the quilt fall from her chest. 'I'm a prisoner here. They're holding me against my will.'

Nick laughed, then stopped abruptly to ask, 'Are you being serious?'

'Of course I am; they've kidnapped me.'

'They?'

'Clate, Jay, Mich and that old man.'

Nick shook his head in disbelief. 'Why would Clate do that? You're his niece, right?'

Jenny shook her head. 'I'm not related to Clate. Mich is my stepmother; it was probably her idea; I'm telling you she's in on it; they're keeping me locked up until Daddy pays the ransom.'

Nick silenced her with another Shush. 'Okay. I believe you. Take a deep breath. Calm down now.'

Jenny did as he asked, and the pain, temporarily subdued, stabbed mercilessly at the nape of her back. She started to cry, the coarse feel of cotton pressing into her skin while Nick hugged her. She felt comforted by his touch until his clammy hands lingered too long.

'I'm all right,' she said and pulled away from him.

Nick released his grip, his loosely clasped hands resting upon his lap. 'Let's assume you're telling the truth, we–'

'I am.'

'Fine. Then we need to get you out of here.'

Jenny motioned to get up.

Nick lowered his voice. 'You stay where you are; we can't just go barging our way out; we need a clear head; think this through, right?'

She responded with a nod and, by the amused look on Nick's face, too enthusiastically perhaps. It made her feel pathetic and weak, like a chained dog grateful for any scraps.

As if sensing her chagrin, Nick tried reassuring her again. 'We need to choose our time. Later tonight when they're all asleep.'

The casualness in his voice caused her to doubt his seriousness. She wondered if he saw it as a joke, humouring her in case she became hysterical? Was his nonchalance more caution than concern to protect himself from a highly strung teenage girl with strange delusions? She shifted a little in the bed, lifting the quilt towards her when Nick's glance loitered uncomfortably on her chest.

Nick averted his gaze, plucked a speck of fluff from his trousers, and flicked it onto the carpet. 'You needn't worry, you know. I do believe you.'

Jenny blushed. 'I never said you didn't.'

His face creased into a smile. 'You didn't have to. Worry's written all over your face.' He gave her a pensive look. 'Just be patient, okay. Mich is in her room and the old man's dozing. Let's wait a while until they're asleep. It makes no sense to hurry this.'

'What about Jay?'

With a hint of a frown, Nick pondered the question. 'Don't worry. He won't bother us.' He studied her for a moment. 'You like him, huh?'

'He's the only one who's been kind to me.' She pictured him in her mind's eye and, without thinking, said, 'What happened to his face?'

'Don't concern yourself about that. Don't you go thinking he's kind. He's no different from the rest; you can't trust him.'

Jenny touched her lip. 'Did it have anything to do with Clate?'

Nick nodded. 'Jay stepped out of line.' He rested his hand on her thigh. 'Clate's a problem, that's for sure, but luckily for us, he's out.'

Jenny glanced reproachingly at his hand. 'And where do you fit into all of this?'

Nick narrowed his eyes. 'I'm just a friend. I've known

Clate and Mich since I was a kid. I do odd jobs for him now and again. I thought you were–'

'If they're your friends, why are you keen to help me?'

Nick's eyes widened as he drew back his head. 'Friends don't come into it. Surely, it's what any decent person would do, especially when they're holding a young girl against her will.'

She rested her hand on his. The last thing she wanted was to offend him. Slowly, Nick placed his other hand on hers and caressed her skin with his thumb. Jenny flashed him a smile; the response surprised her; it wasn't a reaction of consent, but something triggered subconsciously, more a consequence of her vulnerability.

Nick licked the dryness from his lips. 'You look so pretty when you smile; I love how it lights up your face.'

Jenny recoiled from the expectant shine in his eyes. She tried withdrawing her hand, but Nick held it tighter. 'What would you have done,' he said, 'if I hadn't come to your rescue?'

It seemed an odd thing to say, especially the way he phrased it. Jenny responded with a cautious shrug. 'Sit it out, I suppose; wait until Daddy pays the ransom.'

'And no doubt Daddy will do that?'

'Yes,' Jenny snapped.

'Sorry,' Nick said, 'seems I struck a nerve. Of course, he will. I should be more sensitive.' He glanced to his left, then, looking into her eyes, said, 'How much are they asking for?'

Jenny shook her head and pulled away from his hand. 'I'm not sure. Is it relevant?'

Her comment stole the smile from Nick's face; he clenched his hand into a fist, but the door swung open before he could answer. Jenny was undecided about what disturbed her more, the way Nick looked at her or Clate's muscular frame blocking the doorway. Nick, following her gaze, remained seated when Clate ordered him to 'Get up.'

Clate drew hard on his cigar. 'Come on, Bryant, you've had your fun. Now get up.'

Bryant rose slowly from the bed. 'I wasn't trying to have any fun.'

Clate sighed. 'What the hell were you doing then?'

'Just talking to her, that's all.'

'Talking to her about what?'

Bryant looked over his shoulder at Jenny and gave her a callous smile. 'Nothing much, just helping her plan her escape.'

26

Degsy never credited Bryant with having much sense. Still, how he manipulated Clate into bringing him into the con was a praiseworthy story in any grifter's book. Degsy decided to get a change of scene. Bryant's smug smile and Clate's unrelenting scowl made the place unbearable. Mich's only course of action was to sulk, although her mood had been sullen for days making it difficult to notice any difference. For once, Jay handled the situation with style. Knowing silence was the best defence, he'd retreated to the downstairs apartment and, like Degsy, sought refuge in quiet contemplation.

Degsy sniffed the air; the aroma of frying bacon and sausages against a blend of hot coffee was the finest thing he'd smelled in ages. Saliva flooded his mouth, and looking over his shoulder, he stared longingly at the counter. A hint of sympathy travelled on the waitress's smile. 'It won't be long, love. I'll bring it straight over.' Degsy answered with an appreciative nod and then turned to face the window.

For Degsy, a cafe was at its best in the morning between

eight and ten. Daily commuters were in full flight, hurriedly passing in and out with no time to chat, forced politeness with every order, eager to leave with their sandwich and coffee takeaway. The construction workers were less rushed, devouring their full English with ease, slurping their tea while contentedly flicking through the morning papers. Degsy also liked to take his time, idly watching the traffic, his face awash with the warm rays of March sunlight. Moments like these brought out the best in him. He felt untroubled and relaxed, but as a grey cloud gradually obscured the sun, like every good thing that passed through his life, he knew it wouldn't last.

Degsy put these feelings of sadness down to age. Nostalgia was a fickle friend, enticing you into memory's summer years before abandoning you in its winter shadows. Somehow he always navigated his way out, but Bryant's presence harried him like a curse. The fear in the girl's eyes and Jay's beaten face added layer after layer of sorrow.

Degsy suppressed the images with a sigh, and as the waitress laid down his plate, he smiled at her with glee, knowing that on a full stomach, a man's troubles could wait until tomorrow.

Degsy ate slowly; like a condemned man, he savoured every moment. Ten minutes later, he stared at his empty plate, wiping it clean with his last slice of toast. The coffee was strong, and he swirled it inside his mouth to dissipate the taste of eggs and bacon. With a creeping air of discontentment, Degsy looked around, fixing his gaze on the woman at the far table. Her hair, short and black, matched the colour of her stained gabardine trench coat. Giving her newspaper a thorough shake, she sighed into it. She caught Degsy's glance. 'It's a sin and a shame,' she said, her pencil-drawn eyebrows making her face look more pinched.

Degsy frowned, tempted to say *What on earth are you talking about*? Not that she gave him a chance. 'It's evil,' she said. 'That's the only way to describe it, breaking into that man's home, and him a judge too, then raping his young daughter. It doesn't bear thinking about.'

Lately, Degsy had taken little interest in the news and was only vaguely familiar with the story. He answered with a concerned nod, which encouraged the woman to continue.

'She'd only just turned eighteen, a virgin too.' The woman shook her head in disgust. 'For two days, they held her captive in her own home. I dread to think what is going through that poor girl's mind. What a horrifying ordeal.' She closed the paper in anger. 'They should be castrated then hung. Even that's too good for them. I hope their souls rot in hell.' Her eyes grew wider with hate. 'What the hell were they thinking? Who, with an ounce of decency, could treat an innocent girl like that? For two days, they let her suffer. Two days locked in her room. What kind of unfeeling bastards would do that?'

Degsy didn't know what to say; he shifted uncomfortably in his chair as her words, having more relevancy than she could ever imagine, felt more like an accusation. He mumbled a response.

'What was that?' she said with a frown.

'Absolutely,' said Degsy raising his voice. 'I totally agree with everything you say.'

She gave him a self-satisfied smile, then broke into another monologue as though Degsy had begged her to continue. 'Five years they got. Five bloody years. The one who planned the burglary got twelve, and he never even touched her. How the hell do you explain that?'

Degsy answered her momentary pause with a shrug.

'Exactly,' she said. 'They need to have a retrial. That poor girl and her family need justice. That kind of experience scars someone for life. It's no different to murder, in a way. It'll haunt her until her dying days. She'll always carry it around with her.' She paused for breath. 'Those who did it won't. Five years. It's a joke. They'll be out in three, bragging about it, no doubt. Scum like that sees prison as a breeze. They'll feel no remorse. Yes, they'll show it to the parole board, but deep down, they're only thinking about themselves. That sort is only out for what they can get. They see others' suffering as a bit of fun.'

Degsy scraped back in his chair, the woman falling silent when he stood. He strolled to the counter and paid for his food, throwing the woman a smile before making a quick exit.

Along the Kilburn High Road, Degsy wandered aimlessly past the shops. He wanted to walk all day. He had no desire to return to that apartment. The air was so much fresher outside. The busy street comforted him with its flow of unknown faces. The woman's words had taken root; he longed to be free of it and would walk all night if he had to.

He thought about the girl in the newspaper, and, on trying to picture what she looked like, he saw Jenny in his mind's eye, her long mousy hair and those brown eyes heavy with sadness. *She's so young*, he muttered under his breath. He felt consumed by her look of frightened vulnerability, his pace slowing as the girls' faces, real and imagined, blended into one.

Degsy slipped into an alleyway, his hand shaking while he lit a cigarette. He took a deep drag and exhaled, watching the smoke drift above the brick graffitied wall. Again, he thought about the woman's words, knowing *their* crime was no different no matter how much they denied it. Kidnapping was all it was. So why try to dress it up in the sophistication of a con? Not that Degsy was any better. He had bought willingly into that lie. Earlston's money was his only hope, and no shame was big enough to deny himself from having a taste of it.

27

Clate took a dislike to Bryant from the start. From the moment he walked into the club, Clate sensed something treacherous in that pale, overconfident face. He marked him down as a fool. But it required cunning to wangle his way into the con, and Clate might have been impressed in better circumstances. The thing that irked him most was that Bryant demanded a cut. He wanted an equal share, which was totally unjustified.

Bryant had done nothing to deserve it except for keeping his mouth shut. Bryant disagreed, resolute in the belief that by keeping Benny Bray out of this, he required no further justification. He made other demands too. When the day arrived for Clate to exchange the girl for the money, instead of waiting at the apartment, Bryant wanted to accompany him. Neither granting nor denying the request, Clate never responded. Obviously, it didn't sit well with the others. Mich seemed the most aggrieved, and even now, while they walked side by side to the telephone box, she was still talking about it.

'It's not, right, Clate. It's bad enough letting his clammy

hands wander all over me. But he can't just poke his nose in like that.'

Clate squinted at the distant clouds and sighed, wondering what annoyed him more, Mich's constant yapping or the cold grey light of early morning. He quickened his pace and, without looking at her, said, 'Well, it is what it is. I'm afraid we need to put up with it unless you want Benny Bray involved in all this?'

Except for a faint sigh, the mention of Bray's name seemed enough to silence her. Somewhat intrigued, Clate glanced at her and smiled. 'You used to work for Bray at the Indigo.'

Mich nodded. 'In the late sixties, I was just a kid.'

'Soho was so different back then.'

'I've blocked it from my mind.'

'That bad, huh?'

Mich narrowed her eyes. 'It's very upsetting. I'd rather not think about it.'

Clate disregarded the comment with a shrug. 'It might serve us well for you to summon a bit of that upset.'

Mich frowned. 'What do you mean?'

'You're the kidnapped wife, remember. We need to keep Earlston scared. A few distraught tears from his frightened little wife won't go a miss.'

Mich flashed him a wry smile. 'You just watch that temper of yours and don't worry about me.'

Clate could have retorted with a list of concerns but, tired of hearing Mich's voice, decided not to answer. Instead, he took out a cigar, holding it unlit in his hand while walking the rest of the way in silence.

Not long now, said the voice inside Clate's head. *A few more days and you'll be free of this.* This city bled him like a curse, and Bryant, Mich, Degsy, and Jay were the leeches who infected it.

Mich paused outside the telephone box.

'It's too close,' Clate said and kept walking. He continued for another fifteen minutes, suddenly crossing the busy road after spotting a telephone box on the other side of the street. Mich held his arm, clinging onto it even when they were safely on the pavement. He gave her a curious look. The hope of something better kept them all moving forward, and Clate felt no remorse knowing that despite all her efforts, Mich would never see a penny.

Clate pulled open the telephone box door and stepped inside with Mich huddled beside him. With his back turned, he could feel the rise and fall of her chest, his skin prickling against her warm breath. Clate coughed to clear his throat, Mich's perfume and the fusty smell of the telephone box getting the better of him.

Clate lifted the receiver and dialled the number slotting in a handful of coins at the sound of the pips.

The voice at the other end was nervous. 'Hello, Hello,' Earlston said, 'Is that you? How are Jenny and Mich? Are they all right?'

Clate answered with a sigh. 'They're all right, for now. Whether that remains to be the case is up to you.'

'Of course,' Earlston said. 'Could I, could I speak with them?'

With a long pause, Clate hesitated for effect. He placed his hand over the receiver and mouthed, 'He wants to talk to you; make it convincing.'

Mich snatched the phone from Clate's hand, and no sooner had she asked if Earlston was all right than she broke into a sob. Clate stared at her in disbelief. Only his previous instruction reminded him it was an act. Otherwise, from the uncontrollable shaking of her shoulders to the thick tears streaming down her cheeks, it remained convincing.

'Stop it, Henry,' she pleaded. 'Please don't cry. Please, Henry or neither of us will be able to stop.' She wiped the wetness from her eyes and cleared her bunged-up nose with a sniff. 'Jenny's fine. No. No, Henry, they won't harm us, providing you do as they say. Everything's fine, all right.'

Mich held the telephone against her chest. She gripped it tighter and slowly raised the receiver to her mouth. 'You can't, Henry, you can't. They won't accept that.'

Clate snatched the telephone from Mich's hand. 'What's going on, Earlston? You'd be a fool to mess us around.'

Earlston breathed deeply. 'I'm not messing anybody around; please, trust me; there's been a slight delay.'

Clate and Mich exchanged a worried glance. Clate sighed into the phone. 'Delay? You've already extended it to Friday.' Clate closed his eyes and paused and, on opening them, said, 'This isn't a game, Earlston; your wife and your teenage daughter will swear to that. Your Jenny's a pretty girl, don't you think? A great figure too. Shame to let it go to waste; the least we can do is let the girl have some joy before she takes her last breath.'

Earlston broke into a sob. 'Please, don't touch her, please. I'd never play games with Jenny's safety. It might only be a few hours' delay. I–'

'Fine,' Clate interrupted. 'Then let's not wait an extra day. If it's only a few hours, we can make the exchange in the early hours of Saturday morning.'

Earlston sniffed back a tear. 'It might take a little longer.'

'Early morning, I said.'

'Please,' Earlston begged. 'Can we agree on Saturday evening, please? Hopefully, it'll be earlier, and if that's the case, then fine, but I'd be lying if I said I could guarantee that.'

Clate glanced at Mich and sighed. 'Saturday it is. I'll let you know the place and time, and there's no going back on that.'

'Thank you, I–'

'Saturday, Earlston. I'll call you Friday to finalise the details.' Earlston attempted to speak, but Clate, close to slamming down the receiver, talked over him. 'Saturday,' he said as calmly as he could, 'or you'll have that girl's fate forever on your conscience.'

28

Clate couldn't bear to look at Mich, let alone speak to her, and returned to the apartment in silence. When he arrived back, the first thing he did was pour himself a whisky, then, resting his weight against the counter, stared glumly through the kitchen window. The sky did little to lighten his mood. The clouds had formed into one, skulking above the city, making the drab buildings appear greyer. Even the drink failed to soothe him, its sweet peaty aroma making him queasy as he swirled it around his mouth. Clate slammed the glass down on the counter and pushed it away from him.

Burying his face in his hands, Clate sighed into them.

'That bad, huh,' said Degsy's annoying voice.

Clate slowly removed his hands and grimaced at the old man slumped in the doorway. The snowy whiskers covering Degsy's face aged him a hundred years. No wisdom shone in his tired, bloodshot eyes. Dirt lined his shirt collar, and just below his mouth, dried egg yolk crusted over his wrinkled skin. It was a pitiful sight, a reminder of all their failings, as though the devil himself was mocking them through this personification of bad luck.

Unable to look at him, Clate averted his gaze. 'Yeah,' he said with a sigh. 'That's an understatement.'

Degsy inched further into the room, dragged out a barstool and sat in front of him. He nodded at Clate's glass. 'It must be bad if that's no help.'

Clate watched with disgust while Degsy's slug-like tongue slithered across his dry lips. 'Finish it if you like. I'm in no mood for drinking.'

Degsy never needed to be asked twice and downed the whisky in one. He gestured towards Clate with the glass. 'Mich mentioned something about a delay. She sounded rattled. It seems she doesn't know her husband as well as she thought.' He glanced into the empty glass. 'What's wrong? Is he refusing to pay?'

Clate shook his head. 'He's too scared to do that. He just needs more time, that's all.'

Degsy frowned. 'How much time does the man need? I thought we'd already given him an extension? He's not repaying a loan; this is the kidnapping of his wife and daughter, for God's sake.'

Clate clenched his hand into a fist. 'Do you think I don't know that?'

Degsy was smart enough not to reply, the small remnants of colour draining from his cheeks while he lowered his eyes in silence. Clate regarded him with a fierce stare. He had grown to loathe the man's presence, the neediness in his eyes, the way he stated the obvious, his every dull word loaded with insinuation.

Clate wondered if Degsy knew. Could he see the hate in Clate's eyes? Did years of experience warn him he was moments away from a good hiding? Seemingly it was the case because Degsy, with his head lowered, eased himself off the stool and walked sheepishly towards the door.

'Where's Scouse?' Clate asked.

'Reading in the lounge?'

'And Bryant?'

Degsy paused and, with a timid shrug, said, 'Talking to the girl, I think.'

Clate stood up and banged his fist on the counter. 'I told him he wasn't to do that.' A sudden pain throbbed inside his head. 'Go get him. Fetch him, I said; why the hell are you hesitating?'

Degsy paused at the door. 'What should I say?'

'Tell him Clate wants to see him. That he needs to come here, now. Tell him if he's got any sense, he won't make me come for him.'

Degsy did as he was told and returned with an annoyed-looking Bryant a few minutes later. Bryant stood opposite Clate, slapping his bony hands on the counter. 'What's all the shouting about, Clate? You're scaring the girl; everyone can hear you hollering down the hallway.'

Clate took a deep breath. 'You stay away from that girl.'

'I was only–'

'Stay away from her, I said. Don't make me tell you again. That girl stays locked in her room until I say.'

'Fine,' Bryant said with a smile. 'No need to get so upset about it.'

Clate opened his mouth to respond, but Degsy spoke over him. 'He's got a right to be on edge,' Degsy said. 'Earlston's requested another delay.'

Clate silenced the old man with a glare. 'Who the hell asked you to chirp in? Don't you need to go and wash or something?'

Bryant glanced at Degsy and laughed, then, losing his

smile, said, 'Earlston's delayed us before?' He shook his head and tutted. 'We shouldn't let him mess us about like that.'

Clate felt his headache worsen. '*We*? There is no *we*. I make the decisions here. It's one day, that's all. Earlston doesn't have the balls to mess us around. He's too scared to mess this up.'

Bryant tilted his head to one side. 'Or maybe that's what he'd like you to think? He's a businessman, right?'

Clate nodded. 'What the hell has that got to do with anything?'

'Maybe he has a business mind? He's probably always negotiating deals, calling people's bluff. Perhaps, these minor delays are part of his strategy.'

Clate shook his head. 'The man's scared shitless, for God's sake. His only business instinct is to err on the side of caution.'

Bryant nodded slightly and, looking across at Degsy, said, 'What kind of business is Earlston in?'

Degsy fumbled inside his trouser pocket and took out a cigarette; he placed it in his mouth. 'Something to do with shipping, a broker, I think,' he said, his gaze shifting between Bryant and Clate as if the answer made him nervous.

Bryant drew the air in through his teeth. 'Broker. Now that changes things.'

'Bullshit,' said Clate. 'Earlston's as weak-willed as they come. Being a broker makes no difference. Anyway, he's a shipping broker; that's nothing to do with the stock market; it's an entirely different thing.'

'Oh, I beg to differ, and no doubt Degsy will back me up on this.'

While Bryant regarded them with a grin, Clate

suppressed the urge to give him a slap. 'Let's hear it then,' he said, reaching for his pack of cigars to try to calm himself.

Bryant gave a nonchalant shrug. 'There's not much to tell. It's straightforward to tell you the truth. These Brokers are of a different ilk.'

Clate drew out a cigar from the pack. 'Is that right, and how the hell would you know?'

'Believe it or not, I worked as a runner for a while. My thinking at the time was if I was going to con folk out of their cash, then I might as well do it in a way that was seen as legal. Naturally, it didn't last long. But long enough to learn that most of them were crooks. They are some of the best conmen I've ever seen. Most of them are scum, of course. But they could talk their way in and out of anything. The good ones would do anything to close a deal if it went in their favour. They're only loyal to themselves. You do that job long enough, and you lose something of yourself. I mean the decent part; Hell, if it meant winning the deal, I reckon they'd chuck their mother under the bus.'

Clate lit his cigar. 'Earlston isn't like that. I've spoken to him, remember. The man scares easily. He's devoted to his little girl. You only have to mention his daughter's name, and he sobs like a baby.'

Bryant gave him a dismissive nod. 'Unless that's what he wants you to believe. I've seen brokers do that.'

'Do what?'

'Change their emotions on a whim. Crying one minute, laughing the next, doing anything it takes to win.'

Clate pressed his thumb into the cigar. 'And you think that's what he's doing?'

'Perhaps,' Bryant said. 'He's already played you for more time, right.'

Clate pressed harder into the cigar. 'He hasn't played me at all.'

Bryant flashed him that knowing grin. '*No*? He's already forced two delays. You should have that money by now. He might be playing you for a fool. You're far too soft with him.'

'Too soft, huh?'

'Yeah, if it were me, I'd shake him up a bit, remind him who we are. We're the ones running the con. God knows what he's up to.'

Clate pushed harder into the cigar, pressing it until it snapped. It dropped to the floor, and Clate crushed it beneath his foot. He strode over to Bryant and grabbed his arm. 'Playing me for a fool, huh?' he said through gritted teeth. Clate tightened his grip and, dragging Bryant towards the hall, said, 'Well, perhaps it's time to remedy that.'

29

The ache in his ribs had started to ease, and Jay could finally read. Unlike when he was a kid, books failed to transfix him these days. He read all the same. The constant flow of words helped him to think. Not that he made much progress. The walls were too thin, making it impossible to ignore Clate's shouting. Jay snapped the book shut and placed it face down on the chair before following the noise into the hallway.

Bryant looked so small alongside Clate, his skinny arm locked in the big man's grasp. Like a vexed mother scolding her insolent child, Clate dragged him down the hallway. He stopped outside Jenny's door, holding out his free hand until Degsy reluctantly passed him the key. He fumbled with the lock. 'Damn thing,' he said, turning the key repeatedly until the door shuddered open. He shoved Bryant forward into the room and followed him inside.

'What's going on?' Jay said.

Clate kept his back turned. 'Nothing that concerns you, now go back to the lounge; this is none of your business.'

Jay remained where he was, turning his head towards

the unmistakable aroma of Mich's perfume. She stood by Jay's side, 'What the hell are you doing, Clate?' the worried look in her eyes undoubtedly matched his.

Clate's shoulders sagged when he sighed. 'Apparently, Earlston's taking us for a fool.' He pushed his hand through his hair. 'He needs reminding that's not the case.' He gazed down at the phone socket. 'Where did you hide the phone? I said where's the phone; it's time Daddy got a chance to talk to his precious daughter.'

When Mich charged into the room, Jay followed closely behind her. Jenny was sitting on the bed, her back resting against the headboard, her freckled arms holding her legs to her chest. Her face looked gaunt and pale, and although only days, it felt like years since they last spoke. The girl with the fire in her eyes was gone; she wasn't how Jay remembered her. Jay gazed at the frightened, innocent face, and the sad, lonely boy from that long hot summer of '76 suddenly felt less distant.

'Don't be so stupid, Clate,' Mich said. 'We're all tired. Come into the lounge. Come on.' She gave Bryant a fierce glance. 'He's only stirring things up. Don't let this runt get to you.'

Clate shook his head. 'Bryant's not smart enough for that. He has a point, though.'

'No, he doesn't,' insisted Mich. 'You're just tired. Stressed. We all are. A few more days, and we're done.' She reached out and touched his arm. 'Come on, Clate, please. Think this through. You're always the same when you've been drinking.'

For a moment, Clate seemed to heed her words. Then a resentful look passed over his face, and with the back of his hand, he smacked Mich across the mouth. 'Keep it shut,' Clate said, 'you're the reason we're in all this mess, stupid whore, stupid conniving whore,' raising his voice over Jenny's screaming.

Clate motioned towards the girl, turning around when Jay grabbed his arm and pulled him back. Clate countered with a right hook, and as stiff as he was, somehow Jay dodged the punch. Clate came at him with all his weight, gripping Jay's shoulders and shoving him towards the wall. Jay pressed his left hand just below Clate's arm, pushed off his back leg and turned Clate on his hip. He pressed his head into the big man's chest, and as Clate titled back, Jay pushed forward and picked up Clate's leg. Jay pulled Clate towards him and lowered his head before the big man could swing a punch. Then Jay dropped Clate on his back and leaned forward with his hands on his knees to catch his breath.

Jay told Clate to 'stay down,' struggling to breathe as he said it, barely getting his words out.

When Jay looked to his left, he caught Jenny's glance. All he could think about was setting the girl free. He didn't know why, tiredness perhaps, the madness of it all, or all the things Jenny reminded him of.

Jay looked at the girl and smiled. 'Jenny, get your things.'

'Stay where you are, girl,' Bryant shouted and helped Clate to his feet.

Jay straightened. 'I'm taking Jenny home. '

Bryant laughed. 'Like hell you are. Degsy, go lock the front door.'

Degsy, with his head bowed, obeyed Bryant's command, never once looking over his shoulder when Jay called out to him. Jay looked at Mich for support. All she did was stand by Clate's side, touching the blood on her mouth, her eyes full of loathing.

Clate's chest wheezed slightly with each breath, and he

wiped the sweat from his forehead using his shirt sleeve. He stared at Jay and grinned. 'The girl's staying put. Seems you've been out-voted.'

Jay glanced warmly at the girl. 'I'm taking her home; it's gone too far.'

'What about the money?' Mich said, 'I thought this was little Jay's big chance?'

Jay shrugged. 'I guess it's not my time.'

Mich forced a laugh. 'It never was; it's never going to be. I knew you weren't up to the con.'

'To hell with the con.' Jay smiled tenderly at the girl. 'I'm not letting her go through the same thing as me. Come on, Mich. You know yourself; Clate was out of control.' Jay nodded towards Bryant. 'You've seen the way this creep looks at her. This isn't a con. Nothing good is going to come from it. Jenny's your stepdaughter, for God's sake. She doesn't deserve this.'

A glimpse of sadness flickered in Mich's eyes. 'No one does, but we need to deal with it.'

Jay didn't answer. Instead, he turned swiftly to his left to face Bryant inching towards him. Bryant gripped something in his hand. Jay thought it was a metal bar at first. But its gleam was more wooden, and the longer he glanced at it, he realised it was a cosh. Jay caught Bryant with a jab, then staggered forward as Clate smashed his fist into the back of Jay's head. The big man followed it with another blow, dropping Jay to his knees, and before Jay could push himself up, Bryant kicked him in the jaw, and this time Jay lay breathless on his back.

Everything blurred after that. The girl's screams withdrew further into the distance as the ringing in Jay's ears grew louder with every kick.

30

For a while, all Jay could smell was petrol. Then, immersed in the odours of silt and wet sand, the water lapping gently against the shore, it was as though he'd returned to the Dee Estuary. Behind closed eyelids, he watched the seabirds glide upon the noontide breeze. They floated towards the horizon until their mewling cries faded into the distance.

Jay saw himself as a boy in that long hot summer of '76. His sunburnt arms matched the colour of his vest, while his sweat-soaked shoulder-length hair stuck to the nape of his neck. Nash waved to him from the coastal path. 'Faster, faster,' he shouted, beckoning the boy closer while Jay ran barefoot across the scorched sands.

Nash greeted him with a smile, the air thick with the aroma of Brylcreem and his favourite brand of cigarettes. Nash sat down on the dry stone wall, patted it with his hand and invited Jay to sit next to him. Jay didn't need to be asked twice. He sat quietly for a while, admiring the whiteness of Nash's shirt, the tan linen suit jacket resting confidently on his shoulder, and the reflected sunlight glinting in his gold-framed Ray-

Bans. This is how Jay longed to look. He wanted it at this moment but knew now wasn't the time and would have to wait until he was older. Jay felt a yearning in his guts and, on catching Nash's glance, sensed Nash knew that. In fact, Nash always knew; he could see into Jay's heart and always knew what he was thinking.

After finishing his cigarette, Nash stood up and turned to face the estuary. Jay did the same, resting his hands on the warm stones. Nash nodded at the small patches of sand, then pointed across the water towards the distant sandstone outcrops. 'How long do you think it would take to get to the other side?'

'Don't know,' Jay said with a shrug.

Nash hoisted himself onto the wall. 'A good while, I reckon.' He pointed at the rocks. 'Let's sit over there and take a closer look.'

Jay quickly followed, holding Nash's arm to balance himself while they stepped carefully across the rocks. They settled down on the flattest rock they could find. It stood higher than the rest, giving them a clear view across the water. Nash took out his pack of cigarettes. 'You know, I couldn't come back here for a long time, too many ghosts. It's only lately that I've realised how much I love the place.'

Jay looked at Nash and frowned. 'I don't understand. What do you mean by you couldn't come back here? I thought this was your first visit, that you came here for your holidays?'

Nash took out a cigarette from the pack. He glanced at Jay and sighed. 'There's more to it than that.'

'You mean you lied?'

'In a way, yes.'

Jay motioned to stand, pausing when Nash grabbed his arm. 'You need to let me explain, Jay.' Nash loosened his grip. 'I'm not the only one who has been telling lies, right?'

'I don't know what you mean.'

'Come on, Jay. We owe each other the truth.' Nash regarded

him for a moment. 'That man you saw fall to his death in the woods.'

'What about him?'

'He was a friend of mine. Well, so, I thought.' Nash held the cigarette to his mouth. 'But a clever lad like yourself already worked that out, right?'

Jay looked down at the rocks. 'Kind of,' he mumbled.

Nash lit his cigarette. 'Bowen was the man's name. Turns out he wasn't a friend after all. Quite the opposite; Bowen stole a lot of money from me.' Nash took a drag of his cigarette. 'It was my life savings.'

Jay immediately raised his head. 'Why didn't you tell me that before?'

Nash shrugged. 'It wasn't part of the plan, I guess.'

Jay felt the tears well in his eyes. 'Mam warned me about you. She said you were a liar. All this time, I thought you were my friend. What kind of friend has a plan? I knew you were hiding something.'

Nash took a deep breath. 'I'm sorry, Jay, truly I am. If it's any consolation, the friend part is genuine; we're best buddies, right?' He drew hard on his cigarette. 'But in all fairness, I haven't been the only one keeping secrets.'

'I don't know what you mean.'

'Really?'

Jay stood up. 'Yeah, really.'

Nash took hold of his hand. 'That money Bowen stole from me.'

Jay tried pulling away. 'What about it?'

'I think you know where it is.'

Jay shook his head. 'No, I don't. Now let go of me.'

Nash released Jay's hand. 'Fine. If that's how it's going to be. I'm sorry I lied to you, Jay. But seeing we're friends, I figured I owed you the truth. In return, I hoped you would have helped me.' Nash took one last drag of his cigarette and flicked it away. 'We're both to blame in a way. But no matter how you look at it. That money still belongs to me.'

Jay watched the discarded cigarette butt spark onto the rocks. He kept silent, staring at the glowing ember until it smouldered out. 'What if I did know,' he said. 'What would you do?'

Nash looked at him and smiled. 'Take it back, of course.'

Jay answered with a nod. 'And where would that leave Mam and me?'

'Still in a better place than where you are now. You and I are buddies; I'll give you a fair share.'

'Promise.'

'Cross my heart and hope to die.'

As try as he might to suppress it, Jay couldn't help but laugh. Then he lost his smile and frowned. 'What about Shane?'

Nash reached out his hand, resting it on Jay's shoulder as the boy sat beside him. 'Shane's the last person you need to worry about. Put that idiot out of your mind. You leave him to me. Do you hear me, Jay? Jay...'

Jay tried his best to respond, but while the images began to fade, Nash's voice drew further into the distance.

Immobilised with pain, Jay lay on his back. Each raw breath scraped against his throat. His limbs were leaden weights, and the relentless throbbing in his head dulled his senses.

Jay attempted to open his eyes, trying harder, when he recognised Degsy's voice.

'Let's just leave him here,' the old man said, 'He's coming around now.' Degsy continued, a growing sense of urgency in his voice until he went silent.

Jay shivered against the cold while the lapping of the waves drew closer. He felt a small coarse hand upon his skin; an air of warm breath carried the smell of whisky and cigarettes.

'Let's not take this too far.' Degsy pleaded. 'Get rid of him is all Clate said. Please, Bryant, please don't; he's barely older than you.' Degsy began to sob. 'Please, Bryant, please. I'm begging you. Let's just leave the lad here. I don't want to be a part of this.'

Suddenly Jay's body turned rigid with cold, his eyes blinded by a harsh white light as he sunk into the freezing water.

PART III

FALL ON ME

1

Afterwards, when Bryant had driven them back to the apartment, Degsy refused to go inside. Even when Bryant threatened him, Degsy remained resolute.

'Clate will want to know what happened,' Bryant said.

Degsy stood in the courtyard, glancing up at the figure standing at the kitchen window. 'Well, you best tell him then, considering you did most of it.'

Bryant glared at him, his eyes widening with surprise when Degsy defiantly stared back.

'I'm not going in there yet,' Degsy said. He meant it, too, unsure whether his lack of fear was down to stupidity or shock. Either way, he no longer cared. At this moment, the hollowness he felt inside enabled him to face the consequences. Oddly, it gave him strength, and Degsy knew from the youngster's face that somehow Bryant sensed that.

Degsy wandered aimlessly along the Kilburn High Road in the early morning hours. Each thought raced onto the next, and try as he might, he failed to silence them. It hindered his every step and intensified the emptiness he felt inside him. Jay might have been older than his years, but the kid had barely lived. All he had to do was play along, but when he suddenly decided to take the girl home, what the hell was the lad thinking?

Degsy shook his head with dismay, not at Jay's stupidity but at his own cowardice. Petrified by fear, Degsy had watched from the sidelines. Surprisingly, he felt proud when Jay put Clate on his back, but to his shame, he looked away when things turned nasty. They set upon Jay like a pack of dogs, although Mich, to her credit, played no part in it. Thankfully, she went to the girl. Even now, hours later, Degsy was undecided about what disturbed him most, the terror on the girl's face or the sense of hopelessness in her screaming.

There was no denying the truth in Jay's words. This had travelled far beyond a standard con, and Degsy knew the blood masking the lad's face and his limp body sinking into the Thames was a scene that would forever haunt him. Bryant wanted to watch Jay drown, but thankfully a car's headlights scared them off. Degsy closed his eyes and sighed. He was a cowardly old fool, begging like a frightened child. *To hell with Bryant,* he shouted into the night, but Degsy shouldered the blame. *You should have jumped into the river straightaway; your only chance to do something decent for once; Jesus, Degsy, you should have helped him.*

Degsy strolled further into the night, his stooped shoulders and frail limbs casting a pathetic shadow beneath the streetlights. A three-quarter moon shone mournfully through the clouds; the pale luminosity of its face was almost lost against the city skyline. Slipping his hand into his pocket, Degsy took out his pack of cigarettes. He placed one in his mouth, cupping his hands around the match's flame, pulling on it until it was lit. Degsy drew the smoke into his lungs and released it with a defeated sigh.

He felt miserable wandering through the deserted street. Everywhere was so quiet. Even the sporadic rush of passing cars accentuated the night's silence. Degsy's sense of isolation had always been a given. He accepted it without protest. Yet, except for the days following his father's death, this was the first time in years that he'd been struck by unshakable loneliness.

Working so many cons after all these years, Degsy was no stranger to life's darkness. But his days had never been this bleak; usually, the worst things ever got hovered somewhere between off-white and grey. Clate and Bryant had changed that. Greed had struck them blind. The girl was only sixteen, nothing but a child. Her best days were stolen, hope replaced by fear, and innocence tainted by violence.

Degsy slowed his pace, then, glancing towards the road, squinted at the police car's flashing light. The car slowed to a crawl, the front passenger seat window slowly winding down as the car pulled up alongside him. 'Hey,' said the officer inside. 'Where are you off to?'

'I'm sorry?' Degsy said.

'You heard. What are you doing walking around at this time? It's three o'clock in the morning.'

Degsy swallowed against the dryness inside his throat. 'Minding my own business and walking in a homely direction.'

The officer stepped out of the car, slamming the door behind him. He looked no older than twenty; his face was mottled pink, the wisps of hair above his top lip desperate to be a moustache. Even without a uniform, Degsy would have known what he was. That sly, accusing look in his eyes was unmistakable. He gave Degsy a sweeping glance. 'What's your name?'

Degsy frowned. 'Why?'

The officer stepped closer. 'Because I just asked you.'

Degsy knew his rights, and unless he was arrested, he was under no obligation to tell him anything. 'Derek Dempster,' he said with a wry smile. The last thing he needed now was to bring trouble to himself. The officer regarded him with a nod. 'That name sounds familiar. Have you done time?'

Degsy shook his head.

'From where do I know you?'

Degsy answered with a shrug. 'I've no idea, Officer. In fact, being a law-abiding citizen, I'm not convinced you do.'

The young police officer glanced at his watch. 'So where have you been?'

'Drinking with some friends.'

'*Friends*,' he said with a nod. 'From where? What's their address?'

Degsy seemed lost for words. He scoured his mind for an answer, hating himself for hesitating too long. 'To be honest,' he said, 'they're more drinking buddies than friends. I barely know them, to tell you the truth. Some people I drink with at the pub. They live around these parts, I suppose. I never asked them for their address.'

'And you?'

'What about me?'

'Where do you live?'

'Bayswater.'

'Bayswater? What are you doing walking up the Kilburn High Road?'

'Trying to sober up. If those drivers see you swaying all over the place, they won't let you in their Taxi.'

The officer gave him an unconvincing look. 'There was a ruckus outside the Queens Tavern tonight. Do you know anything about that?'

Degsy shook his head and laughed. 'Do I look capable of being involved in a ruckus?'

'Folk are capable of anything.' The officer gave him a long cold look. 'What's that stain on your cuff?'

Degsy glanced at the stain, pressing his fingers into his clammy palms. 'I don't know. It's the first time I've noticed it.'

The officer looked at it again, only he studied it closer this time. 'It looks like blood to me.'

Degsy forced a laugh. '*Blood*? It's not blood. Coffee, maybe, more like wine. It's not blood. No. That's ridiculous.'

'Really? You seem very nervous about it.'

Degsy touched his throat. 'Who wouldn't be nervous if they're stopped by the police and questioned.'

The officer looked at him and grinned, 'Where do you live?'

'I already told you, Bayswater.'

'*Where* in Bayswater, smart arse?' The officer took out his notebook, writing down the details while Degsy gave him a fake address. He read it out aloud. 'I hope this checks out if we need to visit you?'

'Of course,' said Degsy as calmly as he could. 'Can I go now?'

The officer released him with a curt nod. Degsy turned around, but even with his back turned, he felt those sly, accusing eyes bore into him.

Having walked a few yards along the pavement, Degsy glanced at his watch. The voice in his head told him he should be heading back. The wisdom of his years played little part in it. This was a fearful reproach aimed at self-preservation. After all that had happened, Clate and Bryant wouldn't allow him to roam the streets. Like Jay and the girl, Degsy belonged to them and resigned himself to his fate. His only option was to return; at least he owed the girl that much. For now, he would keep walking, savouring these last precious hours of peace.

2

That afternoon when he'd visited him at the club, Benny Bray knew, even after speaking with him for less than ten minutes, the kid was onto something. With his tailored suit and manicured nails, his perfectly knotted necktie with a matching handkerchief, anybody with half a brain could see that Bray paid attention to detail; details saved the day, kept you alive, and stopped the wannabes creeping in.

Bray had suspected for some time that Bryant was acting alone. He'd seen the ambition in his eyes from the start. Dempster was heavily in debt, frightened and down on his luck, which, for opportunists such as Bryant, made the old man an easy target. Initially, it was with Clate that Bray had cast his doubts. Bray pondered it for some time, but when the kid told him things that only Clate could know, it made the story of the girl's kidnapping even more plausible.

It was the accusations made against Mich that nettled Bray most. Five years behind bars felt like a lifetime. Rumour had it that he was weakened by his time in jail, although it was the opposite. Endless thoughts of retribution frosted any man's heart. Bray gave the kid the benefit of the doubt. He sensed some truth in the kid's words, and even if he was lying, Bray welcomed even the slightest chance to avenge such treachery. But at what cost? And when the kid had finished talking, Bray asked, '*So what do you want from me?*'

'*That you're there for the exchange. Clate wants to collect alone. Once he has the money, he and Mich will run out on me.*'

Bray had flashed him a rare smile. '*That's a lot of money to take. Of course, I'm grateful for your insights. Let's say Mich does prove to be the one who grassed me up. That's mere droppings compared to what's at stake. I want at least seventy per cent for my involvement.*'

'*Sixty,*' the kid said without hesitation. '*But the girl stays unharmed. What you do with Clate and Mich is your business.*'

'*And Bryant?*' Bray asked.

'*I want him off the old man's back. So I was hoping you could sort that.*'

'*Oh, and one last thing,*' the kid said. '*I told them I was coming here to ask for a job. Naturally, they warned me against it. They told me it wouldn't end well. They still need to believe that.*'

'*Of course, they do,*' Bray said. '*I'm sure Roy and Chad will make it look convincing.*'

It felt like weeks since they last spoke, and when Bray first saw the kid's badly beaten face, it dawned on him it was only a few days ago. He'd bought into Jay's scheme with high hopes. But after Roy and Chad pulled the kid's bedraggled body from the river, Bray was angry and disappointed. Part of him was intrigued. Having set it up so well, how had Jay allowed things to get as bad as this? The other part was less forgiving, the part that would have left him to drown in the river's dark, cold depths.

When Bray entered the small dusty room, Roy and Chad made space for him. Boxes of flyers were stacked high against the wall, layers of dust remained untouched, and the patches of moth-eaten carpet gave glimpses of the creaky floorboards. It was a room among many forgotten chambers in the upper recesses of the club. Bray rested his weight on a wooden chair, staring impassively at Jay's lifeless body lying beneath the eiderdown on a battered old leather sofa. 'Wake up,' demanded Bray, watching as the kid's eyes slowly opened.

The kid tried to move but struggled to sit up, his sigh thick with self-pity and regret.

Bray wiped his hand across his forehead. 'What happened? What happened? I said. When I ask you a question, I expect an answer.'

The kid mumbled something in response, then fell silent while trying to catch his breath. Bray looked at Roy and frowned. 'Sit the boy up; let's try to get some sense out of him.'

Roy nodded, stepped forward and crouched in front of the sofa. 'Let's make you more attentive,' he said, grabbing the kid's shoulders and forcing him to sit up. The kid scrunched his face in pain and asked for a glass of water.

'Later,' Bray said with a sigh. 'You need to tell me what happened first.'

The kid nodded and took a deep breath, speaking slowly while resting a pale hand upon his ghost-white chest. 'Nothing much. Things just got out of hand, that's all.'

'Got out of hand,' Bray said with a laugh. 'Did you hear that, Roy?'

Bray scowled. 'That's putting it lightly, don't you think. Bryant dumped you in the Thames, for Christ's sake.' Bray slapped his hands down on his lap. 'You'd be lying at the bottom of the river if I hadn't sent Roy to watch over you.'

An unsettled look passed across the kid's eyes. Bray had seen the look before on the faces of broken men. Once tasted, the inevitability of your own death stayed with you. Its image plagued you like a curse, creeping up on you unexpectedly, reminding you of the transience of your own feeble existence. The kid might have taken a few beatings. But this was different. He was changed, and that cocky sureness, now absent from his eyes, could find no way back.

Bray looked at him and sighed. 'I'm going to ask you one last time, and if I think you're lying, I'll put you back in the river myself because as smart as you like to think you are, you can only have so many chances.'

The kid tried clearing his throat. Finally, he caught his breath. He peered through swollen eyes. 'Clate's losing his grip, and Bryant's making the most of it.'

'That doesn't surprise me,' Bray said. 'Clate likes to come across all cool, but he's always struck me as a man of little patience.' He held his chin between his bent forefinger and thumb. 'Now Bryant does surprise me. I always knew he was a conniving little shite. But getting into Clate's head, I must say I'm impressed. I didn't think he was as clever as that.'

'There's nothing smart about it at all. Clate thinks Bryant's close to you, so he's trying to keep him sweet.'

'Well, he should have checked with me first. That makes him a bigger fool than I thought he was.'

'Maybe,' the kid said. He hesitated for a moment. 'Can I ask you a question?'

Bray nodded.

'I know Degsy is in your debt, but I'm guessing Clate is too?'

Bray rubbed the tiredness from his eyes. 'Gambling isn't

Clate's thing. Yet,' he said with a sigh, 'like most losers, he seems to believe that continually betting against that run of bad luck will somehow change things. Of course, it never does, and the fact that I own his club and those apartments prove that. Does that answer your question?'

The kid nodded. 'Yeah, it explains why he didn't check in with you first. He was keen not to bring attention to himself.'

'He's keen not to pay his debts off with his cut. That still doesn't shed any light on what happened to you. I'm guessing it's linked to something about Clate losing it?'

The kid nodded, wincing as he shifted his position on the sofa. 'He thinks Earlston's messing him around.'

'And is he?'

'He's delayed payment a few times. But it's a lot of money to raise–'

'What does Mich think?'

'She reckons Earlston wouldn't have the courage to mess Clate around, seems confident that it's all legit.'

Bray nodded, looked over at Roy, and asked, 'What do you think?'

Roy answered with a shrug. 'Delays put the pressure on, I suppose. But Clate's a pro. I've seen him deal with worse things in his club. I know he has a foul temper.' He gave the kid a sweeping glance. 'I find it hard to believe that a slight delay would force Clate to lose it. What else happened, kid? To push Clate over the edge like that?'

Bray stared into the kid's eyes. He'd better choose his words carefully. Just because he'd fished him out of the river once didn't mean he couldn't recast his nets and throw him back in. It would only take seconds for him to decide. All he needed was to sniff a lie or the kid to give him the wrong answer.

3

_____

J ay had endured some unpleasant experiences over the years, but sitting naked and beaten, shivering like a drowned rat, was undisputedly one of his worst situations. Benny Bray questioning him didn't help. Overweight and immaculately groomed, Bray sat there like a grand inquisitor, his round-shaven face giving nothing away, watching with his shark eyes.

'Lots of things,' Jay said. 'Tiredness, Bryant constantly in his ear. Being cooped up in that apartment hasn't helped, and neither has Clate's constant drinking.'

'Okay,' Bray said with a nod. 'But they beat you unconscious, threw you in the river; I know you said Earlston's stalling. But why take it out on you? You must have said something?'

Jay winced as he shifted position. Bray seemed eager to spot a lie. So Jay's best option was to tell the truth, leaving out the parts that would be viewed less favourably. 'Clate was out of control–'

'You've already mentioned that,' interrupted Bray. 'How exactly?'

'Like I said before, he thought Earlston was playing games; Bryant was in his ear; he'd spent the whole day drinking. He just flipped, decided to teach Earlston a lesson, show him we were serious.'

Bray studied him through narrowed eyes. 'How?'

Jay swallowed against the raw taste of the river burning against his throat. 'He was going to call Earlston, then put the girl on the phone, frighten them both by slapping her around, or something worse.'

Bray shrugged. 'Makes sense. If things were lagging, it might have helped shake things up.'

Jay shook his head. 'Frighten the girl, yes. But Clate was out of control. He was going to hurt her bad. I couldn't let him do that.'

'You're a kidnapper,' Bray scoffed. 'All you should care about is the money. Your conscience will get you killed, as will seeing yourself as some kind of saviour.'

'It wasn't like that.' Jay said. 'Admittedly, I felt the girl had suffered enough. But there's no money if you've nothing to exchange. I was frightened as to where it would lead. Clate was about to do something stupid. I was protecting our interests.'

'Fine,' Bray said, 'So you intervened, and I'm assuming Clate didn't like that?'

Jay nodded. 'Yeah, it ended up in a fight, and Bryant decided to help him.'

'What happened?'

Jay pointed at his face.

'Obviously, it didn't end well. But I'm interested in the details. Tell me about it.'

'The fight?'

'Yeah, the fight. If you can call it that. I'm interested to know how it panned out.'

Not only did Bray watch him, but Roy observed him too. Both men stared at him. Their unforgiving eyes rarely blinked. Neither of them cared about what had happened. Their only interest was in what he had to say. The truth was all he had, and his every word would be a test for him.

Suddenly aware of his nakedness, Jay pulled the eiderdown closer to his chest. 'It was just a scuffle at first. Clate threatened me and pushed me against the wall. Fortunately, he was sluggish after the drink, so I threw him onto his back.'

At first, both men laughed; then Bray leaned closer and regarded him with a long silence. 'Luckily enough, I believe you.'

Roy shook his head with a mix of admiration and disbelief. 'I won't deny I'm impressed; it seems you've only got yourself to blame. You drop a man as handy as Clate, then you better make sure he doesn't get up.'

'I know that now,' Jay said, 'but that wasn't my intention at the time. All I wanted to do was calm him.'

'*Calm him*,' said Roy with a grin. 'And how did that work out for you?'

'Okay, at first–'

Bray quickly stood up, sniffed disparagingly at the stale air, and, with a ponderous expression, strolled over to the window. After drawing back the stained, orange polyester curtains, he turned to face Jay, standing with his hands clasped behind his back, his grim expression accentuated by the greyish light. A questioning look settled in Bray's eyes. 'What I fail to understand is how it all kicked off again?'

'It just did,' Jay said with a shrug. 'Clate caught me unawares. I thought we'd settled things, but he was still angry.'

'Still angry, huh,' Bray said with a nod. 'What did you do?'

'What do you mean?'

'What did you say to piss him off?'

'I didn't say anything.'

'I find that hard to believe. You said Clate was okay after you dropped him on his back. But then he came at you again, with Bryant's help. Something must have triggered it?'

Jay lowered his eyes, focusing on the bloodstain on the carpet. He'd been truthful so far, but he sensed Bray closing in on his quarry, and this time, like others before him, the truth might be the wrong answer. 'I tried to take the girl.'

'Take her where?' Roy asked.

'Somewhere safe, I guess. Clate meant her harm, and as for Bryant, he–' Jay paused for thought.

'He what?' Bray said.

Jay hesitated for a moment. 'I don't like the way he looks at her.'

Bray and Roy exchanged glances. 'I heard Bryant likes girls that age,' Roy said. 'Rumour has it the police have cautioned him about that.'

Bray answered with an exasperated sigh, walked towards Jay, and sat back in front of him. 'Where were you going to take her?'

Jay shrugged. 'I don't know,' he lied. 'Somewhere safe, I guess.'

Bray slowly nodded his head. 'Somewhere safe. Hmmm. That safe place wouldn't have been her home, right?'

Jay shook his head. 'No. No, of course not.'

Bray glowered. 'Well, for your sake. I certainly hope so.' He removed a metal comb from his back pocket and smoothed his hair back, fragments of Brylcreem glistening on his long, feminine fingers. 'The thing is, chivalry's all well and good, but it's pushed you and this little scheme of yours into an awkward situation.'

'I'm sorry to let you down, Mr Bray. Things got out of control. This was Mich's scheme, not mine. And as for this situation.' Jay pointed at his beaten face. 'Look at the state of me. It's probably best if I'm no longer a part of this.'

Bray flashed him a half-smile. 'In principle, it's hard to disagree. But with Mich, Clate and Bryant's deceit, a lot is riding on this. Revenge is a grand reward. But it doesn't buy you squat, and I'm a businessman at heart.' Bray narrowed his eyes. 'That ransom money is a tidy sum, and I want my share of it.'

Bray leaned forward, and Jay coughed at the strong smell of his cologne. 'Walking away isn't an option. A pro wouldn't have got beat up. It made sense to have you on the inside, but now–' Bray sighed. 'But now, whichever way you look at it, you messed up, and you need to make amends for that.'

Jay answered with a nod. Judging by the expression on Bray's face, it seemed wise to keep his mouth shut. Bray tilted his head slightly to one side. 'We need to know when and where they'll make the exchange. But after you decided to take a swim, we'll struggle to acquire that information.'

Jay looked at him and frowned. 'Can't you find out from Clate?'

'How do you mean?'

'You know what they're up to; where they are. Perhaps it makes sense just to confront them, take over the operation.'

'*Operation*?' Bray said with a wry smile. 'To be honest, I did consider that. But sadly, it's not an option.'

'How do you mean?'

'I sent Roy to sniff around Clate's apartment. Seems they've suddenly cleared out. God knows to where. And no one's seen hide nor hair of Clate in that club of his. So the question is, what are we going to do now?' Bray looked over at Roy. 'What do you think?'

'We could try to find them.' Roy said with a shrug. 'Degsy's place, perhaps? No one seems to know where Bryant lives.'

Bray shook his head. 'No, we don't have the time. The money would have exchanged hands by the time we've traipsed all over the place.'

'Hmm,' Roy said, pondering the dilemma with what looked like a rehearsed exaggeration. 'Well, the only way we're going to know is to speak with Earlston.'

Bray flashed him a conspiratorial smile. 'Indeed. That's exactly what I was thinking.'

Jay decided to play dumb. 'You're going to see him?'

Bray slowly shook his head. 'Not we, *you*. It's time to introduce yourself. Like I said before, you need to make amends. So you and Earlston need to have a chat.'

'What am I supposed to say?'

'You don't mention us for a start. All you need to do is find the time and place; how you do that, I'll leave to your imagination.'

'What about my car?' Jay said.

Bray frowned. 'What about it?'

'Any chance I can get it back?'

Bray shook his head. 'Not at the moment. They think you're dead. Let's not do anything to make them doubt that.' A coldness settled in Bray's eyes. 'Don't be getting ideas about running away. I've been asking around. I know all about you, Jay Ellis. Me and Terry Jackmond go back a long way.' Bray gave a callous laugh. 'Look at the kid's face, Roy. I didn't think it was possible, but he's turned paler.' Bray shook his head and smiled. 'Terry's a businessman like me.

He can forget about his grudges for the right price. You give him a cut of that ransom money, and you might buy a ticket to redemption.' Bray rose slowly from his chair. 'That's very charitable if you ask me, and I'm sure your folks back home would agree with me.'

4

Earlston was unsure what ailed him most, the worry, the heartbreak, the fear and starvation, or lack of sleep. Either one was enough to break any man, but combined, they turned him into a wreck. Somehow he found the strength to continue. At one point, he feared it would come to a tragic end, especially when he told the kidnapper about the *complication*. The man's voice was laced with menace, and it shocked Earlston how quickly his demeanour turned from calmness into anger.

Earlston felt ashamed after letting Mich hear him sob. The poor woman was suffering enough. On hearing her voice, all he could think about was Jenny, and he became overwhelmed with emotion. The man's threat only made things worse. How dare they talk about his daughter like that. Jenny was barely sixteen and, as far as Earlston was aware, never had a boyfriend. Earlston shuddered while he recalled the man's words. Clenching his hand into his fist as the vile images plagued his thoughts like a cancer.

All he could do now was sit and wait, feeling more cowardly with each slow tick of the clock. In these moments of desperation, he considered calling the police. A stupid idea the more he thought about it. Things had gone too far. The horror was too real, and only a fool would see a way back.

Earlston paced the room, pausing to gaze through the large arched window. The city knew no sleep. The cars passed in an endless rush, the noise rarely dissipating, only offering a brief respite in the quiet hours of early morning. Earlston glanced at his watch. The night had passed him by unnoticed, as had the dawn, and it was almost ten o'clock.

Today, even the spires and the scattering of leafy trees looked sullen beneath the cloud-laden sky. Earlston took in the scene, his gaze following the slow flight of grey birds and, on losing interest, skimming across the rooftops and terracotta chimneys. He glanced down at the road, following its trajectory until focusing on the young man leaning against the railings at the corner of the pavement. His suit looked wrinkled and unwashed, and if not for the severe bruising on his face, Earlston wouldn't have noticed him.

Earlston watched the young man, his curiosity increasing the longer he studied him. His suit looked crumpled beyond repair, as though he'd recently dried himself beneath the sun after being caught short in a heavy downpour. The man's stance also seemed odd. The shoulders were slumped, yet the eyes remained alert, the forced nonchalance of a watcher rather than someone casually waiting.

The young man looked up, causing Earlston to move away from the window. He hid behind the blinds, peering gingerly through the gap. Surely, he was being stupid, acting irrationally. Earlston would never give it a second thought in normal circumstances. But normality had long passed, and since Jenny's abduction, any horror seemed conceivable.

Initially, he thought of Hoffman. Perhaps he'd hired somebody to keep an eye on him. Even though he'd completed the transaction with little protest, Hoffman was no fool. Earlston sensed his suspicions for days now. He cast the notion aside. 'Don't be so stupid, man,' he said aloud, moving from behind the blinds and standing defiantly in the window.

Much to his relief, the young man had gone, and gazing aimlessly at the road, Earlston found brief solace from the day's tedium. The moment was short-lived. Thoughts of Jenny quickened the beat of his heart, gaining momentum at the high shrill of the doorbell.

Earlston edged quietly into the hall and paused outside the front door. 'Hello?'

'Henry Earlston?'

'Yes, who is it?' he said, cringing at the pathetic frailty of his own voice.

'The name's Nash.'

'I don't know anybody by that name. I'm swamped with work. Tell me what you want, and I'll get back to you.'

'I'd like to come in.'

'Well, that's not going to happen.'

'Please, Mr Earlston, Henry. It's about your daughter Jenny and your wife, Mich.'

'What about them?'

'We both know they're not here. And we both know why. If you want to keep them safe, invite me inside and let me speak with you.'

Earlston shut his eyes, fear holding him silent while he tried to compose himself. He released the latch with a trembling hand and opened the door, almost slamming it shut when he saw the dishevelled young man from across the street standing before him.

The young man stood silently watching him as though waiting to be invited in. He looked younger this close, in his early twenties perhaps, not bad looking, although the bruises on his face and the swelling around the eyes prematurely aged him. His shirt was tide-marked and thin, and his crumpled suit was tarnished with a fine layer of sand-like dust. Earlston stared at him, his fear diminishing while the unkempt figure before him grew less imposing. 'You mentioned my wife and daughter, Mr Nash. What is it you think you know about them?'

Nash answered with a sigh. 'I know they've been abducted, and you're about to pay the ransom.'

For reasons unknown to him, Earlston's first instinct was to lie, call the notion ridiculous, and slam the door shut. Instead, he motioned Nash inside, convinced by the look in his eyes perhaps, the certainty in his voice, or the chance to share the burden and find that one last glimmer of hope.

5

J ay was wise enough not to give his real name but was curious why he instantly chose Nash. Undoubtedly, Mich would have reminded him why. But Jay refused to delve that deep. He had been thinking about Nash of late. So naturally, it was the first name that came to mind.

Following Earlston into the lounge, Jay caught his reflection in the mirror. The image made him cringe, and it would have broken his mother's heart to see the bruised and battered face staring back at him. Even Earlston looked concerned, watching while Jay eased himself into the chair before asking, 'What happened to you?'

Jay attempted a nonchalant shrug. 'Let's just say I had a slight accident.'

Earlston regarded him with a severe look. 'I take it my daughter and wife are somehow connected to it?'

'Yeah,' Jay said with a sigh.

Earlston clenched his fists. 'I swear to God if anything–'

'They're fine,' interrupted Jay. 'For now, at least, and

providing you don't do anything stupid, they'll stay that way.'

Earlston slumped into his chair. 'How's Jenny and Mich?'

'They're doing well, considering.'

Earlston nodded. 'Of course. Of course, they are. Mich is strong. I'm sure she'll help Jenny pull through this.'

For a moment, Jay was tempted to tell Earlston the truth: that his wife was a lying whore who had deceived him since they first met. She was the reason behind his furrowed brow, the gaunt face and shaking hands. The catalyst of this endless nightmare. The sole reason his daughter had to endure this. Jay kept silent. Earlston was to know nothing more than he already did. That was Bray's strict instruction.

Jay lowered his eyes. 'Yes,' he lied. 'She's a great comfort to her.'

Earlston's face softened with relief. 'So why are you here?'

'To keep an eye on things,' Jay said. A lame excuse, but after pondering the question all morning, it was the best he could come up with. The only other option was to watch and wait, but he felt beaten and tired. Besides, Earlston might have given him the slip, and with Bray needing to know the drop-off point beforehand, Jay couldn't afford to take the risk.

A defeated look settled in Earlston's eyes. 'I'm doing everything you've asked. What else do you want from me?'

'We need to make sure you're not playing games.'

'*Games*?'

'Yes, you're always asking for more time. We're worried you've informed the authorities, lying even, especially with all this dubious hesitation.'

Earlston stood up. 'That's ridiculous. What kind of man

do you think I am? Why would I do that? This is my daughter's life, for God's sake.'

'It is indeed. So I'm here to keep an eye on you. Give you a chance to explain the delay.'

Earlston sat down, buried his face in his hands, and then dropped them onto his lap. 'It's a lot of money. These things take time.'

'I'm sure they do.' Jay narrowed his eyes. 'It's an odd delay, though, don't you think? I understand you want more hours. But where is the advantage on the weekend? The banks aren't open on a Saturday.'

Earlston released an irritated sigh. 'I'm not using a bank. This is a cash deal. I've sold shares to raise that amount. This kind of deal needs to be a private transaction.'

'I'm with you,' Jay said with a smile. 'And the extra hours–'

'Are to allow for any unforeseen circumstances.'

'And are there?'

Earlston shook his head. 'Not yet, no. Well, none that I can foresee.'

'Glad to hear it,' Jay said, hesitating before asking his next question. 'I take it you don't have the money now?'

'Of course not. As I've already told you. At best, it'll be sometime on Friday or, at the latest, Saturday.'

Jay concealed his relief. Earlston might have been a coward, but any weakness in the man's character was partly rectified by foolish honesty. It might even have saved him from the cruellest fate. Bray showed no interest in what happened to the girl. He instructed Jay to find out the truth. If the money was already in Earlston's possession, Bray would have abandoned this little scheme and gladly taken it. Yet there again, possibly not. There was a slyness to Bray's smile. A malevolence in the eyes. Perhaps he wanted to teach Clate, Bryant, and Mich a lesson, taunt them to the very end, allow them to dream, snatching it from their grasp the moment they came close.

Earlston frowned. 'It still doesn't make sense.'

'What doesn't?'

'Why you came here. You could have called. I can iden-tify you now. It puts you in an awkward situation.'

Jay puffed out his cheeks and sighed. 'It was decided you needed to be watched from the inside. I drew the short straw.' Jay pointed at his face. 'As you can see, I disagreed at first. Believe me, I'm sitting here under duress.'

'What happened?'

'That's my business. All you need to know is that I'm still a part of this, and until it's all over, I'll be watching over you.'

Earlston pressed his lips into a fine line. 'Seems I have little choice.' He narrowed his eyes. 'I still find it hard to believe. You could be anybody for all I know. Perhaps, you got wind of something somehow. I mean, look at you. You look more like a vagrant than a kidnapper. Maybe you're just some chancer making the most of a sick opportunity, Mr Nash.'

Being referred to by that name held Jay silent. He almost didn't respond, tempted to look over his shoulder to see if Nash's ghost stood behind him. It was a momentary lapse, and, holding Earlston's stare with his own, Jay said, 'Would a chancer know that Jenny and Mich went on a *girly couple of days*? Bonding, I think they called it, visiting museums, art galleries, a health spar, window shopping and all that kind of stuff.'

Something registered in Earlston's eyes, encouraging Jay to continue. 'Would a chancer know she likes to wear a black polka dot skirt and a paisley blouse and packed the rest of her clothes in a green canvas rucksack? She likes indie music, reading too, and she's currently on page one hundred and eighty-six of *The Cider House Rules* by *John Irving*.'

Tears welled in Earlston's eyes. 'Enough,' he cried. 'Enough, you've made your point.' He wiped the tear from his cheek. 'Have any of you hurt her?'

Jay shook his head and, to remedy the lie, said, 'Not at the moment. Let's hope it stays that way. The kindest thing you can do for your daughter is to do as you're told without complications. She's not having a good time of it.'

Earlston got up, strolled across the room and stood with his back to the window. Jay didn't know Earlston's age, but the stooped, ravaged man in front of him looked in his seventies. Earlston sighed, staring at Jay with those tired, defeated eyes. 'You could keep the money for yourself. All you need to do is tell me where they are.'

'I thought you didn't have the money yet?'

'I don't,' Earlston said. 'You have my word. I swear to God, I'll still pay you.'

Jay shook his head. 'Do you not think they've already considered that? There's a lot of money at stake. They would have moved your wife and daughter soon after I left. I won't know where they are until after the exchange.'

6

They covered Jenny's face with a blanket and kept her blindfolded throughout the entire journey. She felt the steady motion of the car alongside the bumps in the road. The oncoming traffic hurried past; music jumped from one tune to the next, familiar pop songs, as someone kept changing channels on the radio.

Jenny tensed at the sound of Clate's aggravated sigh. 'For God's sake, Bryant, just find a channel and settle on it.' His voice sounded tired and raspy, no doubt worsened by the previous night's shouting. When Clate had stormed into her room, Jenny thought she was going to die. Fear held her motionless on the bed, and she dreaded to think what Clate might have done if Jay hadn't intervened.

When Jay told her they were leaving, she was filled with a sudden feeling of hope. She felt foolish now she thought about it, like a neglected child thankful for the slightest hint of affection. It was an optimism doomed not to last, the prospect of escape made more poignant by its transience.

Jenny couldn't have made a difference even if she'd tried. Jay's face grew bloodier the longer she looked. Clate and

Bryant kicked and punched Jay until they were breathless, a merciless beating as relentless as Jenny's screaming. Mich had stood and watched, a hint of gratification in her eyes. Except for Jenny's distress, the old man's silence conveyed the only sign of remorse.

Degsy seemed different since their arrival at Bryant's flat. He was quieter, more discrete, with a constant sombreness in his eyes, suggesting the previous night's horrors had somehow changed him.

Stifling and poorly lit, Bryant's flat looked a mess, the hall's moth-eaten carpet and scabby wall languishing in self-neglect. Jenny wasn't allowed in the lounge and only caught glimpses of the turquoise-painted walls and a heavily scuffed tan leather sofa. The place smelled musty and unclean, a nauseous mix of old food, unwashed clothes and stale cigarettes. Jenny's room was worse, grotty and dimly lit, the thin pastel blue bedspread in keeping with the heavily stained green carpet.

Jenny sat on the edge of the bed; although exhausted, she couldn't bear to lie on it. She stared aimlessly at the door, alone again in another room. Only now, she'd lost all hope, her spirit exhausted by defeat, and all she could think about was how to end it.

As though hearing her silent prayer, the door slowly opened, and Degsy holding two chipped mugs, stood watching her in the doorway. He looked at her and smiled. 'Brought you a cuppa soup. It's all I could find; I thought you might be hungry.'

He offered her the mug, but Jenny refused it by shaking her head.

Degsy nodded with a smile, 'I'll leave it here just in case,' and placed it on the bedside table. He sat beside her on the bed, slurping his hot soup, the loud sound interspersed by faint wheezing from the rise and fall of his chest.

Degsy rested the mug on his lap and, without looking at her, said, 'It won't be too long. Another twenty-four hours, and it'll all be over.'

Jenny fixed him with a stare, his silence awaiting a response, but she didn't answer.

Degsy looked at her and sighed. 'I'm sorry for the way things turned out. It's all a bit of a mess. No one was meant to get hurt, especially you.' He stared into his mug. 'Not that it's any consolation.'

Jenny took a deep breath. 'No, it's not.' She closed her eyes for a second. 'Did you see the state of Jay's face? They're nothing but animals.' A tear rolled down her cheek. 'How could anyone do that?'

Degsy answered with a shrug. 'Crazy things happen in the heat of the moment. Things got out of hand.'

'Out of hand.'

Degsy glanced down at the carpet, choosing silence over another stupid answer. Jenny watched him while he sat, a sudden shine in his tired eyes, his leg uncontrollably shaking. At first, she resisted the urge to speak, the thought of what happened to Jay so dire that she struggled to get her words out. Eventually, she broke. 'What did you do with him?' she asked, her voice trembling.

Degsy rubbed his thumb along the rim of his mug, grimacing as he stared into it. Slowly, he took a sip and placed the mug on his lap. 'It's best you don't think about that.'

'I can't think about anything else. Jay was the only one who tried to help me. He looked so lifeless when they dragged his body out of here.' She shuddered at her next thought. 'I'm assuming he's dead, right?'

Degsy remained silent, but in the deep pools of his eyes, she found her answer.

Jenny motioned to stand but stayed put when Bryant swaggered into the room.

Bryant glared at Degsy. 'What are you doing here alone with my Jenny? You filthy old goat. This all looks a bit cosy.'

Degsy stood up. 'All the filth's in your head. This girl hasn't eaten for days. I'm just making sure she's all right.'

Bryant glanced at Jenny and grinned. 'Well, I'm here to do that. Clate put Jenny under my care. So you can go now.'

Degsy frowned. '*Your* care. Mich is the best person to do that.'

'Mich is flat out. Anyway, that shag-happy old drunk can't be trusted.' Bryant pointed his thumb over his shoulder towards the hall. 'I told you to leave. Go on, skit.'

Degsy remained where he was for a moment, then, with his shoulders stooped, he trudged to the doorway. Bryant grabbed Degsy's arm as he passed. 'Did I see a bit of attitude in your eyes?'

Degsy shook his head.

'Good,' Bryant said. He glanced at Jenny and winked. 'Now get out of my sight and let me talk to my girl here.'

7

Jenny longed for Degsy to stay where he was. Her heart sank when he stepped into the hall, the hopelessness she felt inside expressed through his weak dejected look. She didn't dare to speak, tensing her body when Bryant sat beside her. He smelled of hair gel and cheap cologne. When he sighed, his breath breezed warmly across her neck, followed by the smell of his last cigarette.

'Sorry about that,' Bryant said. 'You call for me the next time that old man bothers you.' He placed his clammy hand on her forearm, stroking a long bony finger over the goose pimples prickling her skin. 'I'm sorry about the heating. The boiler's been playing up for days.' Bryant stood up, strolled over to Jenny's rucksack, and pulled out her cardigan, resting it across her shoulders. 'This should help. We need to keep you warm. We don't want you catching a cold.'

Jenny remained silent, staring at the door, listening to her heart beating wildly in her ears and throat. Bryant sat on the bed, this time edging closer. 'You can look at me,' he said. 'There's no need to be scared, you know.'

Jenny slowly turned her head and, unable to match his stare with her own, lowered her eyes, focusing on the carpet.

Bryant released a sigh. 'Are you angry?'

Jenny shook her head.

'What's wrong then? I heard you talking with that old fool, but you can barely look at me. Have I done something to upset you?'

Again, Jenny shook her head.

Bryant persisted. 'Tell me what's wrong then?'

'Nothing. I. Nothing. I just feel a bit down, that's all.'

'About what?'

Jenny suppressed a sigh. Inwardly she screamed. *What do you think, you idiot? You. This place. Holding me against my will. What a stupid question.*

'About what?' Bryant asked again, this time his voice sounding more impatient.

Jenny shrugged. 'I just want to go home,' and then, catching the angry disappointment in Bryant's eyes, said, 'and about what happened to Jay, I suppose.'

Bryant gave a smile. 'I thought as much. Stuff like that's never nice. But Jay was out of control–'

'He tried to protect me.'

Bryant shook his head. 'That's what he wanted you to believe. Oh, I know Clate was mad. But it was only words. I wouldn't have let things go too far. You and I are friends.' He dropped his hand onto her thigh. 'I'd never let anyone hurt you.'

Fear held her motionless, although she only wanted to recoil from his touch. His hand smoothed further up her thigh, stopping before her waist, and then he raised it slowly and pushed the strands of hair away from her face. He tilted his head to one side. 'That's better. It's a sin to hide such a pretty face. It's a shame you want to go home. I had hoped you and I could get closer once all this was over.'

Jenny failed to suppress her frown, wondering if his words were designed to trick her or were said through genuine delusion. 'I don't understand; you'll have your money then. That's what this is all for, right?'

Bryant stared at her until his expressionless face broke into a sly smile. 'At first, that was the case. That was before we connected. Sure, the money's still the prize, but as to what happens afterwards, our friendship has changed all that.'

How gullible did he think she was? To a rational mind, his words made no sense. Yet when she raised her head, something in his eyes convinced her he believed them. She was lost for words. But Bryant kept staring, the expectant look imploring her to answer.

'I don't see how it does,' came Jenny's sheepish reply.

'How do you mean?'

'It'll be too dangerous for you all. Once Daddy has me home, he's bound to tell the police; they'll come after you.'

Bryant laughed. 'Bound to, but I'll be somewhere hot and sunny by then, and with any luck, you'll be with me.'

'Daddy wants me home.'

'Sure he does,' Bryant scoffed. 'You keep telling yourself that.'

It was an odd thing to say. But here, in this godforsaken room, anything seemed possible. Fear and tiredness clouded her mind. Why had her father not paid the money sooner? What were the reasons behind his delay? Perhaps all he wanted was Mich? Jenny shut her eyes in denial. No, she was her father's world. He would do anything to get her back. But doubt had found a way in. Conspiring with the hunger and cold and those long lonely hours to make Bryant's cruel words more believable.

Jenny began to cry.

'Hey,' Bryant said. 'Hey, stop that. Shush now. Nick's here to take care of you.' He opened out his arms. 'Come on, shush now. You're a girl who needs a hug.'

With his arms wrapped tightly around her and her head pressed firmly against his chest, she felt only revulsion. She listened to the hurried beat of his heart and the deepness of his breath, longing for both to stop.

Bryant sniffed her hair. 'Feel better now? Course you do. You seem tired. You need more rest. We can lie down on the bed if you like?'

Jenny shook her head, her voice quavering as she said, 'No, I'm fine. No, thank you.'

'No, you're not. Come on, let's lie down and rest.'

Resisting with all her strength, Jenny tried to pull away. 'No, please. Let me go. No, I don't want to.'

Bryant tightened his grip. 'Want's got nothing to do with it. Let me decide what's best. Trust me, you'll feel much better afterwards.'

He forced them down onto the bed, whispering into her ear, then quickly freeing her from his grasp as Mich's unmistakable voice screamed his name from the doorway.

Mich rushed over to the bed, grabbed Jenny's arm, and pulled her to her feet. She glared at Bryant. 'You leave this girl alone. Do you hear me? Now get off that bed and get out.'

Bryant sat up and began plucking the fluff from his suit with an ugly grin. 'You're nobody to be giving orders.' He glanced around the room. 'You seem to be forgetting who owns this place.'

Mich shook her head and scowled. 'Oh, there's no

mistaking that. It's easy to see who owns a shithole like this. Now get up and get out. Get out, I said before I call for Clate.'

At first, Bryant ignored her with a shrug, springing immediately to his feet when she began hollering Clate's name. Bryant shoved past her on his way out, stopping to look over his shoulder when he reached the doorway. He looked at her in disgust. 'I don't recall you ever saying no. Like mother like daughter if you ask me.'

'Clate,' Mich cried. 'Clate, Clate,' falling silent as Bryant's shadow faded down the hallway.

Mich gave Jenny a look. A look that was judgemental and loaded with blame. The look she always gave her whenever anything bad happened between them. Mich lowered her eyes and sighed. 'Are you okay?'

'Yes,' Jenny lied. Mich was the last person in whom she would confide.

Mich nodded at Jenny's rucksack. 'You best get changed. Jeans and a jumper. Get out that dress and blouse. It's not wise for you to dress like that.'

Jenny stared at her. 'I didn't do anything.'

'I never said you did. I'll be sleeping in here until the exchange. Scum like Bryant needs little encouragement.'

8

Earlston made no effort to conceal his aversion for Jay. It was written all over his face. An expression that became graver with time, intensifying to the loud, slow tick of the clock. They waited in the lounge. Earlston kept fidgeting in his chair, constantly sighing, intermittently pacing the room or staring through the window.

Earlston's behaviour put Jay more on edge. Jay tried talking to him a few times, but the man either ignored him or grunted a response, the disapproving look in his eyes complimenting his reluctance for conversation. Jay didn't need to ask why. He was nothing but an intrusion, one of the reasons why Earlston had been dragged into this mess.

Being ignored was a sufferable rebuke. Jay had survived worse and was happy to endure the silence. The only downside was his thoughts, his mind jumping from one worry to the next. Jay thought about home, the fern-clad slopes of the valley, and the estuary's gleam quickly morphing into his mam's tearful, troubled face. He glanced at Earlston's phone, his conscience giving way to good sense as he resisted the temptation to call her. At least Bray had afforded him more time, but with Terry Jackmond involved, the question was, for how long?

Leaning back in his chair with his hands behind his head, Jay tried casting out his inner demons with a sigh. Some of them refused to leave, but thankfully, they were easily distracted by the shrill ringing of Earlston's telephone.

Earlston jumped up from his chair, hurried over to the phone and picked up the receiver. He pressed it against his ear. 'Earlston speaking.' His shoulders sagged. 'Ah, Charles, what a relief. I hoped it might be you. No nothing. There's nothing wrong at all. I'm just relieved everything went so smoothly, that's all.' Earlston glanced at his watch. 'I suppose I could be at yours in the next hour–' He fell silent as Jay vigorously shook his head.

'Bear with me a moment, Charles,' Earlston said, placing his hand over the receiver. He gave Jay a fierce look. 'What on earth is the matter?' he said, lowering his voice to a whisper. 'I thought you'd be pleased. The transaction's complete, and the money received. All I need to do is collect it.'

'Not a good idea,' Jay whispered. 'You need to be here when they call. We can't have you traipsing across the city. He'll need to bring it here.'

'Charles will never agree to that.'

Jay shrugged. 'Persuade him, and if you can't, I'll fetch it if I have to.'

Earlston looked at him with contempt. 'That'll raise his suspicions. Look at the state of you. I would have collected it if you hadn't arrived. Why should your presence change that?'

Jay looked at him and frowned. 'Things have changed since then. I'm sure you want to keep your daughter safe.

Like you said, look at the state of me; people are obviously getting jumpy.'

Earlston didn't reply, silenced by Jay's answer. He lifted his hand off the receiver. 'Sorry about that, Charles. Something's come up. I wondered if you could do me a huge favour. Normally, I wouldn't ask, but I need to stay here for a while, I'm afraid.' He let out a nervous laugh. 'So, one could say I'm desperate.' He hesitated for a second. 'I wondered if you could bring the money here. Yes. Yes, I know, of course, Charles. You're an extremely busy man. It pains me to ask, and I wouldn't dream of mentioning it if I had any other option.' Earlston went quiet, the elongated pause feeling like a lifetime. He broke the silence with a sigh. 'Oh, thank you, Charles. Thank you so much. I'm forever in your debt for this one.'

After five more minutes of grovelling, Earlston eventually hung up. He slunk into his chair and buried his face in his hands. As pathetic as Earlston was, Jay couldn't help but feel sorry for him. A week ago, he was just an ordinary husband and father. Now he was a broken man caught in an endless nightmare. Jay considered offering him some kind words, but he felt it wise to keep his mouth shut. Instead, he sat down on his chair, awaiting the doorbell's ring while surrendering to the anxious silence.

Charles Hoffman arrived an hour later. Earlston insisted Jay shouldn't be seen, ushering him into the spare bedroom before letting Hoffman in. Jay caught a glimpse of him passing through the hall. A tall man with blond Brylcreemed hair, wearing grey gabardine trousers and a navy-blue blazer, its top pocket embroidered with a crest.

Earlston led him to the lounge, with Jay creeping into the hall when he closed the door.

~

EARLSTON KNEW he looked on edge. It didn't require any skills in observation to see that. Naturally, Hoffman saw it too. A response he failed to conceal as he shook Earlston's hand and scanned him with a troubled eye. 'Are you feeling all right, Henry? If you don't mind me saying, you look exhausted.'

'I'm fine, Charles. I'm fine. It's been a hectic few days, as you well know. I'm just a little tired, that's all.' He glanced at the briefcase in Hoffman's hand. 'Here, let me relieve you of that. And again, let me express my deepest thanks. You're a good friend Charles. This is a tremendous help to me.'

Hoffman accepted the compliment with a shrug. 'I'm glad to help.' He flashed him a warm smile. 'Providing you don't make a habit of it.'

'Quite,' Earlston said with a laugh, easing the case from Hoffman's grasp and carefully placing it on the table.

Hoffman took a seat and, glancing at Jay's empty cup, said, 'Are Jenny and Mich around?'

Earlston shook his head. 'No, they're away for a few days. Why do you ask?'

Hoffman grabbed the cup. 'No reason. This tea's still warm, so I assumed you had company.'

Earlston sat down. 'Oh, that. That was just... er... It was one of the estate agents. I needed to sign some paperwork.'

Hoffman looked unconvinced. 'Interesting. They don't usually leave the office for that. In fact, you're honoured they came to the house. Is that why you were indisposed?'

'Sorry?'

Hoffman put the cup down and nodded at the briefcase. 'Is that the reason you couldn't collect it yourself?'

'Oh... er... No. That's a different engagement.'

Hoffman leaned back in his chair and steepled his fingers. 'Well?'

'Well, what?'

'Are you going to count it?'

Earlston flipped open the briefcase, breathed deeply, and stared at the neatly stacked notes. Sensing Hoffman watching him, he slowly closed the case. 'There's no need. All seems in order.'

'That's very trusting of you, Henry.'

Earlston frowned slightly. 'I'm presuming you've taken your fee?'

Hoffman nodded.

'Good,' Earlston said. 'Then there's no need to check. We've known each other for years. Trust doesn't come into it.' Earlston glanced at his watch. 'Charles, thanks again for all your help. I know you're extremely busy, so I won't keep you.'

Hoffman narrowed his eyes, folding his arms across his chest. 'Because we *have* known each other for so long, you'll forgive me when I say your behaviour seems a little ungrateful and rude, don't you think?'

Earlston's eyes widened at Hoffman's sudden outburst. He opened his mouth to respond, but Hoffman spoke over him before he could reply. 'The thing is, Henry, I traipse across London at short notice to help you, and all I get is a quick thanks. You haven't once asked after my family, glancing at your watch, suggesting I leave. You don't even have the decency to offer me a drink.' Hoffman sighed. 'This whole thing's been off from the start. Obviously, I advised against it; it's your money; you can do what you want with it.' Hoffman regarded him for a moment, then, in a lowered voice, said, 'This just isn't like you, Henry. I've had my suspicions for a while.'

'Suspicions about what?'

'That's something wrong.'

'Everything's fine.'

'Really? One only has to look at you to know that's not the case. You look awful. And as for today's debacle, to describe it as odd is an understatement.'

Earlston rubbed his eyes and sighed. 'I'm sorry if I appear a bit off; truly, I am. Admittedly, I'm tired. Yes, this whole thing is stressful, and a bit rushed. But other than that, I can assure you nothing's wrong.'

Hoffman stood up. 'Goodbye, Henry. Best of luck with everything. And while I'm here, I think you should get another financial advisor.'

Earlston rose quickly from his chair. 'But why?'

'Because it's a relationship founded on trust. There's no point in continuing if you're going to lie to me.' Hoffman motioned towards the door, stopping when Earlston blocked his way. 'I'm not lying to you, Charles.'

Hoffman shook his head and sighed, 'Fine,' then tried to move past him.

Earlston held out his hands. 'All right, all right. Things aren't going too well at the moment. It's a difficult time for me.'

Hoffman gave him a sympathetic nod. 'Listen, Henry. I don't mean to pry. I'm just worried about you, that's all. There's no need to struggle through this alone. You can talk to me.'

Staring into Hoffman's eyes, Earlston saw genuine concern. It felt good to hear a friendly voice. This burden was too big for him alone. It reminded him how vulnerable he was and awakened that debilitating cowardice that had plagued him since early childhood. It had shown more of itself this past week, creeping from the recesses of his heart. Even now, during his one chance to confide in another, it robbed him of the grace of confession and held him fearfully silent.

9

C late didn't want to go over it again, but they kept asking. The plan didn't favour Degsy and Bryant, and each rendition drew more attention.

'So where's the exchange taking place?' Bryant asked.

Clate glanced at the floor, hoping to avoid the question through silence.

'*Clate*?' Bryant persisted.

'What?' Clate said with an aggravated sigh.

'Where's the exchange?'

'I've a few places in mind. I haven't decided yet.'

Clate lit a cigar, watching as the lighter's flame highlighted the doubt and mistrust in Bryant's eyes. Degsy was harder to read. He wore a blank expression. The old man was a pro. Years of deceit had taught him never to show folk what he might be thinking.

'Run it by me again,' Bryant said.

Reluctantly, Clate agreed only this time with a mind to sugar-coat the answer. 'Mich will accompany me to the exchange. She'll be handed over to show good faith, and once I have the money in my hand, I'll call you to release the girl.'

Bryant narrowed his eyes. 'Earlston will want to see the girl.'

Clate dismissed Bryant's concern with a shrug. 'Like I said, he'll have Mich. Reuniting him with his wife will soften the blow. He can see it as a fifty per cent down payment. Once the transaction's complete, he can get the second part of it.'

Clate's flippancy wasn't well received. Bryant was quick to voice his concerns. Whereas Degsy listened in silence.

Bryant stood up, pacing the room while he spoke. 'And we're supposed to believe that? You have the money for yourself while we sit here waiting like a pair of idiots. Then we tell Earlston where she is, and the police come knocking at my flat.'

Clate took a drag from his cigar, frowning while blowing out the smoke. He watched it drift into the room, rising slowly until it disappeared towards the ceiling. With the cigar smouldering in his hand, Clate pointed it at Bryant, its thin ribbon of smoke curling through his fingers. 'Hopefully, you won't be here. You'll drop the girl off at the other side of town. She can call her daddy from a phone box, and he'll come running to pick her up.'

Bryant stopped pacing the room, his pale hand rubbing the nape of his long, skinny neck. 'And then what?'

'We'll meet up–'

'Where?'

'Out near Richmond. I'll write the address down for you.'

Bryant and Degsy exchanged glances. 'Then what?' Bryant said.

'We'll divide the money, and each of us gets their cut.'

Bryant forced a laugh. 'Sure, and we're just supposed to believe that.'

Clate took another drag from his cigar and stood up. 'Faith brings salvation to the soul. You can believe what you like. But that's how it's going to be.' He stared at Bryant and smiled, opening his mouth to say something but falling silent when Mich interrupted him.

'I don't like leaving Jenny here alone.' Mich said. She gave Bryant a fierce stare. 'He's been sniffing around her like a dog. I caught him lying next to her on the bed. God knows what might have happened if Degsy hadn't woken me up. He's the vilest wretch I know. I don't trust him.'

Clate couldn't disagree. Bryant's presence was like the dirt beneath his nails, the grime across the sink, a constant reminder of the squalor in which he bathed. For now, it was a sordidness to be endured until those clear Spanish waters could cleanse him. The girl was a means to an end, too late to save, perhaps. Clate had warned Mich this was a journey without return. If Mich genuinely cared for the girl, she shouldn't have turned her into a victim. Bryant was the type of lowlife that no one could ever trust. It was a burden they had to endure. Everything came with a cost. Clate had no delusions. One man's fortune meant another girl's misery.

Clate pretended to respond. 'What were you up to, Bryant?'

A surprised look passed across Bryant's face, usually reserved for seasoned liars and those truly innocent. 'Nothing, Clate. I promise. The girl looked down. There's no point in making this any harder for her. With Mich flaked out and Degsy as useless as he is, I was trying to comfort her.'

Clate rode along with the lie. 'And you'll leave her alone once we leave?'

Bryant frowned, the offended look on his gaunt face almost convincing. 'Swear to God.'

Clate threw Mich a smile. 'There you go. I'm glad that's all sorted.'

Mich remained unconvinced, but this was her only way out, so she had the good sense to keep her mouth shut, although it never stopped her from having a dig. 'I'm glad to see you've calmed down, Clate. What was the other night all about? A bit crazy, don't you think?'

Clate didn't reply.

'One minute, you're calmly laying down the law,' Mich said, 'and the next, you're beating a boy to death and threatening to rip the girl's heart out.'

Clate took another drag from his cigar. 'Booze, tiredness, and stress can kill a man before his time. Thankfully, after a long rest, I'm back to my old self now.'

Mich was wise enough not to respond, and Clate, conscious that the old man had remained quiet throughout, focused his attention on Degsy. 'Cat got your tongue, Degs?'

Degsy shook his head.

Clate considered him with a smile. 'It sure as hell seems like. I thought you'd be the first to comment on this.' Clate caught Degsy's glance, and for the first time since he could remember, those sleepy eyes were not awash with fear but what appeared to be a newfound hatred. The moment quickly passed, Degsy suppressing his aversion with a smile as though realising Clate had cottoned on to him.

Degsy shrugged. 'Bryant does have a point. We'd be sitting here like a pair of fools, blindly hoping for your call.'

Clate strolled over to the ashtray and slowly flicked the ash from his cigar. 'What do you suggest I do?'

Again Degsy shrugged. 'Added security might help.'

'I've given you my word. What more security do you need?'

'I know, I know,' Degsy said like a drowning man grasping for dry land. 'And it's not my intention to disrespect you.'

Clate read the hesitancy in the old man's eyes.

'The thing is,' Degsy said, 'when I spoke about security, I was thinking along the lines of some kind of deposit, something a little more... tangible.'

Clate had known Degsy for years. One thing had always struck him about the old man. Behind the shabby suit with its fraying cuffs and the haggard face's subservient veneer was a tendency to be unpredictable. Clate was witnessing that inclination now, registering the scheming look in Degsy's eyes just as he had when Degsy visited him at his club a few weeks ago. Clate stared at him, knowing the best way to deter Degsy from pursuing this idea was through intimidation. Only this time, bullying wasn't enough. Bryant stood by Degsy's side, the look in his eyes expecting a convincing answer.

Clate broke into a smile. 'It's a fair point, and to be honest, I've been expecting it.' He took a few more drags from his cigar and then stubbed it in the ashtray. He strolled over to where his jacket was slung over a chair, slipped his hand inside the pocket and took out three envelopes. He tossed them onto Degsy's lap. 'Here, perhaps these will help to ease your doubt.'

Degsy looked at them and frowned.

'Deeds to the club and the apartments,' Clate said, anticipating the question.

Bryant sucked the air in through his teeth. 'They're just pieces of paper. They don't mean squat. It's not as if Degsy and I can stick around if you and Mich decide to do the dirty on us.'

'That's not going to happen,' interrupted Mich. 'God knows what you'd do to Jenny if we did. Regardless of what anyone thinks, I want the girl back home safely.'

Clate stared down at the floor, hiding his incredulous look. He glanced at Degsy browsing through the documents, wondering if, like Mich's sentiment, they were equally unconvincing. Clate had brought them here by chance, gathering them up while clearing his desk. He knew they had no worth and questioned why he'd taken them. He'd done so subconsciously, perhaps, nostalgic souvenirs to remind him of the unfulfilled promise of the past.

Degsy placed the papers down on his lap. 'They appear to be legit. But they're all in Clate's name. We'd need a lawyer to sign them over if we were to have any legal claim over them.'

Bryant shook his head. 'That still wouldn't be enough. He's already used them to pay off his debts. Benny Bray owns them the last I heard.'

Clate gave Bryant a fierce stare, holding it until Bryant paled, and his scrawny neck sunk into his sagging shoulders like a tortoise retreating into its shell.

'Bray has a stake in it, yes,' Clate said. 'But these debts are being paid, and these still remain my business.' He reached into his back pocket and slammed his wallet on the table. He followed it with a set of keys, keeping the car key in his fist. 'That's all I got, driving licence, national insurance, credit cards and the keys to the club and apartments.'

The look in Degsy's and Bryant's eyes seemed more convinced, faltering slightly when Bryant said, 'Passport?'

Clate gazed sternly into his eyes. 'I've never been one for travelling. In fact, I've never ventured out of the country.

Never had a mind to, so I don't have one.' His words seemed to appease any last traces of doubt, his tone so convincing even he almost believed it.

'Well, gentleman,' Clate said, glancing down at the table. 'You have my whole life's worth in your grasp. So, hopefully, that provides you with enough *security*?'

No one offered a reply. 'Good,' Clate said with a smile. 'Then, if it's okay with you, I'll make that phone call.'

10

They waited anxiously all day; then, like a harbinger of doom, the phone rang as the afternoon dwindled lazily into the early evening. Earlston picked it up after two rings. 'Hello? Hello?' he kept saying, casting his troubled glance towards Jay while he waited for an answer.

Earlston held the receiver closer to his ear and mouth. 'Yes, I do. Yes, all of it.' His shoulders tightened, the colour draining from his face. Everything seemed so still; the walls, the clock, and the traffic outside, as though sympathetic to Earlston's plight, waited with bated breath.

'Of course, I'll come alone,' Earlston raised his voice, 'but what about?' breaking off in mid-sentence when Jay vigorously shook his head.

Earlston sighed. 'Nothing. I wasn't going to say anything. I just got a bit upset, that's all.' He nodded towards the phone. 'Yes, yes. I know that. Of course, I'm listening. I just want my wife and daughter back safe. I want an end to this.'

Earlston placed a trembling hand on his chest, listening attentively, the silence broken intermittently by the heaviness of each breath. 'Yes,' he said with a sigh. 'I know Saint Vincent's. It's just off Kings Cross Train Station near the canal.'

Earlston held Jay's glance with his own, then averted his gaze with a frown. 'Can't we do it now? I have the money; there's no need to wait. Yes. Understood. I'll do exactly as you ask. Saint Vincent's Methodist just after midnight.'

Earlston stood motionless until Jay took the receiver from his hand. Jay held it to his ear to confirm that Clate had hung up. He grabbed Earlston's arm and slowly guided him to his chair. 'I take it you're going to drive?'

Earlston nodded. 'Of course, the traffic's quieter at that time of night.' He slumped back into his chair and rubbed his eyes. 'Several more hours,' he said with a sigh. 'I'll be glad when this bloody nightmare's finally over.'

Jay didn't respond. Not that any words were suitable. Earlston had been through hell. Jenny had suffered more. But all the man could do was sit and wait. Jay slapped his hands down on his lap. 'I need to spend a penny,' he said and stood up. He strolled out to the hall, closed the lounge door, and quietly used the telephone in Earlston's bedroom.

The phone rang for what felt like an age, and when a sleepy-sounding Roy finally answered, Jay was just about to hang up. Jay wasted no time. 'It's Jay,' he said in a lowered voice. 'The exchange is happening tonight. St Vincent's Methodist Church, King's Cross.' He waited for a response.

'What time?' came Roy's tepid response.

'Just after midnight.'

Neither man said a word, and Jay hung up after a moment's silence.

When Jay returned to the lounge, Earlston, now at the far end of the room, stood facing the window. His dark silhouette stayed motionless against the fading light while the sun, receding shyly beneath the city, cast his elongated shadow. Jay wondered whether he should say something but was reluctant to disturb him. Thankfully, there was no need to try, as Earlston, with his back still turned, broke the silence. He began with an irritated sigh, then said, 'You know, when a guest normally uses the bathroom, they have the common decency to flush. They also wash their hands if they have a mind to.'

Jay suppressed his smart reply as Earlston slowly turned around and pointed a gun at him. The way the gun rested awkwardly in his hand, it was clear he was unaccustomed to using it. Not that it gave Jay any reassurance. Earlston had been through so much, a man driven over the edge who seemed capable of anything. 'What are you doing, Earlston? Where the hell did you get that?'

Earlston gave the gun a disapproving glance. 'I found it when going through Mich's things. God knows where she got it from or what she intended to do with it.' He tightened his grip, raising his arm to level the barrel with the centre of Jay's chest. 'What are you doing here?'

'I thought I'd already explained.'

Earlston shook his head. 'No, it doesn't make any sense. Even less so when they called. You seemed desperate for them to believe I was alone. Why didn't they mention you?' Earlston regarded him with a frown. 'And more importantly, who were you calling from the bedroom?'

'It was a personal call.'

'To whom?'

'Put the gun down, and I'll tell you.'

Earlston forced a laugh. 'I know you people think I'm a fool. But I'm not as stupid as you'd like to think. Everything I've done has been for my family.'

Jay watched the tears well in Earlston's eyes. For a

moment, he was tempted to tell him the truth about his wife but hesitated, concluding Earlston would learn that before the day was out.

For now, Earlston needed to hold on to the little strength he had, partly for his own sake but primarily for his daughter's. There was something wretched about Earlston's look. Although he held the gun in his hand, it was to himself where he posed the greatest danger. His finger loitered clumsily over the trigger, one slip away from shooting Jay or himself. Jay knew Earlston wouldn't deliberately pull the trigger. Such a deed required guts. Even when Hoffman offered himself as a confidant, Earlston declined. Perhaps hesitant to take the risk or too cowardly to face the consequences.

Jay edged forward, wincing at the sudden pain in his ribs. He would have swiftly snatched the gun from Earlston's hand in better health. But the last beating slowed him down. It clung to him like an unshakable curse. A constant throb in his head and an ache in his bones gave him an invalid's lumbering gait. 'Give me the gun, Earlston. You're so close to getting Jenny home. It makes no sense to ruin that.'

The gun trembled in Earlston's hand. 'Who were you calling?'

'My mother, back home. I was worried about her. I wanted to see how she was.'

Earlston looked partially convinced. 'You could have called her from the lounge. All you had to do was ask.'

Jay gave a shrug. 'I guess I wanted some privacy.'

'*Privacy?*' Earlston echoed the word with a tone of resentment. 'Why should you have any, seeing as you stole mine from me.' He tried steadying the gun in his hand. 'It still doesn't explain why he never mentioned you.'

Jay considered telling him the truth, but with Earlston's finger still resting over the trigger, he thought it best to run with the lie. 'The guy you spoke with is called Bryant. He doesn't know I'm here. This arrangement is strictly between me and the guy running things.'

'Does he have a name?'

For some reason, Jay hesitated. It was of no consequence for him to refer to Clate by name. He had already mentioned Bryant, but he found himself saying, 'You don't need to know.'

Earlston shook his head, his deep sigh loaded with frustration. 'I thought I was the one who was playing games. You people never let up. All I asked for was a name. You owe me that much, at least.'

'His name is Clate.'

Earlston gave an appreciative nod. He studied Jay for a moment, his eyes tracing over Jay's face until resting on his cuts and bruises. 'Did Clate do that to you?'

Jay glanced down at the carpet. He didn't answer the question, and from the look of fearful repugnance on Earlston's face, there was no need to. Tears welled in Earlston's eyes, his shoulders shaking as he lowered the gun. He broke into a sob. 'You people are animals. I pray for Jenny's sake she's unharmed.'

Jay eased the gun from Earlston's hand; he offered no comforting words, but inwardly he prayed for Jenny too.

11

─────────

The old church in King's Cross was a quiet spot during the day. Flanked by twisted blackthorn, the adjacent derelict warehouse and the graffitied padlocked garages beyond made it a place where few would wander after midnight.

The sheltering hedgerows made it the perfect place from which to watch. Clate could skulk unseen within its shadows, and once the money was his, easy access to the canal provided a quick exit. Even Mich appeared subdued by its dark seclusion, remaining silent while the breeze carried the canal's musty aroma.

With the money almost in his grasp, Clate wanted to laugh, shout against the night sky, celebrate beneath the stars and bask triumphantly. Silence prevailed, and only a fool would show himself. He needed to remain hidden. Only the thick beat of his heart raged against the silence, the longing inside his stomach so strong he could almost taste it.

Before Clate and Mich left Bryant's flat, Degsy had asked

about the girl. 'Keep her locked in her room,' Clate told him. 'Then release her after I call.'

Degsy didn't reply as though the sudden revelation of Clate's deceit had reduced him to abject silence.

DEGSY FELT anxious when Clate left, smoking his way through his pack of cigarettes beneath the slow tick of the clock. Before leaving, Mich locked Jenny in her room and placed Degsy in charge of the key. Bryant tried to intervene, but Degsy, with the key clenched tightly inside his fist, remained oblivious to his protests.

Degsy paced the room, releasing a heavy sigh after every couple of steps. He had been running cons for over fifty years, and in this godforsaken flat, waiting blindly like every sucker he'd duped, was all it led to. He was undecided whether to laugh or cry. Instinct told him Clate would never call, but the desperate hope that he might was all Degsy could cling to.

He sensed Bryant felt it too. Not that Bryant would allow himself to admit it. Clate's deeds and his wallet, which Degsy knew to be worthless, gave Bryant that needed feeling of reassurance.

EARLSTON DROVE SLOWLY through the city, keeping to the speed limit. Jay found it odd that the man could remain so calm considering everything he'd endured. The city lay in a half-sleep, like a beast at rest, lulling you into a false sense of security, waiting, watching with one eye open.

While waiting for the car to warm, Jay turned his collar

against the cold. Earlston stared towards the road, his face mostly in shadow, glowing beneath every intermittent sweep of light.

~

FINDING THE SILENCE INTOLERABLE, Jay turned on the radio. He wondered if he should have asked, but Earlston's face stayed impassive with any reservations he might have expressed through a faint sigh. Jay remained unconcerned, his sense of isolation suddenly heightened by the sad romantic song on the radio. Late-night shows always had that effect. Their sad songs latched onto the lonely and the weak, taking root in the crevices of their heart. Some were vessels for the emotions stored within, while others offered the promise of salvation.

Since he could remember, Jay had had a soft spot for sublime ballads. Only ten years since its initial release, *You Just Might See Me Cry* by *Our Kid* was now considered a golden oldie. Jay hadn't heard the song for years, its catchy harmony taking him back to that long hot summer of 76. All it took was a few notes, each melodic verse triggering so many memories.

~

HIDDEN among the tangled shelter of the hedges, Clate watched the car's slow approach. Mich quietly acknowledged the green Ford Orion. It wasn't what Clate had imagined. The way she spoke about Earlston and his job in the city, Clate pictured him driving a Bentley or a Jag, something so much grander.

From all appearances, Earlston was alone. Clate couldn't

see the man's face. But even in the shadows, Earlston looked defeated. The head was bowed slightly, the shoulders stooped, forming what Clate could only describe as a pathetic silhouette.

The engine died, and Clate retreated further into the dark when Earlston killed the headlights. Clate grabbed Mich's arm and pulled her closer. He pressed his lips to her ear, pausing for a moment at the floral aroma of her perfume. Something stirred in his loins, a sensation he immediately suppressed, its memory soon forgotten as he whispered. 'As soon as Earlston walks onto the lane, step out from the hedges and go to meet him.'

Mich responded with a nod. 'What do you want me to say?'

'Make a fuss of him first; pretend you've missed him. Then take the money and bring it to me.'

'He'll want Jenny.'

'Then he'll have to wait.'

'What should I say?'

'Exactly what we agreed. Tell him once we've confirmed all the money's there, we'll call him and give him the girl's whereabouts.'

'And will we?'

Clate shrugged. 'You're his wife, the girl's stepmother; it's up to you and your conscience.' Clate gripped Mich's arm. 'And don't go thinking confession's good for the soul. You bring that money to me. Otherwise, I'll make a fuss. No last-minute changes of mind. The last thing we need is you getting sentimental.'

12

The young man instructed Earlston to drop him a few streets away from the church. Earlston willingly obliged, although he found it strange that his fellow reprobates wouldn't expect him. The young man assured him everything was fine. 'They want you in the car alone. You go on ahead. I'll be right behind you.'

Now, parked alongside the church, Earlston checked the rearview mirror, trying to catch sight of him. There was no sign, except for the damp lingering smell of his clothes, nothing to indicate he'd ever sat beside him. Perhaps he was never there, a figment of Earlston's imagination. Anything seemed possible for one so desperate.

Earlston stepped out of the car and strolled among the shadows. These midnight hours harboured the unseen. But spectres and ghouls were for the highly strung. Earlston's hauntings were real; there was something so much more physical about his ghosts.

JAY SLOWED his pace walking towards the church, although with Earlston's car clearly out of sight, he'd found it easy to keep his distance. The shadowy presence of St Vincent's, with its portico of four columns and looming tower, was an ominous spectacle, made more threatening by the three eerie-looking Caryatids watching judgementally through a veil of amber light.

Jay looked over his shoulder, watching the deserted road, intermittently glancing from left to right. Bray's lot was nowhere to be seen, and the closer Jay got to the lane, he suspected they had abandoned him. He scoured the surrounding buildings and the alleyways for a sign. Then, it showed itself through the unmistakable echo of high heels click-clacking in the distance.

WITH THE BRIEFCASE held firmly in his hand, Earlston watched silently while Mich emerged from the shadows and slowly walked towards him. He dropped the case to the ground, tears welling in his eyes, and held out his arms. She seemed reluctant at first, then, without saying a word, she pressed her face into his chest. Her skin felt cold, and her body was shaking. He placed his hands on her cheeks and lifted her face to his.

'Thank God,' he said, trying hard not to sob. He kissed her on the lips, recoiling slightly at the smell of stale wine lingering on her breath. He gave her a curious look, burying the notion deep in his mind. The poor woman had been through enough. The last thing she needed, especially in this moment of reconciliation, was to be asked if she'd been drinking.

Mich drew back her head, and Earlston rested his hands

on her shoulders. He studied the worry in her eyes. 'Where's Jen?' he said. 'Where's my Jen? Is she all right?'

Mich took a step back. 'She's fine, Henry.' She glanced down at the case. 'I'm to take the money to them. Once they're happy it's all there, they'll release Jenny.'

Earlston frowned. 'When? How?' He picked up the brief-case, tightening his grip. 'No. I want to see her now.'

Mich shook her head. 'No, Henry. They won't allow it. Please, just do as they ask. These people are serious.'

Earlston regarded her for a moment. 'How will I know where she is?'

'You're to go back home; they'll call you.' Mich reached out and rested her hand on his. 'Please, Henry.' She dragged the briefcase from his grip. 'Let me do as they ask. I'll give them the money. Then I'll return. And we'll get Jenny back together. Let's put an end to this.'

Earlston, noticing the shine in her eyes, answered with a reluctant nod, remaining silent when she turned her back on him. He watched her hurry down the lane. Mich glanced over her shoulder before disappearing back into the shadows.

DEGSY MUST HAVE DOZED off because one minute, he was sitting on the sofa watching the phone, and the next, he'd awakened to his own snoring. He glanced down at his open hands, and then as the stark realisation grew less fuzzy in his mind, he began frantically searching for the key. He immediately stood up, checking all his pockets until lifting all the cushions from the sofa and tossing them onto the carpet.

Degsy tried to retrace his steps. The action didn't take

much effort. Except for a brief visit to the toilet, he hadn't ventured further than the lounge. He did it all the same, pacing the room until it dawned on him to check if the girl was all right? He hurried to the bedroom, pressing down on the handle, growing more anxious as the door swung open.

Bryant lay on the bed with Jenny beside him. Jenny was sat up, her back resting against the pillows. Bryant lay on his side, his head propped by one hand while the other rested on Jenny's lap.

'What are you doing?' Degsy said.

Bryant turned his head and gazed indifferently at Degsy standing in the doorway. 'I'm having a chat with my girl.'

Degsy frowned. '*Your* girl? About what, exactly?'

'Oh, this and that. Private stuff. Things that have nothing to do with you.' His smirk changed to a scowl. 'Go on, skit.' Degsy remained still. 'Shift yourself,' Bryant said. 'Go on, you heard. Make yourself scarce. Quickly, on your way now.'

Degsy didn't move, undecided whether fear or stupidity kept him rooted to the spot. 'Mich said we were to leave the girl alone. You shouldn't have taken the key. I'd come on out of there if you know what's good for you.'

Bryant sat up. 'Have you been drinking, old man? Because it sounds like you're threatening me?'

Degsy shook his head. 'I wouldn't dare. I just think you should leave the girl alone. We're almost done now. I reckon Clate would be quite unforgiving if you do anything to jeopardise it.'

Bryant stood up, strolled over to Degsy, and pushed his face close to his. 'Clate doesn't care what happens to the girl. What happens to her now is up to me, especially once we receive Clate's phone call.'

Degsy didn't know how to respond. He glanced down at the floor, trying to stop his hands from shaking.

'Well?' Bryant said. 'Well?' he said again, raising his voice against the silence.

Degsy gave a shrug. 'Well, what?'

'Well, if you've got nothing else to say. What the hell are you still doing here?'

Degsy felt his chest tighten. 'I think you should leave the girl alone and come into the lounge.'

Bryant shook his head. 'No. I'm going to stay here with my girl unless you're going to stop me from doing that?'

Degsy shook his head.

Bryant grinned. 'Just as I thought. You grubby little loser. It should have been you we threw in the river. I'm sick of seeing your tired old face, smelling that old man smell. Go on, skit.' He shoved Degsy towards the wall, 'Don't go disturbing me again.'

Degsy nodded, glimpsing the look of terror in the girl's eyes as Bryant slammed the door in his face.

13

E arlston waited for his wife to return. The minutes felt like hours, and he quickly lost patience. 'Mich,' he called gently. 'Mich. Is everything all right?'

Only the soft echo of his voice answered. He edged forward, watching for any movement in the hedgerows, his heart thumping wildly against the silence, more so when something stirred within the shadows. Earlston ventured beyond the lane, pushing cautiously through the leaves. 'Mich?' he said again, 'Mich?' raising his voice as he grew more frantic.

She was nowhere to be seen. For a moment, Earlston questioned if she'd ever been there, her image summoned by a desperate imagination. He shook his head in self-mockery as the faint traces of Mich's perfume brought him to his senses. Earlston broke into a jog until the sudden realisation of Mich's deceit stopped him. Earlston fell to his knees, gazing beyond the tangled branches at the distant silhouettes hurrying along the canal.

~

AFTER SNATCHING the briefcase from Mich's hand, Clate quickly checked the money from his hiding place. Everything looked fine. There were no dud notes, as far as he could tell. All he had to rely on were his instincts, and although Earlston waited patiently like a fool, it still didn't give Clate enough time to count it.

On catching Mich's glance, Clate wondered if the greedy look in her eyes also lingered in his.

'I want my share now,' she insisted.

Clate refused. 'Let's get out of here first,' gesturing towards the canal.

They hurried along the path, Mich lagging behind, hindered by those stupid heels she wore. Clate took no heed. He was almost free. Petty grievances belonged in the past; such things were below him now. Suddenly he was aware of the briefcase in his hand. He resisted the urge to laugh aloud; they were fools, every one of them. On reflection, his worries were for nothing. He was smarter than them all; it all seemed so easy now that he had some distance.

At the thought of Degsy and Bryant waiting patiently for his call, Clate smiled. They were losers clinging to a dream. Even Degsy, who Clate knew had seen through his lies, believed what he wanted to. The old man had repeated the same mistakes for years, swallowing the same old lies, too frightened to admit all was lost. Even when Degsy visited Clate at the club, his head was full of stupid notions, the old fool still trying to cling to something. Mich was no better, and staring towards the mouth of the tunnel thirty yards ahead of them, Clate took consolation in knowing he would soon be rid of her.

∼

JAY'S BODY was still not fully healed, and running full pelt towards Earlston's cries left him breathless. He found Earlston on his knees. A defeated look haunted his eyes, and his ashen skin looked ghostly in the darkness. 'What's happened,' Jay asked, lifting Earlston to his feet when the man refused to answer.

Earlston gave him a fearful look, the expression on his face growing more wretched, like a man who had witnessed the tragic horror of his own death.

Jay glanced at Earlston's empty hands. 'You've made the exchange? Well?' He grabbed Earlston by the arms. 'Answer me, for God's sake. Who took the money from you?'

Earlston closed his eyes, keeping them shut as though the information he was about to convey was too much for him. 'Mich,' he said, opening his eyes. 'Mich took it.' A sudden realisation flashed in Earlston's eyes. 'You knew, didn't you?' It was more a statement of fact than a question.

Jay looked down at the ground.

'Didn't you?' Earlston continued. 'What kind of person lies like that? Mich has been part of this all along.'

Tears ran down Earlston's face. 'Help me, please. I'm begging you. I don't care about Mich taking the money. All I want is Jenny. If there's any good in you. Please, help me get my daughter.'

Jay turned his gaze towards the hulking shadow of the hedges and tried peering through the leaves. He pointed to where the lane tapered onto a narrow footpath. 'Is this where she went?'

Earlston nodded. 'Yes,' he said hoarsely. 'It leads to the canal.'

Jay broke into a jog, following the path through the leaves, gaining momentum as he neared the canal, unaware if Earlston followed behind him.

∾

AT FIRST, Degsy stood outside the bedroom door, his heart thumping in his throat, his mind haunted by the terrified look on the girl's face. He thought he heard her cry, but pressing his ear closer, all he could make out was the low mumble of Bryant's voice. Degsy closed his eyes, resigning himself to his cowardice with a sigh.

With his shoulders slumped, he trudged along the hallway and wandered into the kitchen. A half-empty bottle of whisky stood facing him on the draining board. Degsy reached out his hand and picked it up. He poured some whisky into a glass, swirling it around before he drank, watching the amber liquid glint beneath the halogen strip light.

He emptied the glass with one gulp. A feeling of shame tarnished the pleasure, as did the burning sensation in his throat. He poured himself another glass. Why not? It was all a tired old conman could do.

Degsy dropped his chin to his chest, wiping the wetness from his eyes as thoughts of Jay took hold of him. That night, after they tossed the kid's body in the river, Degsy swore he would never be a party to something like that again. It tarnished his soul and filled him with feelings of wretchedness and self-loathing. Yet here he was again, a spineless old fool destined to make the same mistake.

Degsy broke into a sob as his cowardice overwhelmed him. Sniffing back his tears, he looked towards the window, staring in disgust at his reflection. He had been a good-looking kid. The soft round face and the brown eyes of his youth were a sharp contrast to the sad weathered face gazing back at him. He wondered what he might have been, what path he might have taken, if, by some perverse accident of fate, he'd glimpsed his future self all those years ago? Maybe he would have done the same. A man predestined for failure whose biggest con was against himself.

Degsy closed his eyes and sighed, opening them to the girl's shrill scream. He let the glass drop from his hand, opened the drawer, and took out the largest kitchen knife he could find. Even frightened losers got a second chance. He strode out into the hall and pulled open the bedroom door. He knew the odds were stacked against him. But seeing Bryant sprawled on top of the girl, he sure as hell was going to try.

14

On stepping into the darkness of the tunnel, Clate felt the chilled, damp air fall across his skin. He turned his collar to the cold, slowing his pace to allow Mich to catch up, then stopped when she stood beside him. Clate listened to the heaviness of her breath, an anxiousness to her voice as she said, 'What the hell are we stopping here for?'

Clate took out his lighter, flipped open the lid and drew the flame to Mich's face. A look of uncertainty loitered in her eyes. Clate tried easing it with a smile. But her apprehension remained; the yellow flame highlighted the lines on her skin, ageing her, her slim body looking slighter against their shadows.

'You want your cut, don't you?' Clate said. 'Best get it out of the way. This is good a place as any.'

Mich answered with a cautious nod. 'I take it Degsy and Bryant are out?'

Clate grinned. 'They were never in.'

Mich shrugged. 'Okay.' She glanced down at the briefcase. 'Fifty-fifty split, right?'

Clate gestured towards the canal. 'Come over here where there's more light.' Mich did as he asked. He snapped the lighter shut. 'Let it cool for a second. The damn thing almost burnt my fingers.' The press of hot metal weighed heavily in his palm. Clate slyly slipped the lighter into his pocket and rested his hands on Mich's shoulders.

She tried to pull away. 'What are you doing, Clate? Stop messing around, for Christ's sake. Take your grubby hands off me.'

For a second, he thought the sound was only in his head. But when Mich turned to face it, Clate knew it was real. Someone called his name, the man's voice growing less distant. Clate released Mich from his grip, shoved her aside and glanced over his shoulder towards the tunnel's entrance. He considered returning the way he came, quickly changing his mind when he saw the silhouette of two broad figures blocking his path.

With the briefcase held tightly in his hand, Clate withdrew further into the tunnel, breaking into a jog, keeping close to the canal's edge. Conscious of the water alongside him, Clate quickened his pace, small stones unearthed by the heaviness of his tread splashing into the water in his wake.

Almost at the tunnel's end, Clate felt his spirits lift as the darkness petered out into a dull light. The men chasing after him called out his name. Clate didn't respond. He gazed towards the towpath, mindful of the sloping grassy bank, feeling the sweat seeping through his shirt. The overgrown brambles reached out to him, seeming desperate for his touch, while he strode through their prickly shadows.

A dead rat held petrified in the fork of a fallen branch caught Clate's attention. It was almost as though it was frozen in time. Its glazed eyes seemed expectant, the body wholesomely rigid, as though waiting for its stilted heart to suddenly beat. Clate was so engrossed by the dead rodent that he barely noticed the two men walking towards him. On looking in their direction, they were instantly recognisable. They wore their gelled hairstyles and taupe double-breasted suits like a coat of arms, which for those in the know, was like having the words Benny Bray's lackeys written all over them.

One of them stood in his way. He was the older of the two. Clate had seen him in the club, Ray or Ralph somebody, but his actual name escaped him. Clate had no time to fathom why they were here. But the way they eyed the briefcase told him it was no coincidence.

Clate tried to walk around them, but every time he did, they blocked his way. Clate greeted them with a frown. 'You're in my way, fellas. I'd move to one side if you know what's good for you.'

The older one held out his hands. 'Hey, don't be like that. It's Roy Cullen, Benny's pal.' He nodded at the young brute standing next to him. 'You remember Chad, right?'

Clate shook his head. 'No, I can't say that I do.' He glanced over his shoulder, catching a glimpse of Mich in the distance. He wondered why she'd gone quiet, finding the answer in the two men walking alongside her. Clate didn't question how they knew. Such a luxury would have to wait. All he wanted was to get out of there.

Roy nodded towards the briefcase. 'I take it that's a gift for Benny, finally paying off your debts, with an extra bonus to apologise for trying to run out on him.' He regarded Clate with a smile. 'No need to take it yourself. Hand the case to Chad; we'll save you a journey.'

Clate swung the case up to his chest, gripping it with both hands and rammed the edge into Chad's throat. He didn't wait to watch the dope fall, shoving Roy aside before running along the canal. They were nothing but a glitch, and once again, he felt an impulse to laugh aloud, misguided fools, every one of them.

Clate broke into a sprint, feeling closer to it now; the ocean, the sands, and the Mediterranean coastline filled him with energy, a sensation that felt both superior and triumphant.

At first, he thought it was a small stone bouncing up from the path and hitting him casually in his lower back. Clate felt numb in the spot where it struck, a numbness that spread across his body. Feeling the sudden dampness of his shirt, he glanced down at it and saw that it was covered in blood. He was determined to run it out; the numbness turned into a burn, the sensation intensifying until it felt like a hot poker relentlessly prodding him in the back.

Clate swayed as he ran, then crumbled to his knees, the excruciating pain proving unbearable.

With his body soaked in sweat, Clate released the brief-case from his hand; he rolled onto his side, shifting near the water's edge, watching the rippled surface while his free hand dangled in the canal. Clate felt a hand on his back, another on his legs, holding him down while someone pressed his face into the water.

15

To begin with, Jay couldn't get the image of Clate from his mind; the big man's body was sprawled across the edge of the bank, his face immersed in the water. Although it was only minutes, it felt like hours watching him lie there. Then he was gone, almost as though he never was. They weighted his body with stones. Then, with one thoughtless shove, they tipped him over the side, dumping him like the carcass of an old dog, watching him sink until he lay forever lost at the bottom of the canal.

It unsettled Jay to see Clate's life so easily discarded. Yet, the look on Mich's face haunted him most. She had watched in silence while Clate's body disappeared beneath the water. Two of Bray's men stood on either side of her, the stark paleness of her skin looking spectral among the shadows.

Moments later, after carelessly disposing of Clate's body, Roy Cullen approached her. He wore his usual affable smile. His casual demeanour gave no hint as to what had just taken place; the serene look in Cullen's eyes suggested he'd erased all traces of Clate from his memory. He took his hand from his pocket and beckoned Mich closer. Mich barely moved, inching forward with a few reluctant steps. On catching sight of Jay, Mich looked startled. It lasted only a moment until she gazed beyond him, dismissing him with a glance just as she had done with Nash, Pete, Shane and countless other unwanted ghosts.

Cullen narrowed his eyes. 'You need to come back with us. Benny wants to chat with you.'

Mich didn't answer at first. But eventually, she asked, 'why?' her voice, inflected with a strained alarm, almost a whisper.

Cullen flashed her an amused smile. 'Do you really have to ask that? He wants to talk about old times. The days you worked at the Indigo just before Benny got sent down.'

Mich glanced down at the ground. 'I don't remember much about that time. It was years ago.'

Cullen shrugged. 'Yeah, I suppose. But Benny's keen to hear more about that chat you had with the police. I'm sure we can help to jog your memory.' He glanced over his shoulder. 'And there's your involvement in all this. Benny's never keen on having too many witnesses.'

Mich gave no reply, allowing Bray's men to guide her along the path, her tall, slender figure and pale, expressionless face reflected in the canal. Jay watched in silence, calling out to her when hearing the shrill sound of a police siren growing less distant. 'What about Jenny?'

'What about her?' Mich said.

'Where is she? You can't just leave her like that.'

For a moment, there was a slyness to Mich's smile. Her eyes shone with cold detachment. It was the same cruel look she had given Jay when she abandoned him all those years ago. Then her expression changed. Perhaps this was her last chance to do something good, a moment of selflessness before the dark inevitability of her fate. She fixed Jay with a stare. 'Jenny's at Bryant's flat,' and reading Jay's questioning look, said, 'thirty-five Rouchard House, Clapton Park.'

Jay frowned.

'Hackney,' Cullen said. 'I need to speak with Bryant anyway. Come on, I'll drive you.'

Then Mich gave him one last glance, the sadness in her eyes muted by fearful hesitation.

IN THE QUIET hours after midnight, Cullen took advantage of the near-deserted road and pressed down on the accelerator. Much to Jay's annoyance, Cullen waited at every set of traffic lights, slowing down at the known police spots so as not to draw attention to himself. From the casual way he drove, no one would have guessed that he'd just committed murder. But Jay saw the menace in his eyes, making Cullen's casual manner more frightening.

Cullen lifted one hand off the steering wheel, slipped his hand into his inside pocket and took out his pack of cigarettes. He placed one in his mouth, then pressed in the car lighter, resting his hand on the gear stick until the lighter sprung back up. He plucked it from its slot, holding the heated end against the cigarette's tip. Smoke filled the car, and quickly winding down the window, Cullen said, 'Do me a favour, kid, put that lighter back for me.'

Jay did as he asked, then started fanning the smoke with his hand until Cullen got the hint and blew each mouthful through the open window. He threw Jay a glance. 'You're very quiet. There's no need to fret over what happened to Clate. Trust me, it was long overdue. To be honest, I thought you'd be pleased, considering what he did to you?'

Jay shrugged. 'I don't know how I feel, to tell the truth.'

He wondered if Cullen spotted the lie. Could he tell that Jay felt sick to his stomach? Did a haunted look in his eyes betray his forced nonchalance? Or was there something that kept Cullen unsure? Something recognisable told him this wasn't the first time Jay had seen a man fall to his death. Misfortune followed him like a curse, and inwardly he prayed, a longing in his heart, hoping that Jenny would be all right.

Cullen took three deep drags from his cigarette, then flicked it out the window. He placed both hands on the wheel and focused on the road. 'You look a little pale. You know, I thought you were made of stronger stuff.'

'I'm fine, just a bit worried about Jenny, that's all. Can we get a move on?'

Cullen shook his head. 'What the hell are you worried about her for? I thought you were playing us at first. But I'm starting to believe you're a soft touch, and you weren't kidding when you told us that you weren't cut out for this.'

Jay responded with a sigh. 'Mr Bray has everything he wanted, Mich and the money. There's no point in the girl suffering any more than she has to.'

Cullen nodded. 'I totally agree. But knowing that deviant Bryant, as well as I do, there's a hollow feeling in my guts that tells me we're already too late.'

16

A cross the partial hush of the city, they drove in silence. The buildings passed Jay by in a blur. The tarmac road gleamed in the aftermath of the rain while the sheen of the lighted shop signs fell softly upon the glossy pavements. Mostly the streets were deserted. Occasional people wandered into sight, and the lone figure of a man, ambling along the curb caught Jay's eye. Jay's gaze followed him along the path, thoughts of Earlston filling his mind as the man faded into the shadows.

Jay shot Cullen a glance. 'Did you see where Earlston got to before we left?'

Cullen narrowed his eyes. 'Earlston?'

'Mich's husband.'

Cullen sighed. 'With all that fuss with Clate, I forgot about him.' He shook his head. 'Benny won't be pleased, especially how things turned out with Clate; it doesn't pay to have any witnesses.'

'I doubt if Earlston saw anything. No one heard a shot. He was at the lane near the church last I saw him.'

'What was he doing?'

'Sobbing his heart out. He realised Mich was behind it all.' Jay fell silent, undecided about what sickened him more, his part in all this or the wretched look on Earlston's face.

Cullen forced a laugh. 'The poor deluded fool. His wife took his money and daughter.' He shook his head and sighed. 'Jesus. How does a man come back from that?'

Jay stared at his hands and, picturing the girl, hoped he would find the answer.

～

THE ROUCHARD TOWER block reminded Jay of the Moor Estate with its red bricks, dirty windows, and grey concrete balconies. The murky graffitied foyer smelled of urine and damp. Jay took the stairs while Cullen, who displayed no signs of urgency, waited patiently for the lift.

On reaching the third floor, Jay hesitated. The night's stillness, aided by a burgeoning feeling of apprehension, held him temporarily spellbound. He quickly shook it off, hurrying towards Flat thirty-five, a sense of emptiness in his stomach when he found the front door half open.

Jay gave the door a shove and inched into the hallway. The dimly lit flat reeked of that odious blend of stale ciga-rettes and cheap alcohol. Blood smeared the wall, and Jay, following its trail, found Bryant lying on his back in the kitchen doorway, his head resting heavily on the floor tiles while his legs were stretched across the carpet.

Bryant's shirt, once white, was drenched in blood, and as though caught midway in a scream, his mouth was wide open. His bony hands, lightly clasped, rested upon his wound while his dead eyes stared up at the light.

Jay rushed into the lounge. 'Jenny?' he cried. 'Degsy? Are

you all right.' No one replied, and on hearing the faint groaning, Jay followed it into the bedroom. He found Degsy slumped on the floor, his back resting against the end of the bed. The old man's face was masked with blood; he held a knife in his hand; the only indication he was still alive was the sound of his chest wheezing. Jay glanced around the room, taking in the rumpled sheets, the smashed lamp, and the upturned table before crouching beside him.

Degsy peered at him through swollen eyes and, taking hold of Jay's hand, whispered, 'I'm sorry, kid. I'm so sorry. But I'm happy you're here to greet me.'

Jay gave him a tender smile. 'This isn't heaven, Degsy. It's far from it. Neither of us is dead yet.'

A questioning look flashed in Degsy's eyes. Then he broke into a sob.

'Hey,' Jay said. 'Hey, stop that; shush now.'

Degsy squeezed Jay's hand. 'I don't know how you're here; all I know is I'm glad to see you.' He tugged weakly at Jay's hand, drawing him closer. 'I couldn't let Bryant hurt the girl. Do you know what that sick bastard tried to do to her?'

Jay gave him a knowing look. 'Is she all right?'

Degsy answered with a slow nod. 'I told her to go. Leave, I said. Run home to your dad, and don't look back. You get the hell out of here.'

Jay regarded him with a smile, noticing Cullen watching them from the doorway as he glanced over his shoulder.

'This old man's full of surprises,' Cullen said. 'Seems he's done Mr Bray a favour.' He glanced around the room, focusing on the canvas rucksack in the corner. 'Hopefully, she'll go straight to her dad. But there again, she might go to the police.' He stared at Jay and frowned. 'You and your buddy need to go. We'll catch up later. I need to make some calls, get someone to tidy up this mess.'

Jay had no inclination to disagree, and grabbing Degsy by the waist, he lifted the old man onto his shoulder.

17

Jay thought about little else. Whenever he closed his eyes, he imagined that pale distraught girl running scared through the deserted streets. He pictured her banging on doors, screaming for help, seeking refuge from strangers. In his mind's eye, each scenario faded into the next. He saw her flagging down a taxi, sitting quietly on the tube, the knot in his stomach tightening as he pictured her describing him to the police. But mostly, he saw her in Earlston's arms, a silent knowing between them, reunited at long last, closer now perhaps, their bond tightened by a savage experience.

In the days that followed, Jay heard no news about Earlston and his daughter. Bray had moved Jay and Degsy into the rooms above the Indigo, giving them strict instructions to keep a low profile. Jay was in no position to disagree. From Clate's apartment to this, he seemed trapped in a never-ending confinement. Not that he could go anywhere, even if he had the choice. His spell in London had left him broke. Even if Bray decided to give him his cut or what was left after paying off Jackmond. It would be weeks before he could go anywhere; he didn't even have a passport.

Degsy's situation was worse. Battered and tired, he spent most of his days drifting in and out of sleep, lying on a bug-infested mattress. He was like a dog on its last legs; if it had been left to Jay, he would have taken the old man to the hospital. Not that Degsy would have gone. Jay had grown used to his curmudgeonly ways. But Degsy seemed broken inside; his spirit diminished. Even now, as he sat up, he looked dejected. His thin lips were caught in a permanent grimace. He wore the look of a man who had failed to seize his last chance, forever cursed to carry the weight of his mistakes.

Jay strolled over to where Degsy's jacket was slung over a chair, reached inside the pocket and took out his pack of cigarettes. He placed one in the old man's mouth, staring into his rheumy eyes while he gave him a light.

Degsy took a half-hearted drag, releasing the smoke with a sigh. He plucked the cigarette from his mouth and offered it to Jay. 'Here, take it, stub it out.'

Jay took the cigarette from his hand. 'What's got into you?'

Degsy frowned. 'I'm thinking about quitting. Plus, I'm not enjoying it.'

Jay did as Degsy asked, and after resting the cigarette in the ashtray, he dragged over one of the battered old bar chairs and sat beside him. Degsy leaned forward, curiosity burning in his tired eyes. 'Is that a new suit?'

Jay shook his head. 'It's one of Cullen's. It's a little loose. But at least it's clean. The other one got ruined when Bryant dumped me in the river.'

Degsy lowered his eyes at the mention of Bryant's name. He went quiet for a moment, his breathing growing heavier as though he was using each deep breath to suppress every awful memory. Degsy wiped a tear from his eye. 'It broke my heart that did. I thought we'd lost you. I should have done something. I'm nothing but a coward, leaving you–'

'Helping the girl made amends for that.'

'Maybe,' Degsy mumbled with a shrug. He let out a wistful laugh. 'What kind of kidnappers are we? God knows what Bray thinks about me now. I'm supposed to be a seasoned conman. I'm nothing but a soft touch.'

Jay nodded with a smile. 'You were right all along about me trying to be like Nash. Who am I trying to kid? Like you said before, I'm nothing like him. I'm just not cut out for this.'

Degsy looked at him and smiled. 'I don't know. That deal you made with Bray duped us all. It was a brilliant con if you ask me, and if you hadn't tried to take the girl, who knows, you might have got away with it.'

'Hindsight's a wonderful thing,' Jay said with a smile, pausing as he caught sight of an immaculately dressed Roy Cullen watching them from the doorway. Cullen stepped inside and dropped a package on Jay's lap.

Jay stared at it and frowned. 'What this?'

Cullen grinned. 'Surprisingly, it's your cut. Granted, it's a lot less than we agreed. You can thank Terry Jackmond for that.' Cullen glanced at the package and shrugged. 'It's better than nothing all the same. It seems Benny's taken a shine to you.' He looked over towards the mattress. 'You still hanging in there, Degsy? It seems you're not dead yet.'

Degsy nodded with a smile. 'When can we leave?'

Cullen shrugged. 'It's hard to tell. No one's heard anything about Earlston and his daughter. Maybe shame's forcing him to stay quiet. Who knows? A couple of more days, perhaps. It might even be a few more weeks. I'll get one of the girls to bring you some scran; it'll stop you from looking so glum. A full belly changes a man's perspective; it might even help build your strength.' He nodded at Jay. 'I'll see what I can do about that car of yours.' Cullen turned towards the door, pausing when Degsy said. 'How's Mich?'

Cullen turned around. 'I'll tell you later, old man. As I said, build your strength up first. For now, that's a subject you shouldn't be thinking about.'

After Cullen left the room, Jay and Degsy stared at each other in silence. Not that they needed words. The knowledge of Mich's fate expressed itself through the haunted look in their eyes and their deep regret released through every wistful sigh.

Jay tore open the package, took out the bundles of cash, and divided them into two equal stacks. He placed one at his side, then, rising slowly from his chair, gave the other stack to Degsy. For a while, the old man stared at the money in silence. Then he looked up at Jay, a tremor in his voice as he said, 'What's this for?'

Jay flashed him a wry smile. 'I thought we were partners. Fifty-fifty, right?'

Tears welled in Degsy's eyes.

'Stop that,' Jay said. 'Stop it, now, you stupid old fool. I wouldn't have given it to you if I'd known you'd get all emotional.'

Degsy laughed, the wheezing sound in his chest quickly becoming a cough. Jay hurried over to the sink and filled the discarded pint glass with cold water. 'Here,' he said, handing it to Degsy, 'sip it slowly.'

Degsy did as he was told, then rested the glass against his chest. 'So what are you going to do with the money?'

Jay shrugged. 'Don't know. All I can think about is my mam. Now that Jackmond no longer has a grudge, I'll go home and see her, tell her I'm sorry and hopefully put things right.'

'And after that?'

'Who knows,' Jay said. 'I might join you on your retirement; check out these warmer climes you keep harping on about.'

Degsy regarded him with a warm smile. 'You know, kid, you were right when you said you were nothing like Nash. You're cleverer than he ever was. You've got more style too. Nash was a cold fish who didn't give a damn about anything or anyone except himself. Okay, so he pulled off a few cons. But look where it got him. No, you're nothing like Nash. You've got a good heart, which makes you so much better than him.'

Jay wanted to disagree, but he didn't say a word. Instead, all he could think about was Mich, picturing the terrified look in her eyes and the pale gauntness of her face reflected in the canal. He knew the image would forever linger at the back of his mind, the past catching him unaware and, just like Nash's ghost, haunt him in those quiet hours before sleep.

THANKS FOR READING

Thanks for reading. If you **enjoyed this book,** please consider leaving **a review**. Reviews make a huge difference in helping new readers find the book.

WELCOME TO HOLYHELL

BOOK 1 IN THE HOLYHELL CRIME SERIES

In the sweltering summer of 1976, a drought-stricken town harbours a deadly secret. This compelling, atmospheric literary thriller is perfect for fans of small-town crime and rural noir from the author of *Histories of the Dead* and *Hidden Grace*.

'Welcome To HolyHell has the sharp plotting of peak Elmore Leonard combined with the brooding lyrical atmosphere of James Lee Burke. The characters are all marvelously well-drawn and the sense of time and place is spot on.' *Punk Noir Magazine*

'Math Bird gives us a fine bit of noir in 1976 Wales.' *Murder in Common Crime Fiction Blog*

'A remarkable work that will have you dreading as well as eagerly turning the page.' *Unlawful Acts - Crime Fiction blog*

Lies...

It's 1976, and Britain is scorching amid an oppressive heatwave. Conman Bowen, trying to escape the hustle and bustle of London, returns to his hometown, hoping to start anew. But as fate would have it, things don't always go as planned.

Secrets...

For young loner, Jay Ellis, stumbling across a mysterious briefcase filled with cash is nothing short of a miracle. But the newfound fortune isn't the only thing that catches his attention - the beguiling Nash, who appears to have followed the money into town, is an even greater mystery. Could this mysterious stranger hold the key to Jay's newfound fortune - or will he bring an even greater danger?

Betrayal...

Veteran conman Nash is determined to track down Bowen and retrieve the money he stole from him. With nothing more than a hunch and an old newspaper clipping featuring a boy who witnessed his partner's death, Nash follows the trail. As their lives become increasingly intertwined, Nash must navigate the world of violent drifters and treacherous thieves while questioning whether a man's conscience is his greatest strength or his greatest weakness.

Check out the Ned Flynn *Crime Thriller Series*

Book 1

THE WHISTLING SANDS

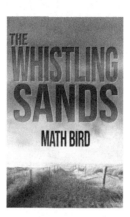

Ex-con Ned Flynn is handy with his fists, but to see his mother looking so frail breaks the big man's heart. He needs money, and he needs it fast. So when a local businessman hires him to find his missing wife, Flynn accepts the job without question. He tracks her down to a remote village on the Welsh coast. But what starts out as a simple errand quickly spirals into deceit and violence.

Book 2

HIDDEN GRACE

Ned Flynn's days are haunted by those who betrayed him, and payback seems the only road to forgiveness. Yet Flynn doesn't know where to start until retired criminal Eddie Roscoe throws him a lifeline. But Eddie's services come with a price, and if Flynn wants the information he seeks, he must help a distraught Eddie find his missing son. As fate brings these men together, the hunt for Eddie's son takes an unexpected turn for the worse, and they become embroiled in an inescapable and violent underworld of forced labour and modern slavery. As Eddie and Flynn fight to survive, each may find that the road to retribution starts within.

BORDERSANDS

A Mabon Pryce Murder Mystery

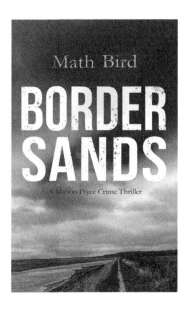

A gripping literary murder mystery that delves deep into the dark secrets of a small town, exploring the complex bonds of loyalty and betrayal and the powerful family ties that shape our lives and remain with us forever. A must-read for fans of Chris Hammer.

ONE BANK HOLIDAY. ONE BRUTAL MURDER.

On a sweltering August Bank Holiday in 1983, the town of Mabon

Pryce's childhood home had much to celebrate - until tragedy struck with the brutal murder of local beauty Mary Reece.

Haunted by the darkness that shrouds the small town, Investigative reporter Mab returns for the funeral and finds himself drawn into the mystery of Mary's death.

As he begins to piece together the events that led to Mary's death, he realizes that the truth is far more complex than it appears. With each new lead, Mab uncovers lies and secrets hidden deep in the town's history. With time running out, Mab must confront his own demons while uncovering the truth about Mary Reece's murder.

Rich with atmosphere, this compelling literary murder mystery from the author of *Welcome to HolyHell* and *Histories of the Dead* marks the start of the Mabon Pryce series and is perfect for fans of Jane Harper and Gary Disher.

ABOUT THE AUTHOR

Math Bird is a British novelist and short story writer.

He's a member of the Crime Writers Association, and his work has aired on BBC Radio 4, Radio Wales, and Radio 4 Extra.

For more information: www.mathbird.uk

Printed in Great Britain
by Amazon

24776798R00202